A
Distant
Crossing

****

By

Thomas Parks

Published in the United States of America

PSS Publishing
P.O. Box 30605
Phoenix, AZ 85046

ISBN #: 0-9676031-0-2

To all the good friends who just wouldn't let it go. Thanks for keeping the gentle pressure on. I needed that.

A special thanks to Todd Elwood .

PROLOGUE

The relentless wind blew icy snow through the crude shelter he had fashioned among the trees of southern Canada. Broken branches, pine needles and twigs were all that separated the man in the ragged army jacket from the fury of winter. He had wedged his makeshift shelter precariously above the mounting drifts in the branches of an old evergreen. There, he would be safe from the wolves prowling the area, though it seemed unlikely they would misjudge the warnings of nature, as he had, and get caught in the storm.

The man had been foolish and careless, and he knew it. That only added to his discomfort. He strayed too far from the small cabin that had been his home those past months, and the North Country was demanding its price. Trying to find his way back against the blinding blizzard would be suicidal. His decision to stay improved his odds only slightly. Maybe, he thought, it was as it should be.

Slowly, he reached for the torn collar of the olive jacket and pulled it higher against the back of his neck. His hollow, dark eyes stared out beneath the bent brim of an old Stetson, searching in vain for a sign amid the dimming light that yet another trial would soon be over. It was not to be. Vision was difficult, hampered by the stinging ice attacking his eyes.

His mind demanded to know how it had come to this. Yet he searched for answers where few existed. He traced over the paths of his life, never seeming to pinpoint where it began to unravel. Maybe he was a victim of a tyranny of gradualism. Whatever it was, his fate now seemed self-evident in that freezing darkness.

His mind wandered to another time – another life, really – filled with promises, high expectations and self-demands. And arrogance, mostly, in believing that what was, would always be. He remembered the impatient faces of those who chose not to consider the possibilities. Theirs was an undemanding faith that the system, however abused and distorted, would always prevail. A generation given the limitless riches in a limitless land. To think, they found the limits.

The once-broad shoulders hidden beneath the heavy clothing rose and lowered slightly. He was tired beyond reason. His mind drifted between stark reality and nonsense. Though the wind seemed to calm, instinct told him to remember the fear and to brace for the long night that waited. Cold hands gripped the jacket tighter around his body. His pale, hollow face nodded. The storm will end, he promised himself. It must.

CHAPTER 1

Dreams of security and of happiness for his family had been tantalizingly close. His stock options, his 401K, the mind-boggling IPO and even visions of swaying palm trees in the sunny Caribbean were all within reality's reach. Then came the collapse. That's when all the oxygen that had powered the hard-charging workers vanished like a wisp of smoke, suffocating lives, careers and dreams. Two days before, dozens of employees hauled away their livelihoods in boxes, but Jim Barnes drew little comfort from collective misery. Today, sitting in the lavish conference room of the Internet company that had recruited him just months ago, he tried to make sense of the cave in. Raking moist hands down his face, he urged his normally reliable intellect to find answers where none existed.

Worse, his mind failed to answer the more important question: "How will I tell Linda and Kelley about this?"

Crushing his wife and daughter's dreams wasn't in him.

Suddenly, the ornate mahogany doors crashed open and Scott Jackson, Jim's former CEO, burst in.

"Argentina's gone down!"

Instantly, Jim pushed aside thoughts of his family. This news was devastating.

"What? Are you serious?"

Jim lifted his six-foot, stocky frame out of the leather chair and stared directly into the panicked eyes of a breathless man trying to maintain footing on an increasingly slippery slope.

"They've repudiated. Folded on their foreign dept. It just came across CNN a few minutes ago. Jesus, this is going to start a financial nightmare."

Scott's words drifted off. Breaking eye contact with Jim, he turned his gaze out of the panoramic window overlooking downtown Los Angeles.

"The world has just changed," he said.

Jim Barnes was quick and smart, and thoughts began careening through his mind like a pinball. He spoke, again coaxing his mind to solve the unsolvable.

"It's half past five here. The East coast exchanges are closed. Thank God! You know the Dow is going to tank. Bank stocks don't stand a chance. Hell, New York is probably holding most of Argentina's paper. If the IMF doesn't step in, Wall Street will be a ghost town by this time tomorrow."

Finally, his mind arrived at something good. It was a small solution, but Jim would take what his mind would give him.

"I've got to start heading back," he told his former boss. "It'll take me three or four days at best to get to Detroit. I can't leave Linda and Kelley there alone. I know I promised I'd help in the shutdown –"

"Don't say another word. You've got your family to protect. Get going before this whole town locks up."

Jim – his brain cranking again for the first time in days – was already onto his next move.

"I've got to get to the bank. There still may be time to get enough cash."

Without hesitating, Jim walked toward the open door.

"It's going to get bad," Scott said. "Be careful Jim. I only wish things had turned out differently."

"Hey, we took a chance," Jim said. At last his mind was clear. "You've got my cell phone number. We'll keep in touch."

Jim walked through the morbidly quiet office. Rows of still cubicles and lifeless computer monitors sat perfectly aligned like deck chairs on the Titanic.

Jim rushed past them, beginning a race with time to get home. An international house of cards was about to crumble and he didn't want to get caught at the bottom of the pile.

****

Only one man stood in the dimly lit situation room at Kirtland Air Force base in Albuquerque, New Mexico. Colonel Jennings Colton shifted impatiently in the soft, leather chair, waiting for the signal that the teleconference with Washington was beginning. He knew why the meeting had been called and was filled with a controlled excitement at the prospect of more power coming his way.

A large man, in both stature and ego, the colonel arrived at this posting in Albuquerque three years earlier. Adjusting to life in the West wasn't easy. Coming from the eastern seaboard, where he spent his youth among the wealthy and privileged, Colonel Jennings Colton was a military man, a West Pointe graduate. He didn't understand the civilians here. They were at once bumpkins and independent thinkers. They were a problem. But that didn't matter now. He had finally achieved the position and power to make his difficulties someone else's problem.

At the far end of the room, a massive video display with one large screen in the middle, surrounded by 20 smaller monitors, flickered to life. Each small screen showed one of Colton's military counterparts around the country waiting quietly to begin. In a way, it reflected what had become of the United States. Everything orbited around Washington. No aides were present. This was the top of top secret.

The oversized center screen zapped on. Staring back was National Security Advisor E. Fife Lindsey IV sitting at the head of a conference table deep in the bowels of the White House. He cleared his throat.

"Gentlemen," he started, eliminating any formality to open these now-familiar meetings. "As you know, the president gave this group the responsibility of developing contingency plans for the transition to martial law, should the worldwide financial situation deteriorate. That day has arrived. We are facing a crisis. We are moving ahead with Operation Patriot."

His words were met with cold silence.

"The domestic situation has deteriorated rapidly in the last few weeks. We have received word that Argentina has repudiated its debt. That move, frankly, will take down the top five commercial banks in this country. More countries will follow their lead, and a number of other banks teetering on the brink of insolvency will follow. The FDIC is woefully inadequate, even bankrupt, and there is no hope of stemming the panic on the part of depositors, which is sure to come.

"The world's financial system, as we know it, is no longer viable. We have contingency plans in place to re-structure this fiscal nightmare, however the immediate dislocations will be traumatic. Violent confrontations and civil unrest are a certainty, as the public will move quickly to withdraw funds, which essentially no longer exist. Reasoning with a well armed, infuriated citizenry will not work. It is your job to ensure the welfare and continued operation of the government of the United States. All of you have participated in the operational planning of Patriot, and you know your responsibilities. Before you are sealed envelopes. They contain orders and the authority you need to control the military districts you have been assigned. Congress and the Judiciary have been informed. Shortly, the president will go before the nation.

"Now, gentlemen, let me be brutally frank. We must be prepared for years of upheaval. You have been given extraordinary powers. Use them to their fullest."

Jennings Colton rolled those words over in his mind. "Extraordinary powers," he thought, his face flush. "At last."

Lindsey finished, "Good luck to all of you, and say a prayer for the United States of America."

E. Fife Lindsey IV, grandson of a governor, son of a senator and ambassador, archetypal representative of the patrician governing class that had taken Washington D.C as their own, exited the room. To his core, he believed the system would be preserved, but at what cost to those beyond the Beltway?

Colonel Jennings Colton eyed the large envelope before him and the corners of his mouth rose in an ill-concealed smile. His turn at bat had finally arrived.

"Thank God," he whispered.

****

The roar of motorcycles and a parade of half-naked, buxom women clinging to the ample bellies of leather clad, self-styled renegades was nothing new to the people of the small town of Bruneau, Idaho. It was fall, and that meant the Aryan Brotherhood was in town for a week of hell-raising.

Annually, the quiet community fell to a siege of smoky pickup trucks, Confederate flags and tattooed skinheads. An aura of hatred and fear shrouded the town. For the locals, the rally couldn't end soon enough. Fortunately, this was the last night.

Arthur J. "Artie" Stubbs, self-described "rising star" in The Brotherhood, sat in the abandoned barn that served as their makeshift headquarters. He reveled in the activity around him. Undoubtedly, he would someday lead this group, he thought, if for no other reason than his IQ approached triple digits, unlike everyone else within shouting range.

Violent men filled the large room. Artie, at only five-foot, six-inches, was one of the smallest of the group. Among present company, though, his verbal skills became his brawn. These guys needed leadership and Artie could incite a riot at a Girl Scout meeting.

Empty beer cans were strewn about and a pungent haze of smoke filled the air. In a far corner, an old TV played "The Gong Show," entertaining the few Artie couldn't rally. A handful of others shuffled haphazardly, murmuring into cell phones. News of violent outbreaks across the country reached even them.

For Artie Stubbs, a small town welder from New Mexico, this was as close to heaven as he was ever going to get. He cleared his throat and spoke.

"It's coming down, I tell you. The shit's about to hit the fan."

Some in the room nodded. Others couldn't care less.

"We've got to be ready. We've got the guns and the manpower to do a number on all the bastards that have been giving us shit. When law and order falls, WE will be the law!" he said, raising his Colt .45 caliber automatic to emphasis the point.

Suddenly, a young, pale man rushed into the room. His needle marked arm dropped, still holding his phone clutched between thin fingers.

"The Feds! The Feds are on the way!" he shouted, wrestling attention away from Artie.

"Where? When?" someone snapped.

"It's some kind of convoy up on Eagle Mountain Pass. They're headed this way, probably about 40 minutes out. My buddy just called. He was on his way home early when they passed. They tried to stop him, but he took off on his cycle and outran them! Hell, they even took a couple of shots!"

This was his moment. Artie seized control. "Grab everything you need! Don't leave anything they can hang us with later. We've got to bust out of here, or ALL our asses will be locked up!"

A burley Vet with huge shoulders and a graying beard thundered, " If it's a fire fight they want, we'll give it to 'em."

A huge roar went up, but Artie Stubbs wasn't having any of it. If they wanted a firefight with federal officers, it wouldn't be his funeral. There would be other groups of idiots to lead. He raced out to the old Chevy van parked under some shade trees.

Sitting with his back against the rear tire whittling a stick, the other member of the traveling party froze. Moss Willis turned his stubbled face to see who approached. He was a dark, wiry loner who trusted nobody. Few knew, or cared to know, anything about him. He had the charm of a coiled rattlesnake. Moss chose to be alone, toying with the switchblade he handled so well, rather than sit in large groups.

"Fire up this piece of shit! The Feds are on the way," Artie screamed as he drew within earshot.

Moss Willis was a drifter, wandering from place to place, familiar with most of the jails in the Southwest. Artie had made him a personal project, giving him a place to stay. He was sure that he could control Moss with his intellect. In return, Moss gave Artie something he lacked: the ability to inflict fear.

Moss had known other men like Artie. He pegged his "buddy" to be a blowhard from the beginning, but he chose to bide his time and go along with the charade. His patience was wearing thin, though, from the verbal beatings he took from Artie. Moss knew the time for Artie's re-education, at his hands, was fast approaching. Moss Willis was a ticking time bomb.

For a filthy, stringy man, Moss moved with speed and grace when he was properly motivated.

"Feds, huh? What the hell do THEY want?" he grumbled as he grabbed camping gear on the fly and throwing it into the back of the van. Inside was an old, torn mattress covered in candy wrappers and beer cans.

"They want us in jail, you MORON! Better yet, DEAD!" Artie screeched as he stored the last of his gear by the passengers seat. "Now GET THIS THING STARTED!"

Moss didn't need to be told twice. He twisted the key and the engine roared to life. Stomping on the gas, the red and gray bondo-covered van lurched forward, tires spewing gravel as it careened down the one lane road through the woods.

Behind, chaos waited for those who couldn't, or wouldn't get out in time. For the two in the van, the same lay ahead.

CHAPTER 2

In the Century City, California hotel suite that had been his home for the past few months, Jim dashed around the dimly lit room gathering his clothes, papers and personal effects. The TV flickered with another national address by the president. It was his third in as many days. And with each speech came more rules for a panic-stricken populous.

"In an effort to preserve the rule of law, I have made the tough decisions which will best serve the interests of the citizens of this country. Large-scale troop movements have begun to fortify the military districts, which were authorized by me on a temporary basis. The troops are there to help and protect you. There is no need for panic."

The president continued, now requiring all citizens to register their firearms. "Any breech of the public safety will be dealt with in the most severe terms," he said. "The interstate transportation of food and other important supplies will take priority over ALL other commerce, which will be suspended for 10 days. A new currency will be put into effect, but until that time, all currency must be brought to federal buildings over the next 30 days to be exchanged for temporary script."

And as Jim closed and latched his suitcase, the president warned, "Personal travel should be limited and will be subject to security considerations."

"Sorry, Mr. President," Jim said. "Can't do that."

A calm was beginning to set in, just as it had in many other stressful situations throughout his career. The fact was, Jim could focus and react when things were bad.

He had been able to withdraw the balance of his checking account, so money was no longer a problem, assuming the green paper would still be honored. That remained to be seen. The "full faith and credit of the U.S. government" was not quite what it use to be.

As he turned toward the door, his cell phone rang. The green display showed it was a call from home. The soft, still-childlike voice of his 15-year-old daughter, Kelley, came on the line.

"Daddy, have you left yet?"

"I'm heading out the door right now, honey. It won't be long. A couple of days, and I'll be there. How've you been?"

"Scared. Billy says there is nothing to worry about, but I'm still frightened. He says he'll take care of us until you get back."

"Look. You and your mother just hang tight, and stay close to home. Things will be back to normal before you know it. And tell Billy he's only your boyfriend, not your savior."

Thankfully, this drew a small laugh and an "Oh, daddy" from his daughter, breaking the building tension.

"Put your mom on, OK?"

Kelley paused. Finally, she spoke, "She's gone down to Detroit with a bunch of her old college friends to organize a protest rally. She said she'd be late, and that if you called, to tell you to be careful, and that she loved you. She would have called you on her cell, but her service carrier has shut down."

Jim Barnes had a side to his nature only a few had ever seen. It was a white-hot temper not easily stirred. The news that his activist wife was treading in troubled waters, oblivious to the potential danger, set him off in a staccato burst of epithets.

"You tell your mother to keep her butt at home before she gets it shot off! This isn't college protests, or a NOW rally, for Christ's sake! There IS no first amendment protection. These are serious times, DEADLY serious, and I want her in one piece when I get there."

"She knew you'd be mad," Kelley replied. "Mom said it was something she had to do."

Jim felt blood rushing to his head. He wanted to yell, but the wrong woman in his life was on the line. He did what he could to check his anger.

"Kelley, tell her I said the fun and games are over, maybe for good. No more issues. No more marches. No more sit-ins. These people are serious. They don't give a damn about the rights we THINK we have. Their only interest is to keep everyone contained. Believe me, they don't care who they destroy. Will you talk to her?"

"Sure, dad. Look. Don't worry about us. We'll be all right. Just get home as soon as you can, OK?"

"I'll get there, honey, count on it. Believe me, if I could sell my car and fly, I'd do it. I've got my laptop with me, so I'll e-mail you guys every night." Then Jim added, "I love you both very much. Never forget that. Never."

He hung up the phone, took his car keys from the counter, and walked across the room. He stopped for a moment, struck by the thought of the words he had just spoken. They seemed so distant, so final. Darkness invaded his soul. He hoped he was wrong.

Standing at the door, about to begin one journey and end another, Jim glanced back over his shoulder and caught sight of the now-silent television. He shook his head, thinking back to the barrage of triviality emanating from the mass media, and its 24-hour news cycles.

"We're drowning in our own bullshit," he muttered.

****

Night was falling as a battered van and its two passengers careened south on narrow mountain roads. They were just outside Wellington, Utah, and headed for New Mexico. In the back, propped up on his elbows on a stained mattress, Artie Stubbs pressed the buttons of his GameBoy.

"Slow down, damn it!" Artie bellowed toward the front. "You're throwing my ass all over back here."

Moss had been waiting for his opportunity to break the bad news. "You probably didn't notice, but this piece of shit van just blew its engine. You got your wish, Artie. We're going to go slow – REAL slow – as in stop."

Artie fired the videogame against the side of the van. Little red buttons and broken glass flew in every direction. "You've gotta be kidding! We're in the middle of nowhere and you total the fuckin' engine? You stupid asshole!"

Moss turned, glaring at Artie. His patience was thinning. "You forgot one thing. We're broke, too."

The gray and red van coasted to a stop on the gravel shoulder of the road. Artie unlatched the back doors and stepped out. A quick gust of cold mountain air swirled up and caught him off guard. Reaching for his leather jacket, he put it on quickly and walked toward the front of the van. Suddenly, he was seized with a burst of anger, striking out with his left foot at the side of the crippled vehicle. Naturally, the metal refused to budge, snapping his ankle to one side. The pain shot up through his leg and he fell to the ground in a heap.

Moss came around from the front but abruptly froze in his tracks. Artie, curled up in pain on the gravel, leveled the barrel of his .45 automatic at Moss' chest.

"I ought to blow your ragged ass away, you stupid bastard!"

Moss Willis was many things, but he was not a complete fool. He lived his whole life around men like Artie, whose emotions could transcend logic in an angry instant. So he stared down at the fallen man and said absolutely nothing.

Seconds of silence seemed like an eternity. Then, as quickly as the confrontation began, it ended. The deadly look on Artie's face faded, and the gun dropped. Moss remained silent, promising himself that he would never be caught so helpless again. Not with Artie, anyway.

"I'm going to see if I can find some help," Moss said slowly.

Moss started down the dark road toward some faraway lights in the valley. As the damp chill of the air penetrated his clothing, the frustration began to burn in the pit of his stomach. At that moment, Moss made a simple promise to himself: Artie was a dead man. It was just a matter of when and where.

About a mile and a half away from the van, his pace quickened as he saw the source of the lights. It was an old, white-slated wood farmhouse, sitting back from the road. A dirt driveway wound its way to the house and an old green Buick station wagon rested like an obedient dog alongside.

Moss approached the house cautiously. It was the dead of night and he didn't want to be welcomed by a shotgun. Glancing around, he crept up on the old porch, the splintered boards groaning under his feet. Peering through the kitchen window, Moss could see an elderly man in a chair reading the paper. He had heard the boards creak, and looked to see who was there. Moss knocked lightly on the glass.

The man walked over slowly, and turned on the yellow porch light. He studied Moss for a moment then cautiously opened the door, leaving the steel latch chain in place.

"Something I can do for you, young man?" he asked in a deep, wary tone.

Moss had nowhere near Artie's flair for bullshit, but he did what he could to muster politeness.

"Yeah, ah, our van's broken down up the road. I need some help so we can get it to the nearest town," he said.

"Well, there's nothin' I can do for you at this hour. The missus is feelin' poorly, and I can't leave her. Up the road about two miles, there's a gas station. They'll help you."

With that, the old man began closing the door.

So much for politeness, thought Moss.

"Wait a minute, old man," Moss shouted, blocking the door with his foot. "How about letting me use your phone? I've walked a long damn way. I'm freezing my ass off out here. I don't want no trouble, I just —"

The farmer cut him off. "Don't 'old man' me, you miserable Mexican. I told you where you could get help. Now get off my property!"

He slammed the door the rest of the way, rattling the loose frame on its hinges.

Instantly, an explosion burst in the depths of Moss' soul. Without thought or care, he crashed a fist through the windowpane and closed his grip around the collar of the startled farmer. With one violent jerk, he yanked the man's head back through the opening. As the helpless old man stared up into the eerie yellow light, eyes wide with fright, Moss leaned close to his ear and hissed, "I ain't no Mexican."

Grabbing a fistful of gray, wispy hair, Moss slammed the old man's head down, impaling his neck on the razor-sharp pieces of glass stuck in the wood frame. Blood erupted from his throat, spilling red on the flaking white door. Moss crouched as the man's blood pooled at his boots, and he stared up into the wide, disbelieving eyes of a man dying.

In seconds, the old man's eyes glazed over and his feeble old body let out a gurgled sigh.

Total silence descended on the farmhouse. The anger inside him peaked, and he felt a strangely satisfying calm.

It didn't last long. From upstairs, Moss could hear the voice of a woman calling out. He knew he had to act quickly. The car, he thought. Find the keys to the car.

He reached inside, unlatched the chain, and pushed the door against the weight of its dead passenger. Frantically, he scanned the room for the car keys. Nothing. The sound of light footsteps upstairs drifted toward him. Don't come down, old lady. Don't come down.

He noticed a desk in the corner and raced over to it, pulling out drawers and scattering papers in his panic. Nothing.

A trembling voice called out, "Herb? Herb? What's going on? Are you all right?"

Damn. Where are those keys? Moss looked back at old man dangling like a side of beef on his front door. The pockets! Check his pockets, he thought. With two strides, he was alongside him, his bloody hand searching the corpse. Eureka! He touched some jagged metal deep in the man's pocket and withdrew a large key ring.

Just as Moss was about to escape, he caught sight of a shotgun barrel shaking violently, coming through the far kitchen door. His right hand instinctively found the switchblade in his rear pocket and snapped it open. Instantly, Moss hurled the knife toward the doorway just as the ashen, terrified face of an old woman came into view. With a sickening thud, the blade buried itself in her skull below her right eye. A surprised, bewildered expression came over her as she fell backwards, dead before she hit the floor. The impact jerked her finger, and the shotgun exploded, shredding the kitchen walls with pellets.

Moss was not hit, but froze in his tracks. He always knew murder was in his blood, but this? …

Struck with panic, he shook himself to gain control. Quickly, he moved to the woman, pulled his knife from her skull and retreated out the door into the night. The cold air was a welcome relief from the stifling heat in the farmhouse.

In seconds, he had the green Buick's engine roaring. Moss slammed it into gear and buried his foot to the floorboards. The bulky wagon surged forward, gravel spraying from its back tires.

Artie Stubbs was massaging his swollen ankle when the headlights of a car raced up the hill toward the crippled van and its equally crippled owner.

The car skidded to a stop. Moss emerged.

"Where the hell have –" Artie started. Moss' wild eyes and the drying blood on his hands and clothes told Artie he'd be wise to taper his comments.

Moss wasted no time. "Get your shit together," he ordered. "We're outta here!"

Against better judgment, Artie tried to regain control. "Wait a minute –"

He didn't get a chance to finish.

In one swift movement, Moss wheeled around and snatched Artie by the throat. He had the look of a maniac in his eye.

"This car is hot, REAL hot. There're two dead bodies down the road that say I ain't lyin'. Now MOVE!"

He pulled Artie to his feet, at the same time snatching the .45 from his waistband.

"OK, OK," screamed Artie.

"Good. Now get your shit into the car. Make sure there's nothing left that can ID us."

Artie did as he was told. His days leading violent men – or at least this one in particular – were over.

Once both men were inside, Moss spun the screaming car around on the gravel shoulder, and pointed it south for the New Mexican border. It was just the beginning of the longest night of their lives.

****

According to the road sign, Williams, Arizona was the next stop. Jim Barnes figured it was as good a place as any to get some food and gas. Pulling off Interstate 40, he soon came to a stop at the Grand Canyon Cafe just off the exit. It was time he tried out the green paper in his wallet.

Jim walked into the restaurant and surveyed the large room. Typically Western, with deer heads mounted on the wall and Indian trinkets cluttering the counters. Other than a couple of truckers watching their rigs as they plowed through greasy meals in the window booths, the joint was empty. Jim wandered over to the deserted counter and took a stool. He didn't plan to stay long; just enough for a quick bite before getting back on the road.

The middle-aged, obviously exhausted waitress approached. She managed a smile.

"What can I get you?" she asked. The pink shade of her lip-gloss matched her uniform.

"I'll have a cheeseburger, fries and coffee," Jim said.

Then, a new twist on the familiar scene.

"Hate to ask you, sugar. But how you planning to pay for it?"

"Cash, if it's still good," Jim replied.

She smiled, obviously relieved. "Yeah, it's good. Plastic is out, though. That's why we've got to know."

He thought back to his former boss' words. The world has just changed.

Across the room, the door to the men's room swung open and a lanky man around 45 years old stepped out. He wore a faded green army jacket and slung a blue denim knapsack over his shoulder. He adjusted the belt around his slim waist and deftly checked his fly, not really caring if anyone noticed. Then, with a hop on every other step, he bounded across the room, full of energy, heading straight for the counter.

Jim spotted him out of the corner of his eye and watched as he sat down two stools away. The blond stranger had a rugged face.

"G'day, love," he said, addressing the waitress as he straddled his seat. "How's about a drop of tea? Hot tea, that is. You bloody Yanks try to poison me every chance you get, but I'm on to you!"

His whole face lit up into an infectious grin that seemed to brighten the room.

The waitress spun around and looked at the stranger with the twinkle in his eye. Clearly taken with his devil-may-care smile, she tried to regain her balance by asking the same question she posed to Jim earlier, but was cut off.

"Let's see, love, right now Visa is no place you want to be. MasterCard used to be for everything else, but now it's for nothing at all. How about Australian Express? You know the one. Go 'head and leave home without it, 'cause it's bloody useless anyway!

Whad'da you say? No, I can see you've got a heart colder than a well digger's bum. Well, cash it is, then."

"If that's all you want, tea's on the house, sweetie," she answered, laughing.

"What? What's this? Kindness to a stranger in a distant land? I'll never forget you, er ... what's your name?"

"Julie," the waitress answered, now with blushing cheeks to match her uniform.

"Like I was saying, this is something I can tell me grand kids. Just my bloody luck. All my life, me mates kept saying, 'Go to America, and make your fortune. It's the land of milk and honey.' And what happens? I get here and you bloody bastards go belly up! Not a quid to the lot of you. Well, your kindness makes up for the whole bloomin mess, love, er. ...."

"Julie," she prompted again.

"Right. Too right. Maybe just a spot of milk and sugar, too, if it isn't too much trouble?"

Julie turned to get his tea and the Australian glanced over at Jim and winked.

"Bullshit, mate. Dazzle 'em with bullshit. They love it!"

Jim shook his head and laughed.

"Peter Sullivan's me name, mate," he continued, extending his hand. "Pleased to make your acquaintance."

"Jim Barnes," he said, taking Sullivan's firm grip.

"Tell me Jim, what brings you out on a night like this? I figured most of you Yanks would be home diggin' the gold fillings out of your teeth."

"Oh, I was out driving around lookin' for someone to shoot. This IS the Wild West, you know." It was Jim's turn to snicker after seeing Sullivan do a double take. "No, I'm on my way back east. Got a lot of miles to cover."

"You don't say, mate. You know, Jimmy, maybe this is fate that we should meet. Two ships passing in the bloody night, as they say. By the way, mate, I ain't a poofter. No worries there. But as it so happens, I'm off in the same direction, a place called Cortez, Colorado, to see a sheila I met in L.A. Trouble is, my bloody thumb isn't worth a fiddler's fart this time of night. Maybe I could hitch a ride with you? I'll even shout for some petrol."

Jim's eyes narrowed and he looked at the Australian closely. Dazzle 'em with bullshit, he thought. But the guy had a quality about him, an honest openness. And, it wasn't out of the way. Linda would kill me, he thought, but what the hell.

"Tell you what. Save your money. I'll take you as far as I can. By that time, I want to know all there is about the land Down Under. Maybe I'll chuck it all and move there. Deal?"

A wide grin spread over Sullivan's face. "Mate, you've got yourself a deal. Bloody hell, I'll fulfill my part of the bargain right now. Beer, beer, and more beer. And – " he paused for effect, "an occasional sheila, just for good measure. That's all there is, mate. That's the lot."

The two men laughed. Jim felt the tension in his neck release as the conversation continued. It was good to relax. Soon, they chatted like two old friends.

Neither man could have guessed that in a few short hours, their fates would be forever linked and the bond that remained would never be broken.

CHAPTER 3

Jim and his new Australian friend sped along the dark landscape. The northern Arizona stretch was deserted, interrupted only once by a short convoy of National Guard trucks. Not tempting fate, Jim slowed the car to a reasonable speed. He had better things to do than rear-end the U.S. military.

Once past the line of green trucks, the road was free and clear again. It was nearing midnight but Jim decided to continue on until the sun appeared again. Then they'd stop for a few hours rest.

The ride had been pleasant, marked by the easy banter of the hitchhiker. The Australian had proven to be witty, and he possessed a wealth of knowledge about many parts of the world Jim had only dreamed of visiting. Sullivan roamed freely most of his life, preferring to leave complication to others. His natural charm had served him well as he went "walkabout", an aboriginal reference meaning to wander until the feeling stopped. Jim Barnes had no doubt that his new "mate" would be on the road for many years to come.

Peter felt along the side of the seat for the release handle, wanting to make room for his long legs.

"Never could get use to riding on this side of the car," he said absently.

"That's right, you drive on the left down there."

"Yeah, inherited it from the pommie bastards."

Jim looked at him. "Who?"

"Pommies, the English... Brits. Descended on Australia like bloody locust when they found out how good the beer was. Been trying to get us to drink it warm ever since. Stands for "Prisoner of Mother England". Me great granddad was a convict. Come to think of it, me old man had a few brushes with the law. Must be genetic."

"And you?"

"Nah, just minor scrapes. Closest I came to the brig was in Vietnam. I had this sergeant, and he says to me one day, 'Peter, mate. Shag ass over to the Yank base, and pick up a new starter for this here tank.' So off I went. I used to like going to the Yank base. Craziest bunch of bastards I ever met. So I say to the supply man, 'I'm here to pick up a starter for our tank.' And he screws up his face, looks across the way where the bloody things are parked, and says, 'Take one of them over there. The whole bloomin thing! When you're done,' he says, 'dig a hole and bury it.' Well, good on ya, I thought, and off I go. I nearly shit meself laughing! A few months later, I heard some pipsqueak second lieutenant was looking for me. He could get stuffed for all I cared. I was headed home soon, anyway, so I kept me bloody head down for awhile."

"How long were you over there?" Jim asked.

Sullivan grew serious for the first time. "Too bloody long, mate, that's for sure. I won't soon volunteer for anything again, I can tell you." He seemed to drift off for a moment, and then looked over at Jim in the darkness. "So what's waiting for you at home, mate? You look like the domesticated type. A missus?"

"Yeah, I've got a wife Linda and a teenage daughter, Kelley. Haven't seen them in six months."

"And what are you going to do when you get back?"

"You know, Peter, I just don't know. I suppose there are a lot of guys just like me. You work your ass off all your life, trying to build a future, playing by the rules, and the next thing you know, a bunch of assholes screw up, and it's all gone. Maybe we'll pack it all up and go walkabout. Who knows?"

"Jimmy, me boy, the one thing that war taught me is never rely on anyone else, and you won't be disappointed. If they bugger things up, it's their problem. If you do it, well, that's life. Most of the bastards I've known through the years who THOUGHT they knew straight up didn't have a clue."

"Yeah, we've been getting dazzled with bullshit for years," Jim added.

Up ahead, the state line of New Mexico, marked by a large sign, could be seen in the car's lights. The turn off north to Cortez was a few more miles away, and Jim knew the time was short for making a decision concerning the Aussie. Actually, he had made it hours before. There was no way he could leave the guy off in the middle of nowhere at that time of night. Jim would go north, through Cortez, then on up to Denver, where he could catch the freeway east. It was a little out of the way, but it was the least he could do for a fellow traveler.

Sullivan had seen the Cortez signs, and knew he would be getting out soon, though not really relishing the thought. "Up ahead, there, mate, looks like that's me stop."

"Peter, this is your lucky day. I'll give you a lift up to your girlfriend's place. It'll cost you breakfast, though. Does she know how to cook?"

"Mate, if she doesn't, trust me, I'll teach her. I wasn't too keen on spending the night under the stars. And by the way, did I tell you I'll never forget you, err… ?"

"Julie."

"Yeah, that's right. Blimey, all you Yanks have easy names to remember! That's what I like about America, one big happy family!"

Tired as they both were, they could still manage a chuckle.

The car wove its way through the bends and curves of the two-lane highway that cut through the Navajo reservation. Occasionally, their headlights would pick up the staggering form of an Indian trying to find his way home in the dark, a little too much whiskey in his belly. But other than that, the wind, and the dark outline of hills and mesas in the moonlight were their only companions. They hadn't passed another car in miles.

Suddenly, up ahead, large pieces of metal could be seen strewn across the road. Scrap from a pickup truck, Jim thought. He swerved to miss the largest pile, and, feeling secure, resumed his speed, when a loud, crashing noise erupted from the front end. The two men looked at one another, waiting for something to happen. It wasn't long before their expectations were met. The car began to wobble uncontrollably to the right. At best, it was a flat tire. At worst, ...they did not want to think about it.... Jim hit the brakes, and pulled over into a wide, open area well off the road, gravel crunching beneath his tires.

Sullivan looked at Jim Barnes, and broke the silence. "Today's YOUR lucky day, mate. Why sitting right next to you is the finest mechanic Australia has to offer. Peter Sullivan, in the flesh. If I can't fix it, it can't be fixed. Specializing in wire and tape jobs. I'll have this Yank tank back on the road lickitty split."

For once, Jim hoped he wasn't being dazzled.

****

The green Buick wagon lumbered south, continuing its journey into New Mexico. Silence filled the air, each passenger lost in thought about the mayhem that occurred just hours before.

The atmosphere was morgue-like, dark and foreboding. Death had become the third member of the traveling party.

Moss Willis drove, keeping a watchful eye in all directions for any hint of trouble. He was mentally exhausted, taxing his intellect to the limit trying to devise a safe getaway. From the drama, exhilaration, and release of the kill, he found himself confused as to his ability to lead their escape. But no other option existed. For Artie to gain back control would be the end, and he was not prepared to die. Not without plenty of company, anyway.

The echoes of fear and hatred that Artie Stubbs preached returned with a vengeance to haunt him. He had surrounded himself with violent men, and events had reached their logical conclusion. Artie was unprepared. He sat slumped in the back seat, a prisoner of the actions of a man who had been his lackey hours before. Moss had finally snapped, and he was out of control. Artie wasn't sure he could regain the upper hand from the human detonator.

In the distance, about a quarter mile away, Moss could see the headlights of a car pulled over to the side of the road. He made a quick decision.

"All right," he said, "We're gonna dump this junk heap. They're probably lookin' for it anyway by now." He reached down into his waistband and pulled out the automatic.

"Here, take this back, and don't get any ideas. You cover me."

"All right, all right. You're in charge"

"That's better," Moss replied, "Now, we'll just see what's going on. If it looks good, we grab the car and haul ass. Just don't screw up."

Moss began to brake, and turned off the road to his left, coming to a stop directly in front of the disabled vehicle. He could see two men about to change a tire. As dust swirled around them from the momentum of the stopped car, Moss saw them stand, preparing to meet the late night arrivals.

Jim Barnes glanced over at Peter, and gave him a "wait and see" look. He felt uncomfortable that late at night, on a deserted stretch of highway just off the Navajo Reservation. But his first inclination was that they had stopped to help. Jim could see two shadowy figures in the old wagon. They opened the car doors and stepped out.

"Anything we can do?" shouted the driver, trying to be as casual as possible.

Jim sensed an imbalance between the words and intent of the dark man who approached, but he chose to stay cool. He had been wrong before.

Sullivan, on the other hand, watched the strangers and braced himself for the danger every instinct in his body screamed was near. The air was filled with the same smell of trouble he had known in war. The hair rose on the back of his neck, and his nerves tensed. His eyes fell on the other silent man as he slowly came around the car. At least his hands are empty, Peter thought.

"No, that's okay," Jim answered, "We've got it under control. Thanks for the offer, anyway."

A strange smile came over Moss's stubbly face. "Always willing to lend a hand," he said pleasantly.

In the next instant, Moss flashed open the knife, its shiny blade slashing toward Jim. The movement was so sudden, he had no time to react, and it sliced a small gash in his chin. Then just as quickly, Moss had his arm around the frozen man's shoulders, while the blood-tipped blade came up to his throat. Stunned, disbelieving, Jim Barnes could not move a muscle.

By the time the Australian reacted, lurching forward ready to attack, it was seconds too late. He pulled up, knowing that Jim's life hung in the balance.

"Easy now, easy," Moss growled at Peter, as their eyes locked on to each other. "Back off, asshole. One move, just one, and I'll cut his friggin head off."

Sullivan did not say a word. He was beaten, for the moment.

Moss looked over at his partner. "Get over there and tie his hands. Use his shoelace. NOW!" Artie did what he was told.

Peter's mind raced like a computer. His first thought was to grab the little guy, before he could tie him up. But the odds were that he was a throwaway, and Jim would die, anyway. He would wait, and bide his time.

"Now," Moss continued to Artie, "put your gun on him. If this guy tries to pull anything, blow his brains out." There was no question in Moss's mind, after watching the deadly look in the Australian's eye; he was the one to worry about. He had killed before, Moss knew. "Now," he whispered in Jim's ear as he lowered the knife, "fix the goddamn tire."

As Jim Barnes stooped over to work, the only sound he could hear was his own heavy breathing. Hyperventilating? His mind careened from one thought to another. Death, his family, the pain from his chin. What the hell was happening?

Control. He was losing control, slowly falling over the edge into panic. Stop! He screamed to himself. Hold on! His hands, seconds before quivering, became still. Something deep, almost primal, began to rise. Think! He ordered himself. Think!

Moss looked at Artie and broke the still air. "I've got an idea. If we leave the car here, the cops will think we went south. Instead, we'll head back north and cut over to Farmington. That'll screw 'em up."

Artie looked back, but did not answer. He kept the automatic pointed at Sullivan, but was seriously considering unloading it into Moss, ending the problem. Trouble was, he had never killed before, but only talked about it. The time of truth was at hand. He had no idea what to do.

As Jim was finishing the tire, the pungent smell of gasoline drifted up from beneath the car. He looked closer, and could see a drip in the dirt.

Moss smelled it too, and bent down. "What the hell is that?"

"Gas," Jim replied with a steady voice, "probably a fuel line leak. It's coming out pretty fast."

"Son of a bitch!" Moss shouted. "Okay, let me think." The car was useless, no doubt about it. He didn't want to leave it abandoned. It might draw attention. He had an idea. Looking around, he could see the land drop off abruptly about a hundred feet from the road. A cliff.

"Get your ass in the car, NOW!" he screamed at Jim. Moss looked over at Artie. "We're going to dump the car. If he tries anything, kill him." With that, he jumped in the passenger seat, and put the blade into Jim's ribs. "Drive slowly. Over there." He nodded his head in the direction of the drop off.

Jim started the car, and it began rolling toward the edge.

From his experience in combat, Sullivan knew what kind of man could kill, and who could not. Many times, his life had depended upon it. As he watched Artie Stubbs, he guessed that he was not a man who could cross that threshold. He was the weak link, Peter thought.

"You know that bloke is going to get your bloody ass killed, sooner or later," he began quietly, watching Artie closely. "He's a psycho, mate, no doubt about it."

Artie Stubbs looked around nervously. He watched the highway, scanning the distance for an approaching car. Fidgeting back and forth on his cold feet, the pain in his ankle getting worse, he turned back to Peter. "Well, I've got a surprise for him."

Sullivan seized the opportunity, "The bastard's got the brain of a gnat. Bloody useless. I'd be thinking about ending that bloke's misery and getting the hell out of here if I were you."

Artie looked at him but did not reply.

The wheels in Artie's mind began to turn just as a loud crashing sound rose up in the distance. A burst of light shot up from the cliff, illuminating the still figures of two men standing at the edge. As the darkness descended again, Artie could hear footsteps approaching from the desert.

Jim walked a few paces ahead of Moss. In his mind, the time was near to make a move.

"We're gonna take my friend along as a little insurance for a while," Moss said to Artie. Then he nodded toward Sullivan, "Get rid of him, over there."

The air instantly became electric. Up to that point, there was a chance they would be left alone, slim at best, but a chance. That bubble burst. All cards were on the table, face up.

Adrenalin gripped Jim, and he whirled around on Moss, his right fist slicing through the air. It connected with the startled man's face just below the right eye. The force of the blow was magnified by the rage Jim felt. Flesh, blood, and the sound of bone cracking ripped the quiet, and Moss went down in a heap, crumbling to the dust.

The speed of the attack, and the intensity, froze Sullivan and his captor. He looked at Artie, who was transfixed, watching the scene. With his hands tied, the Aussie was helpless, and Peter did not want to do anything to Artie to set him off. So he watched, his nerves tingling. The Yank, he knew, was fighting for both their lives.

Artie was confused and frightened, caught completely off guard. He stepped back, watching, waiting for something to happen. His gun remained leveled at the Australian, but his attention was on the ground.

Moss Willis had been down many times before in fights, and he was far from out. Staggering, he was still able to deflect Jim's clenched fist as it shot toward him a second time. With one steady motion, Moss rolled to his knees, brought both hands together and smashed them down on the raging man's back. Jim crashed face first into the dirt. Quickly, Jim spun back around and buried his fist in the dark man's stomach. A rush of air escaped Moss's lungs, and he fell forward. The moment had come to end it, to kill if necessary, Jim knew. Dust filled his eyes, as he looked down on the object of his fury, and prepared to finish him. But he hesitated, unable to draw from experience the will to inflict death. Those seconds were all Moss Willis needed.

With the intensity of a crazed animal, Moss lashed out with his foot, and drove it into Jim's midsection. He fell back hard, his head smashing against some rocks. Stunned and bleeding, he lay sprawled on the ground, near collapse. The star filled sky hung above him, broken only by a dark shadow at his feet. Moss Willis brought the large boulder he carried up above his head, ready to deliver the lethal blow. Jim summoned every ounce of strength left in his body to roll to his left as the rock hit the ground where his head rested seconds before. Then, his right hand gripped a small log in the darkness, and brought it slashing back at Moss Willis, striking with a loud thud just above his groin. The crippled man dropped to his knees, eyes bulging, staring at everything and nothing. Slowly, he twisted, and crumbled down.

It was left to Jim to end the fight for good. There would be no hesitation. Once again the splintered wood rose up, as Jim summoned the force to drive it down on the semi-conscious, groaning figure before him.

Then, as quickly as the melee erupted, it ended with Artie cracking the handle of his automatic against the back of Jim's skull. His eyes rolled up, fluttering, and silence closed in. Artie Stubbs had made his choice, for better or for worse.

Seconds passed in desperate quiet for all four men. Moss Willis, dirt and blood clinging to his ragged clothes, was the first to get up. He looked down at Jim, knowing it was Artie who had saved him. His first thought was to kill the sprawled man, but that would wait, he told himself. Turning back toward Stubbs, his voice raspy, he growled, "Now go do what I told you."

Artie glared back at him. For an instant, the barrel of the gun began to turn toward Willis, and then stopped. He had made a mistake, he knew, but would right it at the proper time. Turning his attention back to the Australian, his hand came forward, locking on Sullivan's jacket, and they both stumbled ahead into the brush.

Thinking fast was nothing new to Peter Sullivan, but he was quickly running out of options. Buy time, he kept telling himself, buy time.

"You don't want to do this, mate," came the controlled voice of a man close to death. "You're digging your own grave. Do us all a favor and put a bullet in that crazy bastard. You go your way, we'll go ours. Blimey, no one will know, and bloody few will care."

Artie knew the stranger spoke sense, but some unseen hand kept driving him forward. Events were beyond his control. He was playing out a part in a drama, which could only end in tragedy.

As they approached the edge of the cliff, Sullivan made a last desperate attempt at escape. He stepped back quickly, then drove forward with his shoulder, trying to knock Artie over ahead of him. In the darkness, he misjudged the distance, and only grazed his captor. Stumbling, he crashed to the ground and rolled down over the rocky embankment, coming to rest on a small ledge. Grimacing with pain, and dazed by the fall, his eyes moved, searching the moonlight. Into the stillness above him, a dozen yards away, a hand stretched out, still gripping the cocked automatic. By the open door of the station wagon, Moss struggled to load Jim's limp body in the back seat. As he gripped Jim's legs, and swung them into the car, he heard the unmistakable report of Artie's .45 echoes across the desert. A sullen smile crossed his lips. "Mr. Big Man" had balls after all, he thought.

Artie was in full flight as he covered the distance back to the waiting car. He pulled up next to Moss, with a wild, panicked look in his eye, and said simply, "It's done."

Willis grunted, "Good. Get in the back with this one, and keep your gun on him. If he tries anything, kill him." With that, he ran around to the driver's side and jumped in.

As the car engine revved to life, he spun back out onto the pavement, heading north. If his plan was to work, they had to put many miles behind them that night. Moss's heart pounded rapidly in his chest, and the flush of excitement brought his tired body to life. He was beginning to like the danger he created.

CHAPTER 4

Colonel Jennings Colton, back in the command office outside Albuquerque, shifted uncomfortably in his chair. It was midnight. His body's normal timetable had been thrown off in recent days with the late-night meetings. Long hours were nothing new, but this was a different kind of stress. His orders were coming straight from the president.

Everything boiled down to this: preserve law and order at any cost.

In sector 47 – Colton's watch – which consisted of New Mexico and parts of west Texas, reports of sporadic uprisings were making their way to his desk. With each new case, the colonel grew more determined to deal with them severely and decisively. A bunch of pissed-off hicks aren't about to blemish my record, he thought. The legal system, in his opinion, had become a morass. Cases lumbered through the courts, bogged down in delays, compromises and Constitutional rights. Sector 47 was about to meet the hammer of justice. A wry smile crossed the colonel's face as he thought of the legions of lawyers in the justice system. Their livelihood had depended on the skillful use of language and interpretation. Words came cheap. If the colonel had his wish, their place in the unemployment line would be secure for years to come.

Jennings Colton's staff had directed all law enforcement agencies under his command to coordinate their communications through his office. All decisions, both major and minor, concerning the implementation of policy and enforcement, were to be made through his office. Secure lines for teleconferencing with those agencies were now in place. Fast, clear and decisive action would be directed from his office to squelch any unrest. The turf wars of the past among various police departments were gone. The wagons of authority were circled.

From the instant Operation Patriot went active, his office was a beehive of activity. All stations were manned around the clock. Declaring martial law was only phase I of Patriot, too. As the country fell into full military control, phase II called for imbedding computer chips into all citizens for tracking purposes.

They think things are rough now, Colton thought to himself.

A young sergeant knocked tentatively on his door, interrupting the colonel's thoughts.

"What is it, Anderson?" he barked.

"This fax just came in from Sector 43 in Colorado. I thought you might want to be informed." He handed a piece of paper to the colonel.

Colton's eyes narrowed and his jaw set as he scanned the report. He spoke out loud, but to himself. "Murdered. Found by their grand children. Son of a bitch."

The report advised to be on the lookout for a green Buick station wagon stolen from the old couple's home. The assailant, or assailants, was presumed armed and dangerous.

"I assume you've notified everyone?" Colton asked.

"Well, no, sir, not yet," the sergeant stammered, "We were waiting –"

Jennings Colton cut him off. "Listen, Anderson. Pull your head out of your ass. I'm not going to do all the thinking for this office. If you guys can't cut it, you're out. Understand? Now, I want whoever did this caught. I'll personally string him up by the balls as an example to anyone else defying my...for defying the law. Now, MOVE!"

The young man spun on his heels and walked briskly toward the door.

"One more thing, Anderson. I want to be notified when we have whoever did this in custody. I'll take charge of this one. Should provide a good photo op. Get with Simmons in the press room on that."

"Yes, sir."

"No screw ups, sergeant. This is the kind of high profile thing that could set the tone. Before I'm through, everyone will understand the meaning of the words 'swift justice.'"

The sergeant left, and Jennings Colton resumed reading. His thoughts drifted, though, from the words before him to the dead grandparents in the report. Animals, he thought, we've become a nation of wild animals. The most powerful country in the world was slowly, irrevocably being reduced to its lowest common denominator. Well, he promised, I can play that game too. Only the animals have no idea of the toys we have devised to deal with them.

****

The lumbering station wagon wound its way east along dark stretches of road. Having made it through Farmington, the largest city in the area, the men inside breathed a little easier. At that late hour in this sparsely populated area of northern New Mexico, there was little chance of a confrontation with the law.

Jim Barnes sat upright in the backseat, groggy from the blow to head. Still very aware of the danger around him, he was in no shape to do anything about it. For now, he could only wait, watch and listen carefully. And, above everything, try to stay alive.

That thought nearly made him chuckle. Stay alive? Hours ago he was laughing with a new friend. Now two brutal maniacs held his life in their hands. Suddenly, it wasn't so funny. A hatred bubbled in him again. It was the same rage that helped him beat the man driving the car.

Jim's emotions ebbed and flowed. One second it was self-pity. The next, a fiery anger. Panic was always lurking close, too, threatening to overtake him. They can't do this to me, his mind repeated over and over. This can't happen. My wife, and daughter. ... His body twitched involuntarily, shaken by the chill of his own mortality.

This was not part of the equation. His was a life full of warmth and comfort and security, never straying far from the upwardly mobile profile of his generation. Jim recognized the irony. Those very things – the things he'd strived to achieve – were responsible for dulling his instinct to survive.

That lull has passed, he thought, and he was well into the storm. The time was near to draw on all the tools his human soul possessed. At that moment, he made a silent vow to prevail, whatever the consequences. If it meant killing to survive, then he would kill. All the rules he had built his life around meant nothing. They weren't playing by those rules. Jim Barnes was down to basics.

Artie was quiet, lost in his own thoughts. In the rear view mirror, Jim could see the eyes of Moss Willis, studying his face. The two men glared at each other, an animal hatred surfacing that neither man chose to hide.

"Welcome back," Moss began sarcastically, "the nightmare continues." As no retort came from the back seat, he continued, "Just remember you're alive as long as I say so. Screw up once and you're dead. Artie there will blow a hole in you just like your limey friend, right Artie?"

Stubbs looked over at Jim. "Yeah, anything you say. Just get us out of this mess."

Jim decided to try a little reasoning. "Look, why don't you do us all a favor and let me out? I don't know who you are, or what you've done, and I'd like to keep it that way."

"Not a chance," he answered coldly. "If we run into the cops further up, you're our ticket out. Besides, I've got a score to settle." Just then, the red fuel indicator lit up on the dashboard. Moss glanced at it, and muttered, "Shit. Okay, we've got to find some gas."

"At 1:30 in the Goddamned morning? You can't be serious." Artie said.

"As a heart attack, man. Just keep your eyes open. Check and see how much money our friend has. He's buyin'."

Stubbs motioned for Jim to surrender his wallet.

Pawing through it, Artie clearly was unimpressed. "What the hell? Only 25 bucks?"

Jim remembered when he put most of his money in his luggage, except for a 20 in his shoe, and 50 in his wallet.

"I thought all you exec-types always carried a wad of cash to impress us peons," Moss sneered.

"No," Jim replied coldly, speaking before thinking, "that's credit cards. Something you wouldn't know anything about."

"Well," Moss continued, ignoring the remark, "that ain't gonna do shit for us. We've got to get some cash."

The car fell silent again. Miles passed. The dark countryside, with its pine trees, hills, and stretches of pasture, seemed a blur. Eventually, the lights of the car lit on a crudely built wood sign that read, "Groceries and Gas." Drawing near, they could see the store, set back off the road, obviously closed. But Moss slowed down, turning onto the gravel drive. He came to a stop in front of two old pumps.

Candy Rosario, the owner of the business, rolled onto his back in the bed he shared with his wife, his eyes straining to open. That Goddamned dog, he thought to himself. If he doesn't shut up, by Jesus, I'm gonna shoot him in the morning.

He was nursing the start of a hangover from a night of poker with his friends. The Rosarios had lived in the small adobe house behind the store for many years, and once a week, the cards came out, the whiskey flowed and the laughs roared. Candy had only been in bed for what seemed like minutes when the commotion outside rousted him. At that moment, he would have given all he owned for the comfort of his pillow, but it was not to be.

The barking continued unabated and Candy knew something had to be done.

"Ricky," he called out to the eldest of his six children, "Get up and check out the store. I can't take that yapping no more."

Ricky Rosario was already awake. He shrugged, fully aware that Pop was in no shape to be wandering around in the dark. He jumped down from the warmth of his bunk bed and threw on his clothes. He was a gangly young man of 18, still somewhat naive, and he didn't give a thought to taking his father's pistol with him as he opened the rickety screen door and stepped outside. With a few long strides, he was around the side of the building and staring out through the darkness at the gas island. There, he could see Moss Willis shaking the pump handle.

"Hey, Mister," Ricky shouted across the drive, "the place is closed, locked up for the night. Come back tomorrow."

"No, wait a minute," Moss yelled back, trying to think of something, stalling, "Kid, we've got an emergency. There's a guy here in the car. He's hurt real bad. I've got to get him to a doctor. We're out of gas. Here, see for yourself."

Ricky Rosario's mind was telling him to stay away, but he had a good heart. If someone were in trouble, he would have to do the right thing.

"OK, hang on a second. I'll be right out."

As he walked the few paces to the door, Ricky removed the key ring from his jeans, still in his pocket from locking up the business earlier. Once inside, his hand searched the coarse wood of a familiar wall until he found the light switch and a control module to deactivate the silent alarm. Even in small town America, alarms were a booming business. Not far from the door was the plywood counter and cash register. Below that, on the shelf, was a cigar box containing the pump key and a loaded .38 caliber revolver. As he reached into the box for the key, his eyes settled on the gun. Hesitating, he thought for a moment about taking it with him, but then dismissed the idea. He turned to go back out the door, and was met with the twisted, pained face of Moss Willis glowering back at him.

Ricky jumped back. He hadn't heard the stranger approach. Then, the youth tried to regain his composure. "You all right, mister? Geez, you scared the shit out of me."

"No I ain't all right, kid," Moss growled back, "I twisted my damned ankle in that mine field you call a parking lot."

Ricky eyed the dark man carefully. He was a mess. His clothes were blotched with dirt mixed with what looked like dried blood. His jacket was ripped, and one pocket was torn out completely. Something terrible had happened that night.

"OK, the pump is on," he said to Moss, "Go ahead and get what you need, and we'll settle up when you're done."

Moss grunted and limped back to the car. It wasn't long before he had the pump running and the gallons pouring in. Moss canvassed the dimly lit area as he filled the tank. This place is in the middle of nowhere, he thought. It's going to be a laugher.

Jims Barnes used the time to gather his thoughts. Somehow he had to alert that kid that he needed help. But with Artie's gun pointed at his chest, cocked and ready to fire, there was no chance. He would have to wait, and brace for the trouble that was sure to follow.

Moss covered the distance back to the store with a slight limp. Years of anger seeped out with every step. Once inside, he walked up to within inches of the teenager at the counter.

"You know, kid," he began slowly, looking directly into his eyes, "I've been thinking. I ain't got my lawyer with me so we'll have to settle out of court for the ankle. Give me all the money in the till." With those words, the switchblade in his pocket came out, and snapped open, its tip pointing to the ceiling.

Ricky Rosario's eyes grew wide. His muscles tensed. He couldn't move. He could only stare at the angry stranger. Then, over in the corner by the milk coolers, a low growl could be heard. The head of a large black German shepherd peered around the corner of an aisle, its upper lip twitching, displaying gleaming white fangs. The beast was trained to sense danger and respond. The animal's glassy brown eyes bore in on the man threatening his master.

It was Moss Willis' turn to be surprised. He quickly twisted his head to meet the challenge and a cold panic embraced him. Moss hadn't seen the dog. It was a major error.

The moment gave Ricky his chance. His right hand went down under the counter and into the open cigar box. His fingers circled the familiar gun handle. The youth brought the weapon up and turned to meet his attacker. As he did, he caught a gleam of shiny steel slashing toward him. The backhanded motion passed with a rush of air, and then everything went deathly quiet. His eyes turned slowly downward and he watched with disbelief the huge gash in his throat pouring out his blood.

His once cheerful eyes clouded over, the youthful face turning pale, and he fell to the floor.

Everything happened so quickly, with raw reflex, that Moss Willis hadn't seen the German shepherd make its move to attack. But suddenly, he was pinned under the weight of a furious, growling animal, ripping and tearing at his body, trying to do to him what he had just done to the boy. Shocked, Moss fought back. Flailing with his arms, he tried to keep the deadly fangs away from his throat.

Finally, as the dog's teeth began to take their toll, he rallied all the strength left in his arms, and swung the blade in a wide arcing circle, embedding it up to the hilt in the dog's fur above the shoulder. The dog yelped as the blade sunk into its heart. The deathblow seemed to have no effect for seconds and the dog continued to rip and claw. Finally, he slowed his assault. It was as though the dog grew tired. Staring down at the murderer he had tried to kill, the shepherd rolled to his right and collapsed.

Everything was still except for the pounding of Moss Willis' heart. Mauled and bleeding, he scrambled to his feet and let out a scream. His mind was in chaos and all he could think to do was run. He dashed out the door into the fall air, his legs churning for the car door. Over his shoulder, he could hear a voice screaming, "Ricky? Ricky? What's going on?"

Candy Rosario was running, too, around the corner of the country store, balancing a rifle in his hand. He crashed into the entrance of his store and seconds later let out a cry of anguish that filled the countryside.

Outside, Moss grabbed the driver's door, threw it open, and landed safely inside. He twisted the keys in the ignition. The engine screamed, and he slammed the gearshift into drive. As the car screeched forward, a single rifle shot rang out, and the window beside Moss Willis' head exploded into a million fragments, the bullet passing just behind his bloodied scalp.

Jim Barnes turned to his left, paralyzed with fear, and saw smoke rising slowly from the gun barrel. Behind the leveled rifle glared the crazed eyes of a father who had just found his murdered son.

As the car roared away, Candy Rosario dropped the weapon and cried out helplessly. Then, amid his anger and frustration, he stopped. Scrambling back into the store, he picked up the phone receiver just above where his boy lay bleeding on the wooden floor. Twenty-nine miles to the east was the small Hispanic-populated town of Tierra Amarilla. Candy knew that a car traveling in that direction had to go through it. There was simply no other place to turn off.

He would see to it that his brothers and cousins would be waiting for the murderers when they arrived. In that part of the West, men settled their problems the old fashioned way, without troubling the law.

****

The bank of video monitors at the Army Command Headquarters was alive with scenes from around the military district, taken from satellite feeds from space. The desk watch, half asleep from the late hour and inactivity, jumped at the sound of one particular monitor that showed an agitated soldier describing trouble.

"Command Headquarters. Corporal Goode speaking," he said, switching to two-way communications.

"Let me talk to Anderson, quick. We've got trouble in Section 23 Northwest," came the unidentified voice. The video had come in on one of the army's secure lines, so the corporal assumed it was one of the many patrols out cruising that night.

"Hang on a second, I'll get him," Goode answered. He decided to walk the short distance to Sergeant Anderson's office instead of buzzing him.

He rapped lightly on the glass of the opened door. Sgt Jeremy Anderson shifted his attention from the forms he was filling out to the corporal.

"Yeah, Goode. What can I do for you?" he asked absently.

"There's a video relay for you. Sounds like trouble."

Without hesitating, the sergeant raced to the other room. "Anderson here."

"This is Kowalski in Section 23 Northwest. We've picked up something on the CB channel that I think you should know about. Somebody's been killed. The locals are in an uproar. I couldn't make out all the details because of static, but from what I heard, the description of the getaway car sounds a lot like the one you put out earlier. They're heading east toward Tierra Amarilla. Sounds like they're going to have a helluva welcoming committee waiting for them."

"What's your ETA?" Anderson snapped, quickly becoming alert.

"About 25 minutes, give or take. I'm to the south."

Anderson thought for a moment. "Listen carefully. You're the closest unit around. Get your ass up there and try to head off the problem before it starts. Who's your partner?"

"Pierce," came the answer. "But he's home, sick. I'm riding solo tonight."

"Shit. Watch yourself. These guys have already killed an old couple and God knows whom else. They won't hesitate."

Kowalski chuckled. "Sergeant, I grew up in south Philly. I use to go through punks like these cowboys on the WAY to the fight. Just get me some back up as soon as you can."

"We'll get a bird up to you right away. Kowalski, Colonel Colton wants to make an example out of these guys in the worst way. Get them anyway you can, dead or alive, but don't let them get away. Understood?"

"No problem, Sergeant. Just as long as you know they probably won't be breathing." With that, the screen returned to normal surveillance monitoring.

Anderson jumped to his feet and started down the hall toward Colonel Colton's office. He peered around the corner and saw the man stretched out on his couch, fast asleep. Better leave him that way, he thought to himself. By the time he wakes up, I'll have this all wrapped up.

Anderson retreated back to the main office area. "Get me a chopper up to 23 Northwest with a couple of grunts. Tierra Amarilla. We've got ourselves an old-fashioned shootout and I don't want to miss it. Move! Move!"

The room burst into activity. Green jacketed personnel scurried in all directions. They were trained for trouble. It was time to put what they learned to work. The measure of their competence would be tested in the early morning hours.

****

Injured, exhausted, and bleeding, Moss Willis drove erratically down the asphalt road. Twice he nearly lost control of the careening metal. The passengers in back knew they were in big trouble, heading for an unknown end.

An eerie silence filled the car. Only an occasional thud of a bug splattering against the windshield broke the quiet. Moss Willis' right arm was hamburger. Pieces of torn tissue and blood trickled through the ripped clothing. His ankle was beginning to swell, too, and he was falling into the frenzy of a cornered animal. He was no longer scheming, but only reacting. Putting distance between him and the dead boy was Moss' only concern.

Artie Stubbs spoke first. "We've got to get rid of this car. The whole state's gonna be looking for us."

"NO, GODDAMMIT!" Moss screamed, "We're gonna keep going. We've got gas and we're gonna run until it quits."

"Listen, you moron," Artie shouted back, the panic rising in his voice. "We might as well put neon lights on this piece of shit! I can't take anymore! You've screwed up everything so far! I want OUT! You hear me? First chance, or I swear to God I'll finish you right now."

Artie raised the barrel of the automatic to the back of Moss' head. His grip tightened around the plastic handle and his finger began to squeeze the trigger.

"No, man," Jim whispered forcefully. "It's suicide at this speed. Wait until he slows down!"

Artie looked over at the man sitting next to him. He was another screw up that had to be corrected. But, he also recognized the truth in his warning. Artie would wait. There was another town coming up soon, Tierra something or other, and he would finish it there.

Strangely relieved, Jim watched as Artie turned the gun back toward him.

Minutes passed. The curves and bends in the road began to straighten out as state route 64 turned south. The forest, which had been so close to the blacktop, receded back signaling the outskirts of a town. Lights up ahead confirmed it.

Moss Willis' foot lifted slightly from the gas pedal, slowing the vehicle as it approached the final curve. The tired old car seemed to welcome the relief, as it shuddered to lesser speeds. In the back seat, Artie Stubbs began to steel himself for the task ahead. The gun shook visibly as he changed his aim again toward the driver's seat. Jim, taking in every move, braced himself for an inevitable explosion.

Rounding the turn, the car's headlights picked up an odd assortment of objects in the distance. It looked like a makeshift roadblock lining both sides of the highway. But there were no flashing lights or warnings to stop, only what appeared to be farm wagons and pickup trucks.

The station wagon rolled on, slowing as it went, and the three riders looked out at the unusual sight. As they drew to within 50 yards of the blockade, more than a dozen men rose up from behind the cover, each armed with a rifle or shotgun. The long line of cold gray steel leveled down on the rumbling car.

"Holy shit," Moss whispered.

The three men in the car ducked.

Suddenly, a shotgun blast exploded the front windshield. Glass shattered, flying like confetti.

Then, all hell broke loose.

Bullets ricocheted everywhere with the ting-ting sound of metal piercing metal. Light from the flaming gun barrels looked like a strobe, flashing in the darkness.

Moss rose up slightly and jammed his foot down on the accelerator. Another shotgun blast ripped through the driver's door, and tore into his flesh. Lead filled the interior of the car like fireflies, bouncing in all directions. Another bullet grazed his head, stunning him. The car weaved back and forth, before finally swerving off to the right of the roadblock.

Shots rang out from behind. There was no let up, no quarter given. The two terrified men in the back hugged the floorboards, praying for their lives. It was all-out war and the men firing weren't interested in taking any prisoners.

The wagon rolled down the road, but Jim didn't know whether Moss still had control of the car. For all he knew, a dead man could be at the wheel.

Bullets riddled the car from behind. The hits were fewer, though, as it coasted about 100 yards down the street.

Then a shot hit the bull's eye. Flames burst near the gas tank. Their only means of escape had turned into a bomb. The stench of smoke, gunpowder and death filled the crisp air. Moss mustered all his strength sitting upright, hoping for a chance to run. A single rifle shot whistled though the opening where the rear window had been, and exploded in his upper right chest. Bone cracked, flesh flew, spraying the dash with deep red as the wagon coasted to a stop.

It veered to the right, bumped a curb and halted beside an old hardware store. The smiling face of the True Value hardware man peered down.

The right side of the flaming car was hidden from the men running toward them, still firing. Artie Stubbs, his hands cut by broken glass, and his leg bleeding from shotgun pellets, reached up for the door handle and jerked it. The metal door didn't budge. Suddenly, Jim Barnes' leg crashed past Artie's hand, slamming into the reluctant steel. It fell open with a thud.

The two terrified men scrambled over each other trying to escape. They fell to the ground outside, a tangle of arms and legs. Spinning and slipping, they clawed their way in a low crouch and set off for a nearby field behind the building. Their eyes searched frantically for cover. Anything to escape the slaughter.

Moss Willis, too, had struggled free of the wagon. Stumbling into the street, he turned in a last, defiant gesture to face his attackers. Another shotgun blast roared out, shredding his chest. Rifle and pistol bullets riddled his nearly lifeless body, their force making it move in a weird, ghoulish dance. Then everything stopped. Except for the crackling of the fire beside him, there was no sound. He looked up with a perplexed expression on his face and then slowly crumbled. Moss Willis would never kill again.

Artie and Jim streaked for the safety of the woods nearby, staying low. Artie was in the lead, still clutching the .45 automatic.

Then, without warning, a single shot rang out from the nearby trees. It struck Artie squarely in the chest, ripping pieces of his heart and lungs out through the crater that was his back.

Jim stopped, horrified. He dropped down beside the lifeless body and tried to breath. He couldn't. He tried to think, and that, too, failed. Death was fast approaching. There was no way out. His ears picked up the sound of footsteps coming toward. He looked up in time to see a man in a green Army jacket level his .357 Magnum revolver at his head.

Corporal Kowalski was taking no prisoners and he wasn't about to try to stop a dozen men from their frontier justice.

Behind, in the mayhem, the old Buick finally let go in a roaring blast that lit up the night. Kowalski turned to see the surreal scene of men scattering in all directions, flames shooting up to the night sky.

Inside Jim Barnes, something snapped. A primal rage filled the soul of the innocent victim of fate. His last hope for life rested on crossing an unimaginable threshold. He grabbed the .45 automatic from the dead fingers of Artie Stubbs, twisting the barrel up in the direction of the man who wanted him dead. At the same time, his finger squeezed the blue metal trigger and an ear splitting report filled the air.

Corporal Kowalski turned just as he was hit full in the stomach, his feet rising off the ground, a lifeless form tumbling back into oblivion.

Once again, quiet descended. Jim could only stare blankly at the spot where the soldier had stood seconds before.

Then, suddenly, a whining, screeching high-speed motorcycle, raced across the field behind him, closing the distance fast. It swayed and bounced violently, crossing the ruts and mud puddles. The machine roared up to the startled man holding the gun and came to a sliding halt alongside Jim's leg.

The haggard face of Peter Sullivan, dirt surrounding his eyes, looked down.

"Get on, mate," was all he said.

In a trance, Jim swung his leg over the leather seat, wrapping his arms around the man in front. Sullivan revved the engine and released the clutch. Dirt and gravel sprayed

back from the rear tire, as the two weary
victims raced off into the night.

CHAPTER 5

Jim Barnes tried focusing out of the dust-covered window of the hunting cabin they had come upon hours before. The early morning sunlight struggled to penetrate the majestic pines surrounding the small, stone house. It sat at the base of large, rolling hills. A few hundred yards away, a magnificent green valley stretched out like a lush, green carpet. Just days ago, Jim Barnes would have considered it a vacation home. But now, it was simply shelter and days ago was another lifetime.

With his back propped up against the stone-and-mortar wall, legs brought up beneath his chin, Jim turned his attention to the sparse, one-room cabin. Three feet away, Peter Sullivan stretched out on a crude wooden cot and mattress, similar to the one that had given him a few fitful hours of sleep. The fact that the Australian managed sleep spoke volumes about his past. Without him, I'd be dead, Jim thought.

Jim's eyes drifted back out the window, gazing at nothing and everything at once. Every muscle in his body ached. He was in the middle of nowhere, but he was lost emotionally more than physically. He tried to calculate the hours since he'd last spoken to his wife. He stopped trying when the number grew past 100.

When they first spotted the cabin after following a winding dirt road back into the forest, Jim nearly wept. Imagine that, he thought to himself, middle-aged, tempered by the wars of business, possessor of unlimited potential (or so he was told), and his first instinct after a true crisis was to blubber like a baby. But he held firm.

Sullivan knew Jim's struggle. He had been there before. Pulling the trigger that ends another man's life – even if to save your own – is like living a nightmare. The two strangers, thrown together in a darkened world, were now bonded by that nightmare.

Jim mourned, too. Not for the dead man, especially, but for himself. He knew his life would never be the same.

Lying in the cot last night, death and terror had pummeled down on Jim like waves crashing onto a struggling swimmer. Just as his senses began to reconcile the bizarre circumstances, another fuse would ignite that exploded him into turmoil again. It seemed strange to him that he was alive to hear the early morning chirping of the birds when, by all rights, he should be zipped up in a body bag.

Jim reserved his mourning, too, for the soldier. He was simply there, in a place and time, and he had died. He was innocent.

The other two that had invaded his life uninvited, Moss and Artie, stirred up a new loathing in Jim unlike anything he had ever felt – one that somehow stripped away a protective cloak that covered him.

The quiet of the morning was broken as Peter Sullivan stirred, stretched out his arms and let out a guttural sound from the back of his throat. His eyes popped open and he quickly glanced around the room, trying to get his bearings. As recognition set in, he propped himself up on his elbows.

"For a dead man, you sure look pretty healthy," Jim began.

"One things for sure, mate; I didn't make it to heaven, 'cause this mattress had to come straight from hell." He twisted and turned, stretching out the kinks.

Jim forced a smile, his thoughts still centered on the night before.

Sullivan continued, "Well, as you Yanks say, is somebody going to let me in on the bloody punch line? What a raging joke! I should be waking up next to my sheila in Colorado, with, I might add, a smile on my face."

"It's a good thing you're not. You saved my life last night."

"Well," Sullivan replied, "we'll call it quits. No worries. I was the one that got you into the bloody mess to begin with. If you hadn't picked me up, you'd be almost home by now."

Jim recalled the last time he saw the Australian. "You know, I thought you were a goner. I remember hearing a shot. What the hell happened?"

"Beats the bloody shit out of me, mate," he said, shaking his head. "All I know is the guy has his gun pointed right at me forehead and I figure its time to kiss my bloomin' ass good-bye. Then he raises it a little, and bam! He missed! The bastard missed me! I would have busted out laughing if I hadn't shit meself first!"

Jim wondered if he was serious. The Aussie continued. "After I heard the car take off, I walked due north. Out in the bloody boonies I was! I must have legged it five or six miles when up comes this red Indian bloke in a truck. Half pissed on the grog, he was, too. Well, off we go. Bloody thing was slower than turtle shit. Finally drops me off in some town, and I decide it's either get the coppers or go after you meself. There was really only one way you could have gone. I saw that bike outside a bar. The owner must have been too pissed to drive home. Anyway, I hot-wired it, and the rest is bloody history."

Jim shook his head. "Yeah, but how –"

Peter cut him off. "I just kept going, figuring sooner or later those bastards would mess things up."

"You passed that grocery store further up?"

"The place was lit up like the Sydney Harbor Bridge. I didn't stop. What happened?"

"That son of a bitch killed some kid. I couldn't believe it. There was nothing I could do. I felt like a spectator in a bad dream. Then later on –"

"Like a fire fight in 'Nam. I heard it clear down the bloody road. Expected to find you turned into Swiss cheese."

Jim shook his head. "If that's the way it was over there, thank God for deferments."

"Strange thing is, mate, you do begin to numb up to it all. That is, as long as you keep your bloody head down. Knew a lot of blokes who forgot that simple rule. One too many John Wayne movies. Anyway, you did all right. Rule number one is living to tell about it. You passed that test. Now all we have to do is dig ourselves out of the shit and we're done with it."

Jim looked out at the swaying tree branches. "I might have passed," he said wistfully, "but that soldier I killed sure didn't."

Sullivan sat forward, looking directly into Jim's eyes. "Listen, mate. You did what anybody would have. It was you or him. Any bastard says different, they're just kidding themselves. It's over. Just let it go."

Of course, Jim knew he had no choice. Not letting it go would eat him alive. But this was something he'd let go slowly, a piece at a time.

"What the hell do we do now?"

"No worries, Jimmy. We wait a couple of days. The whole place will be crawling with bloody soldiers or police. Either way, they won't have a warm spot in their hearts for us. I don't know about you, mate, but after what I saw last night, I'm not about to let those bloody cowboys have at me for target practice."

Jim gazed out of the dusty window again. "I don't know. Maybe I should turn myself in. Try to explain. I mean, for Christ's sake, this is still a civilized country. There are laws."

The Australian walked across the room to a sink in the kitchen area. There was a small hand pump. He gripped it and began working the handle.

"You know, mate, a week ago I might have said good on ya, throw yourself at their mercy. But a bloody lot of things have changed, and no matter how much you try to explain, there's still a hole the size of Ayers rock in that dead fella's gut. Take my advice and make tracks, Jimmy."

"Where to and with what?" asked Jim. His rational, get-to-the-point sense that had served him so well in business was starting to hum again.

"Back to Cortez. To me sheila's place. We'll regroup there and you'll be on your way."

Jim contemplated for a moment, weighing the situation. Sullivan made sense. If they got to Colorado, he could contact his wife. His cell phone and laptop plunged off the cliff with his car, so that was out. At least it would buy time until he regained his balance.

Finally, Jim made what he thought might be the best decision in his life.

"You're in charge, Peter."

Sullivan smiled. "That's the spirit, cob bah. Now, by the looks of these bloomin' shelves, there's not a drop of tucker in the place. Maybe I'll make myself useful and scout about."

"If somebody offers you a tank, don't be shy," Jim said. "We might need it before we're through."

Sullivan picked up his army jacket from the table. He opened the door, looked back at Jim and smiled.

"Crazy bloody Yanks."

****

Sergeant Jeremy Anderson waited in the small office used by the local constable of Tierra Amarilla. He knew the call would come soon. The early morning was brutal to the exhausted soldier who spent the last 18 hours trying to figure out what happened the night before. The Hispanic men who blasted a cache of ammunition into a station wagon slipped quietly back home, disappearing like wisps of smoke. Nothing more was said. Nobody knew a thing. Everyone covered everyone else's back.

They exacted their revenge and were content to leave it there. But one body, that of a soldier, had to be accounted for. The angry mob had nothing to do with that killing, Anderson knew, and the colonel would demand answers.

Another green-jacketed corporal, an M-16 slung over his shoulder, appeared at the entrance to the room. "You've got a call from headquarters. It's the colonel."

Anderson nodded and picked up the phone. Before he could begin talking, an agitated voice came barking over the line.

"OK, sergeant, what the hell's going on up there?"

"Well, sir, it's a mess. We've got two civilians down, taken out by the locals. But nobody knows anything and I'm not sure I want to ask. One of ours bought it too. Larry Kowalski, a career soldier. As best as I can tell, there are two gunmen left. Got away on a motorcycle. We've got patrols out all over the place looking for them."

"Where's Kowalski's partner. What does he have to say?"

"Ah, well, sir, he was home sick. Kowalski was alone. He told me he could handle everything until we got here. I guess he screwed up."

"No, Sergeant Anderson, YOU screwed up! Now you listen, and you listen good. When one of my men gets killed because of stupidity, it makes me look bad. You understand? I don't like to look bad, not ever. So if you know what's good for you, and for your career, you'd better come up with those two bastards. Real soon. As a matter of fact, don't come back until you do."

Kowalski was stretched out on a slab, his guts blown away, and this pompous ass is worried about looking bad? For an instant – perhaps all of a half second – Anderson felt like shouting those words. Doing so would undoubtedly sabotage his career, though, so he bit his lip and dryly responded with, "Yes, sir."

"Have you got an ID on either of the two that got away yet?" asked the Colonel.

"No, but we found a burned up wallet in the back seat of the car. The stuff inside is pretty charred, but the lab should be able to tell us something. I'll have it sent down. We'll do a DNA search, also."

"Do that. The two casualties, who are they?"

"Their names are Arthur Stubbs and Henry Willis, both of Belen. From what we know, they were both recently in Idaho at the Aryan Brotherhood compound. There's not much left of Willis."

"Well, that suits me just fine. Now listen, we'll handle the press from down here. Everything at your end is censored. Refer all media to me. Understand?"

"Yes, sir. What do you want me to do with the bodies?"

"Get them on a chopper. We'll contact Kowalski's next of kin and tell them how you sent the son of a bitch in alone holding his dick. That sound about right, Sergeant?"

Anderson didn't know what to say. "No, sir, ah, I mean, yes sir. Whatever you say, sir."

Colonel Jennings Colton's voice grew softer, but it carried the same threatening tone.

"Let me repeat myself one last time, Anderson. If you don't come back with those murderers, I'll have your balls. You think about that the next time you take a piss."

The line went dead and the sergeant replaced the receiver. He had always wanted to be an accountant, and at that moment, he couldn't remember why he joined the army in the first place. Then, the slogan "Be all that you can be," began ringing in his ears. The power of advertising, he thought, shaking his head.

****

The Australian took in the scene in the small diner that doubled as a country store. It was near the town of Tres Piedras, about 40 miles away from Tierra Amarilla. Sullivan was alone in the small room, except for a table of old men – regulars, Peter gathered – seated in their customary place by the corner. From where he sat, Peter could listen to their conversation and still keep his eye on what was going on outside. Cars buzzed by. Few stopped for gas.

A young Chicano girl placed a cup of steaming coffee and two donuts in front of him. He gave her a warm smile. Over his shoulder, the conversation turned to a subject he recognized.

"Heard they took care of those young bucks who've been tearin' up lately," said a gruff, whiskered man at the head of the table.

"My cousin Lupe lives over there. Said it sounded like a war. The lead was flying. Shows you don't screw around with people up here," a dark Hispanic man muttered. His face turned down as he ate the last of his biscuits and sausage gravy.

"I heard they didn't get them all," put in another man.

"There aren't too many ways you can go. Won't be long before somebody spots them and finishes it."

The last comment made Peter nervous. He glanced out the window at the stolen motorcycle parked a few feet away. What a bloody idiot, he scolded himself.

Sullivan quickly decided that he and the Yank were in serious trouble. His thoughts focused. No mistakes. He had to think clearly and plan if they were going to survive.

The Aussie tossed back the rest of his coffee, popped the last bit of pastry in his mouth and left money on the table. He walked a short distance through an open doorway into the general store side and looked around. Canned food, some twine, and tape; that would do for now. With his usual hop as he strode, Sullivan stepped outside in the crisp November morning air. The openness suddenly offered some relief.

The last chore was to top off the cycle. He wanted a full tank to ride as far from the area as they could without stopping. As he began filling up, Peter spotted a police cruiser coming up the highway, heading his way. All he could do was pray it passed.

His prayer went unanswered as the cruiser braked, turned into the diner and came to a stop beside him.

The lone figure in the car wore a Smokey the Bear hat. He opened the driver's door and stepped out, looking back over his shoulder at the Australian.

Sullivan knew what to do. A wide grin came across his creased face and his twinkling eyes set on the patrolman.

"G'day, officer," he began with his best twang. "Top of the morning to ya."

The cop said nothing, but closed the door and moved around his car.

Without hesitating, Peter continued, "A bit nippy out. Like to freeze my bloody ass off."

The cop was a deputy in the local sheriff's office. He eyed Peter carefully. "You English?" he asked.

"No, 'stralian." Sullivan set the hook. "Where I come from, people would take that as an insult. You ever been Down Under, mate?"

"No, can't say as I have. Would like to go, though."

Peter started to roll. "Great place, 'stralia. Land of milk and honey. Greatest beer in the world, I might add. Had my fill of it over the years. Once got so bloody pissed, I boxed a kangaroo, I did. He beat the stuffin' out of me, the bastard. Had a hard time facing me mates. They were shitting themselves laughing."

"Where is it that those critters live?" the officer asked.

"That would be the Outback, mate. One of everything in the world out there that can kill you. Snakes, spiders, you name it. As a matter of fact, that's where a mate of mine, David Windham, came a cropper. Was bit on the head of his pecker by a tiger snake while taking a leak. I was always glad I wasn't there with him, if you get my drift. That would have been one bloody dilemma, that." Sullivan roared with laughter.

He finished with the gas, and put the cap back on the tank, never stopping to let the policeman think.

"Bloody great place, 'stralia. A real man's country. Three women to every bloke. They're on you like flies, they are. In some pubs, I used to pass out numbers. They had to wait their turns." He winked at the stranger. "Mate, could I trouble you to give this five dollars to the man inside for the petrol?"

"Why, uh, sure. No problem."

"Good on ya then. And listen, if you ever get to Sydney, look me up. The name's Ned Kelley. Everybody knows me. I'll set you straight with the sheilas." Sullivan laughed. He had given him the name of a famous Australian outlaw.

With a quick kick of the starter and a wave of his hand, he was off down the road, leaving the deputy standing in the distance. Peter, my boy, he thought to himself, they don't stand a chance when you're in top form, now do they, mate?

****

Hours passed, and the first gray of dusk fell on the woods around the hunting cabin. Inside, Peter Sullivan was opening a can of baked beans with his pocketknife while Jim Barnes stood in the front doorway looking into the distance. There was a small fire in the stone hearth.

"You found some clothes," Peter said.

"Yeah, there's an attic opening over in the corner. Some old pants and shirts, a couple of blankets. Nothing else up there."

"Could I trouble you to do me a favor then, mate? Go on over to that tall grass by the side of the shack and bring me back three or four armfuls of it. I've got an idea."

Later, when he returned, Sullivan had arranged two sets of shirts and pants on the floor, and was busy tying knots in the legs and arms.

"What's this?"

"Need to make a couple of decoys in case we get some unexpected company. Give them something to shoot at besides us. Here, run about thirty feet of twine through the holes I put in those empty cans. We'll string it across the path down by the road. If someone was to show up sniffing around, they'll probably come that way. These will be our doorbells."

Jim finished the job and the two men walked outside, down the gentle slope to the dirt road. There, they stretched out the twine, tying the ends to a couple of trees. Sullivan got down on his knees and dug a small hole underneath each can, placing rocks below them. If the twine moved, the cans would rattle against the stones. Once that was completed, they returned to the cabin, and dined on cold beans and tuna fish.

Between mouthfuls, Sullivan drew up a plan of escape.

"That window over there, out the back. I opened it earlier and it slides easily. If someone shows up, that's our exit. I have the motorcycle parked nearby. Do you still have the gun?"

Jim nodded in the direction of his cot.

"Over there. I think it's got about eight bullets left."

"Good then," Peter answered. "Let me handle the weapons. I've had more practice."

"You won't get an argument out of me. Just one thing: we use it as a last resort, right?" Jim asked.

"Too right, mate. As a last option."

"Good. I'm not looking for any more notches on my gun, if you know what I mean."

"You know," Peter said with a bemused look on his face, "To this day, there are people down in Australia who think all you Yanks carry six-shooters on your hip. Riggy didge."

"Well, that's the way it used to be, I suppose. Hell, who knows? Maybe that's where we're headed again. With all the morons running around, we might just have to start carrying six-shooters. I never would have believed that even two months ago."

"I always thought that's why the politicians started wars. To clean things out a bit. Some of the dumbest bloody bastards I ever met were in those rice paddies. And blimey, I volunteered! I guess that makes me the biggest fool of all."

They both laughed.

"None of it made sense back then. I knew either they were wackos, or I was. So I let them have at it. I minded me business and tried to stay out of the line of fire."

"Yeah," Jim said ruefully, "And here we are, with half the cops in the Southwest looking for us."

"But they haven't got us now, have they? That's part of the fun. I like to think I can stay ahead of all the bastards. If I can do that, I'll die a happy man."

"I'm sure you will, Peter, I'm sure you will."

****

Evening fell softly on Tierra Amarilla, as it almost always does. Pines swayed to the gentle night breeze, crickets chirped their mating call and birds serenaded as the moon rose. The town did what it could to recover from the excitement of the past day and drift back to normalcy.

Seated on a barstool in Gus' Tavern was Sergeant Jeremy Anderson, slowly turning his frosted mug of beer. His thoughts were far from the crowded room. He felt alone at that moment, lost in a crowded bar.

He regained his focus, though, remembering he was on the trail of killers. Letting them slip away would be the end to his already shaky military career.

Through the din of the room, he began to pick up small bits of a conversation two seats away. The big man pouring drinks and a gruff, bearded Anglo dressed in a red checked wool shirt, and green and brown camouflage pants, jawed about unknown guests in the area.

"So where was this again?" asked the bartender.

"You know, south, I don't know, 30 or 40 miles. Where the Rielito River cuts across the open pasture near Kearny Point. Same place you and me went quail hunting a couple of years back."

"OK, OK, now I remember. Near the old Garcia place."

"That's it. See, I was working the high grass down by the river – lots of good birds in there – when I thought I saw smoke coming out the chimney. Could have been wrong, though. These old eyes aren't what they used to be."

"Nobody been at that place for a couple of years, since old man Garcia died."

"That's what I thought. Maybe squatters have taken up there. Anyway, who gives a shit? Get me another beer, would ya?"

Anderson turned to the hunter. "You didn't happen to see anybody, did you? A car or something?"

"No, like I said, mister, only smoke. Thought I smelled it in the air, too."

"Is this Garcia place hard to find?"

"No," he murmured, sipping his cold beer. "There's an old dirt road heading east about eight miles past Melendez's store on 68 south. It's pretty rough. It goes back into the woods maybe two miles, and the cabin is just before the clearing."

Anderson's mind began to click off the possibilities. Up to that point, there had been no sign of the fugitives. The roadblocks placed throughout the area came up empty. It seemed the men simply vanished. But, he thought, maybe they found a place to hold up.

"Could I trouble you to draw me a little map of the area?" he said to the hunter, pulling an ink pen out of his coat pocket. "It's dark and I wouldn't want to miss it."

The bearded man eyed the soldier wearily. "What's in it for me?"

Jeremy Anderson's day had been long, tense and frustrating. He was tired, his career was jeopardized by an egomaniac colonel who constantly hounded him, and he was in the middle of nowhere chasing killers.

"A good night's sleep in your own bed," he shot back, his eyes boring in on the old man's face.

The hunter took the pen without a word and began to draw lines on a bar napkin. When finished he slid it back toward the sergeant.

Anderson stood up and turned toward the door. As he began to walk away, he muttered, "Your country thanks you."

"Saddle up, Romenelli, you and me are going for a little ride," Anderson said the moment his boots touched the parking lot.

"Where to, sarge?" Romenelli answered, firing up the green jeep.

"South about 40 miles. I got a tip. Could be the guys we're looking for. One way or another, I'm not spending my life in this Godforsaken town, so we're gonna check it out."

"Yes, sir," replied the corporal. His right hand moved to the passenger side, shifting the M-16 rifle from between the seats. Anderson felt for the automatic on his hip. It was there, loaded and ready for action. He swung his leg up and pivoted onto the seat. He gripped the army jacket around him tightly. It would be a long, chilly ride in the windowless vehicle, with only the canvas top to protect them from the biting air. But if they found the men they were looking for, it would be well worth the discomfort.

"Hit the road, corporal," he ordered, bracing for another sleepless night.

****

Sullivan's head rested comfortably on his hands, like a contented child, as he lay stretched out on the cot. The dying fire crackled and an occasional gust of wind whooshed outside. He was falling into a deep, restful sleep, the kind every tired body craves. At that moment, the troubles of the world were in another place and time. Peter Sullivan preferred it that way.

Nearby, Jim slept also, but fitfully. His mind couldn't release the violence of the previous day. Instead, it replayed the events over and again, punishing him for straying from the comfort zone that was his life.

Suddenly, the sound of clanking metal broke both men from their lull. The Aussie shot straight up in bed, his eyes wide. He threw off the old wool blanket that covered his legs, and reached across to where Jim Barnes lay. Sullivan clamped his right hand over his partner's mouth, and he, too, came awake with a wild-eyed fury. The two men looked at each other in the darkness, communicating without words.

Down below, where the dirt road met the path to the hunting cabin, Sergeant Anderson silently cursed himself for falling for the oldest trick in the book. He betrayed their presence, losing the element of surprise. If the men he hunted were in the stone cabin, he would have to proceed with a new respect. They were clever and not to be taken lightly.

Corporal Romenelli shifted his M-16 to his right hand, crouched low, and began the ascent up the path. With his left hand, he brushed the ground ahead, feeling for more surprises. Directly behind, the sergeant followed, a long black flashlight in one hand, a cocked 9mm automatic in the other. Beneath the green army jackets, pounding hearts thumped against chest cavities.

They moved silently, except for the snap of a twig or leaf. Those sounds were carried away in the wind. The three-quarter moon brightened their way enough to see, but the darkness in the woods was deep and foreboding.

At the front door, both men stood, their lungs holding breath within. They faced each other, eyes intent, and hands cold. Anderson, his back against the stone, turned to his right, trying to peer inside the dark room through the front window. Everything was black. As his eyes adjusted to the dark, he could make out two large shapes on beds near the back of the room. They were big enough to be the men he was looking for. He gave no thought to the possibly that they were innocent locals camping out for the night. This was it.

The sergeant turned back to look into the wide eyes of Corporal Romenelli. He slowly nodded his head. Both men set their jaws. The corporal backed up two steps so that each man was at the side of the wood door. Then, without a word, they both reared back at the same time and crashed shoulder first into the door. It smashed back on its hinges, slamming into the wall. The soldiers rushed into the room and up to the cots, screaming at the top of their lungs.

"U.S. Army. Don't MOVE!" Anderson yelled.

"NOW! ON YOUR FEET!" ordered Romenelli as he brought the M-16 up to his shoulder, aiming down at the head of one of the figure below him.

But there was no movement, only a sickening stillness. Anderson shot a glance at his partner, as if to say, "What the hell?" and then turned to look again. Still holding the gun outstretched in his hand, he brought the flashlight up. A beam of light shot out, and struck the brown wool blanket covering the still form. With great care, he leaned forward, grasping the corner of the blanket, and ripped it back. There, in the beam of his light, was a pair of pants and a shirt stuffed with grass. The right sleeve was folded neatly across the chest. A makeshift hand of sticks wrapped in twine extended toward them. With the middle finger extended.

"Son of a –" he began to say.

From behind his right ear, a voice whispered to Jeremy Anderson, followed by the metallic click of a gun hammer locking in place.

"Gidday, mates. Welcome to our humble home. Now, we're all going to be nice to each other by lowering those nasty guns to the floor. At a moment like this, when we're all searching for the meaning of life, I wouldn't want to get bloody nervous, if you follow me drift."

The two soldiers froze, their nerves tingling and minds racing. With a slow, deliberate motion, they lowered their guns and dropped them to the floor.

Stillness hung in the dark room like an executioner's sword. The only person certain of the next move was the man who did the talking, and even he was making up most of it as he went.

"Now," Sullivan continued in a controlled, deliberate voice, "I'd like you to meet me mate. Jimmy, here, was probably a Boy Scout, just like yourselves, and he's bloody well going to try to remember all those knots that got him a bloomin' merit badge. So be kind, and both you blokes bring your arms around back, and don't even THINK about being stupid. Roger Dodger?"

The two men did as they were told. Jim came in through the open doorway with the spool of twine in his hand, and began wrapping it around each man's wrist. When they were secured, he motioned for them to sit down and continued at their ankles. Not a word was spoken. Peter

Sullivan's hard stare shifted from one to the other. Finally, the sergeant cleared his throat, and spoke.

"You two have no chance. You're up against the U.S. Army. We've got satellites that can spot a flea on your ass. It's just a matter of time."

"Not if the rest of your buddies are as dumb as you two blokes," Peter laughed, "For Christ's sake, I thought they trained you idiots better after 'Nam. Bloody hell, if we were the VC, you'd be dining on your nuts right now, no worries."

Jim finished and stood up. "I don't know what the hell is going on, but his whole thing is one major misunderstanding."

"I'm sure those old folks in Utah felt the same way," Anderson shot back.

Jim glared down at the man at his feet. "Listen, we didn't have anything to do with people in Utah. Man, this is crazy. You've got to believe me."

"I've got a dead soldier on a slab back in that town you shot up and somebody's going to pay big time. That's a promise. Now, if you were smart, you'd untie us and submit to military justice, because sooner or later we'll find you."

Sullivan cut him off. "Not bloody likely, mate. No, no, no, no. Old Peter here has seen your brand of justice once too many times and it ain't gonna happen again. No, no, no. We'll just be on our way and wish you blokes a nice life. By the way, what might you be driving?"

Romenelli looked up. "An army jeep, up the road a little ways."

"Keys in it, mate? Good tires? Lots of petrol?"

The corporal nodded.

"Well, good on you, then. We'll be off. Jimmy, go out to the motorcycle and take the plug wires off. I really didn't fancy riding that thing, anyway." Jim walked out through the open door and Sullivan backed toward it, never taking his eyes off the two men. Then he stopped. Silhouetted against the slivers of moonlight, he lowered the .45. Silence gathered about the room as the adversaries glared back at each other. In a cold, clear voice, the Australian spoke to the men who hunted him.

"I'm only nice once. The fun stops here. You tell your Yank friends they've made a big mistake and the best thing they can do is bloody well let it go. Find some real bad guys."

There was no mistaking the menace in his voice.

Quietly, he turned and began to race down the leaf-covered path, Jim following closely behind. Once more they would go off into a night that held only the promise of trouble.

CHAPTER 6

It had been only three days since the government declared martial law, but already a dark veil of uncertainty descended on the country. Hope and promise evaporated in the sudden, painful reality. The "new economy," with its flurry of dot-com start-ups and soaring market indexes, grounded to a halt. The most creative accounting in the world couldn't hide the billions in red ink. The complex, worldwide network of international business faltered, too. Americans, for the first time since the Great Depression, weren't imagining a better tomorrow.

The late November days drew colder, too. Everyone expected a long, harsh winter. No one seemed to have an answer. How to fix a world economy? The best and brightest were as confused and frightened for their families as Joe Six-Pack. Although layoffs abounded, cars and buses still plied the city streets and farmers still harvested crops. But an unmistakable gloom transcended it all. It was as though a nation of children were just told there's no such thing as Santa Claus.

They had been betrayed by the system they created.

The government enacted Operation Patriot to maintain control and to established priorities. The free movement of essential items such as food and fuels topped the list. But as soon as shelves were stocked, the populous snatched them clean, hording for the long winter ahead. Movie theaters sat empty. Luxury cars collected dust on dealership lots. Once-bustling restaurants echoed in emptiness. No doubt about it; priorities were established. It was canned food, gallons of sealed drinking water and squirreling away as much cash as possible. The triviality of the past was gone.

But some functioned best in such a no-nonsense world. Colonel Jennings Colton was among them.

As he climbed the painted wooden stairs leading into his command building that November morning, he glanced down at his Palm Pilot one last time to check his scheduling for the rest of the day. He knew the power his presence would have over his subordinates as he entered the room. He smiled, inwardly. He had built an aura of authority around him and he constantly reinforced it. He relished it.

"AttenTION!" bellowed the sleepy-eyed private at the operation's desk as Colton burst into the room.

The Colonel didn't acknowledge the tired young man as he stepped quickly across the large, open room.

"Coffee, black," he snapped at the first female soldier he came upon as he neared his office at the far end of the building. "Staff meeting in 10 minutes in the conference room. I want updates on all operations in our sectors. Come prepared."

More than a dozen military personnel scattered around the room, picking up papers, digging in filing cabinets and searching for note pads.

As the group settled down around the large conference table, Colonel Colton walked in, a cup of steaming coffee in his hand.

"First question: Who made this coffee?" he said, his eye searching the faces in the drab green room.

"I did, sir," replied a small, bookish man near the end of the table

"Stedylmayer, don't ever touch that coffee pot again, understand? I don't care if a nuclear bomb hits this place, and you're the only one left standing, and we're out of fresh coffee. Frankly, I'd rather die that way then to be taken out slowly drinking this piss. Sgt. Hurley, here, is in charge of that operation. If something happens to her, I guess we'll all have to do without."

Normally, such a fanatical speech from a colonel would be taken as a joke. But everyone remained uncomfortably silent. They knew he wasn't joking.

"OK," the Colonel continued as he sat down, "Calhoun, we'll start with you, and work around the table."

The young black corporal began addressing the group, providing details of the past 24 hours in his area. The meeting continued for almost 45 minutes, each taking their turn in a relentless grilling on the major worries of the day, when the subject of Section 23, Northwest, came up.

"What do we hear from Anderson?" asked the colonel.

"Nothing, yet, sir," threw in a sergeant to his right. "He hasn't checked in."

"What?" barked Colton. "When we're through here, check his radio and cell phone. Roll him out of the sack if you have to. I don't know what that son of a bitch thinks he's doing, but he better get his head out of his ass quick."

"Yes, SIR!" came the quick reply. The meeting continued as topics such as food distribution, military-civilian police coordination, essential services, motor pool and information releases were covered. At meeting's end, each man and woman present was prepared to return to his or her computer terminals and continue setting up the new society. As the meeting was about to adjourn, a junior staffer knocked on the open door of the conference room.

"What is it?" snapped Jennings Colton.

"Sir, we've got communications from 23 Northwest. They've found Sergeant Anderson and Corporal Romenelli about 40 miles south of the command post in Tierra Amarilla. They, ah, we're walking alongside the road. Evidently they, ah, lost, ah, their vehicle, sir."

Colonel Colton shot from agitated to enraged in a blink. "Put the call through to my office. I'll be there in a second," he ordered. His dark eyes began to cast about the silent room, leveling on each of the participants, as he desperately wanted to unleash his fury. But no one moved a muscle; no one gave him an excuse.

"Meeting's adjourned," he announced.

Moments later, in the quiet of his office, Colton picked up the receiver and spoke. "This is Colonel Colton. Who am I talking to?"

Static could be heard on the line, obviously a radio patch with a field unit.

"It's Anderson, sir. I don't have much time to explain. We had 'em, sir. Romenelli and I had 'em dead to rights holed up in a hunting cabin not far from here. It was dark, and things got screwed up, and they escaped, with, uh, our Jeep. One of them is a foreigner, probably Australian, and the other is named Jim. You might see if the lab has finished with that wallet yet."

"Yeah, go on," Colton said curtly.

"Anyway, our satellites have tracked down the Jeep. The Global Positioning reading makes them about 100 miles from here to the northwest. Looks like they're taking back roads heading for Colorado. We've dispatched the closest unit – some local blue – to try to tail them. I've got a chopper on its way here right now. I think I can beat them to the border and make the arrest there."

"All right, move out, soldier," Jennings Colton ordered, "And, Anderson? If you fail me again, I will make your life a living hell. Clear?"

"Yes SIR!" Anderson replied, grateful that the conversation would end so quickly.

Colonel Colton hung up the receiver and thought for a moment. Then he looked toward the doorway and called out, "Calhoun, get in here." In seconds, the staffer was at his door.

"Sir?"

"The lab report on that wallet found in the burned out vehicle up in 23 Northwest, has it come in yet?"

"Yes, sir, just a few minutes ago. I was going to bring it in."

"Did they get anything out of it?"

"Yeah, a name. James Barnes, from some town up in Michigan. They have a DNA match, also. I'll get it for you."

"Do that, and also, start a workup on the guy. Find anything you can. We're going to make an example out of Mr. Barnes and I'll want to know everything there is about the guy before I crucify him."

"No problem, sir.

Jennings Colton stared up from his desk at the soldier before him but his thoughts were elsewhere. "One more thing, corporal. Have Orlowski come over from the information center. We're going to want to do this up right when the time comes."

The Colonel knew this was an opportunity to establish his credentials and he would take advantage of the gift.

****

Peter Sullivan turned the wheel of the army Jeep effortlessly as he negotiated the winding mountain roads coming out of the high country of New Mexico. The early morning sun was still low and a brisk chill filled the open vehicle. The tall pines were giving way to the rough foliage of the high desert country. Their destination neared.

"About an hour I figure, mate. What do you think?"

"Sounds about right. Man, I'll be glad when we can slow down and get warm. I'm freezing my ass off," Jim answered.

"Leave it to the bloody army to forget the windows. If they don't kill you with bullets, then how about a touch of pneumonia? Reminds me of the time I drove a big rig across the Outback. That was just before the coppers lifted me bloomin' license. Driving under the influence of the grog, they said. Anyway, I was so bloody tired that I had to keep the windows down to stay awake. When that didn't work, I decided to tie off the blasted steering wheel and get some shuteye.

Bloody road across the Outback was so straight, I figured, stuff it!"

Jim looked at his companion incredulously. "You mean to tell me you drove a truck across Australia sleeping?"

"Only for about 15 or 20 miles. Woke up and found myself plowing through a herd of big blue kangaroos. Had a couple of the bastards on me bumper, I did. By the time I got back on the road, I felt refreshed, what with the excitement and all. Finished driving straight through to Adelaide."

Jim shook his head. "And you think we're the crazy bastards."

"Thing is, mate, out there, you might only pass one car in a day. Odds were definitely in my favor. Give an Aussie odds, and look out! Those blokes down there will bet on two cock- roaches crossing the floor, they will. Sort of a national pastime, just like your baseball."

Sullivan laughed as he drove on, occasionally looking in the rearview mirror. Suddenly, his expression grew serious. Jim noticed it and looked back. "What is it?"

"I'm not sure, but I think it's a copper. He's been dogging our bloody trail now for miles, trying to stay back. Damn, I bet they picked us up with a GPS device on this jeep. We could have us the makings of a problem."

Jim looked back over his shoulder. "Pick up your speed. See if he stays close. If he's on to us, the only thing we can do is make a run for it."

The Australian's foot pressed down on the accelerator and the Jeep shot forward. Behind them, the cruiser mimicked the move and began to close the distance.

"The chase is on, mate! Hold tight! Let's see if we can shake the bugger."

The Jeep careened down the last of the hills toward the flatter plains below. Peter's jaw was set. The landscape flew by, with greens and yellows of the pines swiftly giving way to the browns of the low country.

The white Crown Victoria, now with lights flashing and siren screaming, gained ground on the Jeep. Inside, the officer reached for his radio.

As both vehicles approached 90 mph, the cop tossed aside the handset and gripped the wheel tightly. The two cars raced down the two-lane highway in choreography of speed and death.

Sullivan scanned the horizon for a way out. Giving up was out of the question. This was about survival and he was a survivor.

As the Jeep shimmied at top speed, Jim fumbled with a hand-held radio. Its digital readout was scrambling, trying to lock in a frequency. Finally, a choppy voice broke the static. "ETA is 10 minutes. Stay on 'em. Stay on 'em."

This couldn't be happening, Jim told himself. I'm a businessman. A husband. A father. Maybe it was time to give up. Quit the running. But with all that had happened the past few days, the uncertainty was too great. His inner voice told him to get the hell out of there. By the stern look on the Australian's face, he could tell Peter was in full agreement.

The road flattened out and they could see further ahead. The turns were less severe and the Jeep gathered more speed. Sullivan searched the road ahead intently, looking for something that would give them a chance to escape.

"We're closing in," the voice on the radio announced. "You have full authority to stop them at any cost. This is a matter of national security!"

Instantly, it hit Jim. The voice was talking about them. "National security?" he said. "Jesus. You've got to be kid –."

Blam!

Peter and Jim ducked instinctively. A moment passed and Jim peered over the back seat of the Jeep. The cop held a shotgun out of the window as his cruiser sped down the highway.

Blam!

Only a few pellets found their mark, tinging the shell of the Jeep.

"We've got John Wayne on our tail," Sullivan said. Then, oddly, he smiled.

Up ahead, he spotted something. On the right side of the road was flat grazing land, full of tumbleweed and scrub. A wire fence marked the property. But between the road and the fence was a large drainage ditch,

mounded up on his side. If he hit it just right.
…

"All right, mate, get ready to hang on. We're fixin' to go bush."

Blam!

The men ducked again. Then Peter cranked the wheel and floored it. The Jeep veered off the road, hit the side of the ditch and launched into the air. The engine whined and the wheels spun as it flew. The wire fence passed under them just as the vehicle came down.

The backend of the Jeep crashed down onto the hard desert, followed quickly by the front tires slamming forward. The Jeep bounced three more times, flinging Peter and Jim up into the canvas top and down again like pin balls in an arcade.

"Holy shit!" Jim screamed, releasing the tension that had tightened his body like a vice.

Sullivan grinned from ear to ear. "Good on ya, mate," he said, patting the dashboard, "Short wheel base. Might have been a sticky wicket if this had been a real Yank tank!"

Jim looked back over his shoulder. The police car was stopped alongside the road with the driver standing outside, aiming the shotgun at them. From that distance, not even the Duke himself could hit them. The cop didn't even pull the trigger.

"Where to now?" Jim asked, his voice rising above the noise.

"Well, if we keep heading west, sooner or later we'll hit a road, or the Pacific Ocean. Either way, it'll be bloody fine by me."

"The way my luck's been going, we'll run into the Grand Canyon."

"No worries, mate. Old Peter will jump that, too. The Evel Knievel of Australia, that's what they'll call me. Blimey, that last one was a heart thumper. Near shit me knickers!"

"That makes two of us. I don't need this crap!"

Peter grinned. "Aw, live a little, mate. Just think of all the stories you can tell your grandkids. What a partnership. Why, bloody Butch Cassidy and the Sundance Kid have nothing on us! All this adventure and excitement in the Wild West. Keeps you young!"

"Problem is," Jim retorted, "I'd kind of like to get older. Do me a favor and slow this buggy down, would ya? I think I broke my tailbone."

Just then, the Aussie tensed as he looked into his side mirror. "Bloody hell, we've put our foot in it now!"

Jim turned around again. In the distance, the unmistakable whirl of a green Army helicopter approached. It was closing fast, nose down, blades slashing through the air as it covered the distance between them.

"Well that's that, buddy," Jim yelled over the noise, "We aren't going to outrun those guys."

In a way, he was almost relieved. Surely, he could convince the authorities to check their stories and put an end to the madness. At least, he thought, they would fall into civilized hands, and not some lynch mob.

Sullivan clutched the wheel and stared ahead. Finally, he let off the accelerator.

Up in the helicopter, Sergeant Anderson, and Corporal Romenelli knelt by the open doorway of the craft. The pilot maneuvered them into position above and behind the Jeep as it rolled to a stop.

"Stay about 100 feet back," Anderson screamed at the pilot, trying to be heard above the noise of the rotors, "Remember, they're armed and dangerous. Don't take any chances."

The pilot nodded and moved the bird into position. Anderson picked up a bullhorn with his right hand and cradled an M-16 in his left.

"This is the United States Army. Stop immediately, and throw down your weapons!" He would give them one warning. That's all they deserved, he reasoned.

Romenelli aimed his rifle steadily, focusing the red laser sight on Sullivan's head. He was ready for action. Both men's eyes strained through the rising dust for any provocation.

The two men in the Jeep kept watched the helicopter above them, both noticing the rifle barrels aimed their way. The chopper began to descend and was only 50 feet off the deck. Both Peter and Jim were cautiously tense.

In surrender, Sullivan pulled the .45 automatic out of his army jacket with his left hand and swung it up and out through the open window. It was an innocent movement, but one that would unleash a savage chain of events.

"WATCH THE GUN!" Anderson shouted, panicked by the barrel that seemed to be pointing at him. On instinct, his left index finger squeezed the trigger of the M-16 and a rapid burst of fire shot out of the weapon. The bullets crashed into the dirt all around the two startled men in the vehicle. Their bodies numb with fright and shock, both were frozen in place – sitting ducks.

The only thing that saved Jim and Peter was the copter pilot who violently jerked back on the stick and poured power to the engine to gain altitude. The thrust from that movement sent Romenelli and Anderson tumbling back across the interior of the machine.

The Australian was the first to react from their momentary reprieve. His right foot slammed down on the gas pedal and the green Jeep shot forward. Jim, still frozen from shock, was knocked back into his seat.

"STUFF THOSE BLOODY BASTARDS!" Sullivan screamed as they picked up speed. "That's IT! Now I am bloody pissed!"

Up in the air, Anderson regained his balance. "You Son of a Bitch! If they get away, it's your ass!"

The helicopter swung around in a full 360-degree turn, and dashed off after the Jeep. Anderson looked out and surveyed the terrain all around them. The only chance of escape was into the rocky buttes and foothills about 10 miles in the distance. There, they might be able to squirrel away for a while. It would take men on horseback to drive them out. He wasn't going to let that happen.

"Make a run at them from behind," he ordered, "If I miss, we'll swing around for a frontal assault. And keep this bucket of bolts steady, for Christ sake!"

As the copter roared up from behind, Jim and Peter looked back in unison. The nose of the chopper bore down. Machine gun barrels pointed right at them. Red needles of light from the lasers crossed the jeep, sighting in for the kill.

Before a shot was fired, Sullivan began a high-speed weave, side winding across the desert. Anderson let go a barrage of fire, squeezing down the trigger of the automatic. The shots missed as the nimble Jeep dodged and weaved as it raced across the landscape. The pilot shot past them a good distance before bringing his machine up high and around for another pass. It was a modern bullfight, frightfully deadly and equally disadvantageous to one side.

As their attacker turned up ahead and began racing back, Jim's temper finally got the best of him. He wasn't going to die like a lamb at the hands of some wild-eyed cowboy drunk with power. They had no reason to be firing on them. Hell, he thought, they wouldn't even allow him to surrender.

Jim's jaw clinched in rage. He would not go quietly into that good night. His right hand reached for the automatic that the Aussie had placed between the seats and his fist tightened around it. There was still seven or eight shots left in the weapon and he would put them to good use.

Leaning out the window, Jim thrust his right hand out, drawing down on the approaching machine. At that moment, he was of singular mind. There were no thoughts of his wife and daughter, his career, prison or even death. He was strangely calm, and in a disquieting way, he felt good. Some deep, buried instinct had come forward and he welcomed it.

Anderson steeled himself for the next pass. They came at the Jeep to its right, angling for a clean shot. At about 50 yards off, he and Romenelli began firing bursts. The noise was deafening. Suddenly, a smoking hole burst in the metal door of the chopper. Anderson realized that they were receiving return fire.

Startled, Anderson squeezed off another burst. Then, in an instant, his right shoulder erupted into a mass of tissue and blood. The force of the blow knocked him back into the chopper. Searing pain shot through him.

"You got one, mate! You got the bastard!" cried Sullivan with unbridled joy as the two adversaries passed. "Those bloody pricks will think twice about getting close next time!"

The joy was short-lived. Up ahead, the land abruptly ended, giving way to a dry riverbed canyon about 30 feet deep and 90 feet wide. There was no time to react, let alone stop.

They shot out over the edge just as the Australian was able to yell, "JUMMMP!" The two flying bodies cleared the whining Jeep and all three crashed down, out of view, onto the sand and rock below. A small puff of dust rose up from the jagged gap like a final belch, as the earth swallowed them up.

High above them, the scene had not gone unnoticed by their attackers. Romenelli smiled as he looked over at the pilot.

Anderson, stunned and silent, clutched what remained of his shoulder.

The copter made a sweeping pass over the wreckage. Romenelli could see the mangled vehicle on its side, crushed against some rocks, but the two men were out of view.

"No way they survived that," Romenelli yelled to the pilot. "Set her down."

The copter swung back around and came to a rest on the embankment above. The corporal jumped free of the aircraft, clutched his rifle and crouched away from the aircraft

"You stay here," he yelled back to the pilot, "I'll go down and make sure those pricks are finished myself!" In New York, where Romenelli grew up, there was a saying among his streetwise friends: "Kick the dog while he's down." He planned to do just that.

Jim's eyes flicked open, but he dared not move. The pain was bad. He looked down at his body as if it were detached, belonging to someone else. His head was splitting, but it could have been worse, as he missed a giant boulder by about three feet. Fortunately, where he landed was more sand then rock. He wasn't sure if Peter shared the same fate. He also wasn't sure if he wanted to find out. When it came right down to it, he wasn't sure of anything at that moment.

Carefully, Jim checked to see if all his parts moved. He got up, dragged himself a few feet and slumped down against a boulder. OK, he thought, no bones seem to be broken. He wiped some dirt and sweat from his face, and looked around for Sullivan.

Just then, out of the corner of his eye, he saw a movement. There, standing with a rifle against his shoulder, a soldier aimed down at his forehead. Jim knew he was about to die.

At first, Romenelli didn't speak. He glared at his victim with total disgust.

In a low, guttural voice, he growled, "Kick the dog –"

Jim Barnes braced for the pain. Instead, from nearby rocks, he heard a familiar Australian voice.

"Not bloody likely, mate."

Two shots roared out of the riverbed. Romenelli was lifted up, his chest ripped open and his body deposited in a heap on the rocks. Blood seeped out of his wounds. He was dead before he hit the ground.

As the reports echoed off the boulders, Jim realized that a profound change was taking shape within him. Instead of revulsion, fear and horror upon seeing the violent end of another human being, he felt only cold, calculating anger. That dead man stood before him and passed judgment on his life. Whatever the soldier's motivation, he was not concerned with Jim's wife, his child, or the effects his death would have on his family. He was not concerned with truth, or justice, or fair play, or the tangle of events that had brought them to that place. The day for dialogue and understanding and rights had truly passed, maybe never to return. Jim knew that the sooner he accepted the new reality, the better chance he'd have to survive.

The soldier was simply going to kill, as he had been trained, and nothing else mattered. Fair enough, but he had been killed first. Again, fair enough. Jim's innocence was trickling away as surely as the blood from the dead man's wounds.

Peter Sullivan rose up from the rocks a few feet away, still staring at the lifeless body ahead of him. He was in a great deal of pain, but gritted his teeth. The automatic in his hand dropped down as though it suddenly weighed 100 pounds.

High, gray clouds swirled as the wind picked up across the desert. Sullivan came over to where Jim sat and the two men stared at each other for a long moment. The Australian could sense the change in his friend. He had seen it many times in combat. He knew from that moment on, Jim could be trusted with his life. Peter reached out with his left hand and offered his mate help in getting to his feet. They locked wrists and Jim stood up.

"There's more of them up there, mate. Sooner or later they'll get curious. Let's nick off and get ready."

"How are we going to get out of here? I don't think I can walk very far," Jim said quietly.

"First things first" Peter said, motioning to the embankment and helicopter beyond.

The two men struggled up the side of the riverbank. Once there, they could see the copter. The pilot was just getting out and beginning to walk toward them.

Peter and Jim worked themselves under a small overhang in the rocks and waited for the man to approach. As he neared, they could hear the scuff of his boots as he came to a stop at the edge of the cliff. In a lightning movement, Sullivan sprung up, grabbed the pilot's ankles and jerked him off the cliff. As the man tumbled forward down the rock embankment, the Aussie brought his right hand around and cuffed him on the side of the head with the gun, knocking him cold. It was ruthlessly efficient.

"Bloody hell, mate, let's bugger off. Time's a wasting," he said.

They both rose to their feet and climbed up to level ground.

"What now?" Jim asked.

Sullivan only smiled as he turned toward the helicopter without speaking.

"You've got to be kidding!" the American said.

"I trained to fly them before they sent me bloomin ass to Vietnam. After I got there, the bastards mucked up my orders and I landed in an infantry unit. But like you

Yanks say, it's like riding a bike; you never bloody well forget."

Jim shook his head as the two set off cautiously for the copter. Once there, they could see Sergeant Anderson lying in the corner unconscious, but still breathing.

Jim grabbed a first-aid kit packed behind the pilot's seat. "I'll see what I can do for him."

"Good on ya, mate. I'll get this bird in the air. Might take me a minute to figure out what's what, but then we'll be off. How far's Mexico from here?"

"Mexico?" Jim said. "I don't know, 300 miles, I guess. Why?"

"Cause that's where we're going, mate."

"Are you out of your –"

"Listen, mate, we're really in the shit, now. The boys in green aren't going to be happy. What do you think will happen if we go flyin' into town as big as you please? You think they're going to say `Gidday, Peter, old sport, don't worry about a thing. We understand you had to put two slugs into our buddy. After all, he was a bit rude. Oh, by the way, just park the chopper and leave the keys in it!' No, they're going to grab yours truly, lean my bloomin' ass up against the wall and tell me it will only bloody well hurt for a second. You might have a chance, but not me. Hopefully, we've got enough petrol to get to the border. Once we're across, we'll head east toward El Paso and you can bugger off for home. I've hung in there for you, and now you're going to have to do this for me."

Jim looked at Sullivan. There was no question he was right. "I hope you know what the hell you're doing."

The Aussie climbed up into the pilot's seat and looked around.

"No worries, mate. Always thought I was really good at this. Never could bloody well understand why they kept grounding me!"

Jim gulped and climbed into the back. Sullivan flicked some switches and the rotors began to whirl. Before long, the engine was screaming and helicopter broke its bond with the earth.

"Back in the saddle, again," Peter sang.

Jim Barnes just shook his head.

CHAPTER 7

The threat of sleet and hail clouded over Albuquerque that November morning. The wind picked up, buffeting the army staff car carrying Colonel Jennings Colton. Rain pelted the dark, tinted windows. Winter, it seemed, was on the way.

Colton was on his way to a news conference at the civic auditorium downtown. An army jeep ahead of his, carrying four armed soldiers, moved easily through the half-empty downtown streets. It was a weekday. The stores were open. But demand for their goods was weak. Everything was on hold, waiting leadership, guidance and a measure of hope.

The colonel mulled over his words. Most of them were utter bullshit, he knew, but his goal that morning was pacifying the simpletons, plain and simple. The media hounds, eager for news bites and snappy headlines, would help his cause.

The car pulled up along side of a line of official vehicles and limousines. The governor and his staff, along with many legislators, state and city officials were there. Across the street, TV news vans, with satellites pointed to the sky, filled a parking lot.

The trappings of power were everywhere, but there was emptiness to it all. It was as though no one would admit the emperor wore no clothes. The elected leaders inside refused to give up the symbols of authority they had accumulated regardless of how superfluous they had become. In the same way an aging movie queen continues to apply heavy make-up to subvert the ravages of time, those men and woman would stand defiant against the reality that was now thrust upon them.

Colonel Colton paraded into the auditorium, his military bearing ramrod straight, exuding power, and proceeded directly to the long table, which had been placed on a stage high above the news media below. He immediately approached the governor, smiled, shook hands and repeated the procedure with all the other dignitaries at center stage. Then, he moved behind the podium and began to speak.

"Ladies and gentlemen, as I'm sure most of you are well aware, in the three days since the president announced emergency procedures for the security of the country, rumors and misinformation have spread rapidly and they have caused a great deal of worry. In an effort to dispel some of those falsehoods, a national simulcast news conference has been arranged with Washington D.C. and all military districts around the country. On the screen behind me, we will soon be patched by satellite into that conference. National Security Advisor E. Fife Lindsey IV will make the address and take questions from this and other districts.

"At the conclusion of his remarks, we will shift focus back to our area and you may then ask questions of me or any one of the dignitaries on this stage."

With that, the giant screen flickered on. Lindsey, his face drawn, stood in front of a bouquet of microphones.

"Let me begin by saying that I welcome this opportunity to address all the various groups which are assembled around the country. I will take your questions, and hopefully, provide answers which will explain the efforts which are being made on your behalf."

He continued, "To put the situation in some perspective, we can compare our actions to a company filing Chapter 11 reorganization. We are not bankrupt; we are not without contingency plans. What we need is time and patience on the part of the American public to reorganize our financial systems so that we can get on with life as we know it."

Lindsey continued. Though obviously drained, he tried to project an air of confidence. Finally, he began taking questions.

The first was from a TV news reporter in New York. The satellite feed switched to the reporter. His tie was loose and the shirtsleeves rolled up.

"Sir," he began brusquely, setting the tone for the questions to come, "Can you explain to me and the rest of the country how the top 10 banks in the U.S. were allowed to function when, in effect, they have been broke for the last ten years, by YOUR OWN measurement and regulations, due to non-performing loans to the Third World?"

"The simple answer," Lindsey began, "is that the problem became too big, too fast. The world financial systems, as they were constituted in the past, were extremely complicated and intertwined. Any attempt at rash, quick action would have been a disaster. Now, in retrospect, it can be argued that we should have had the political and moral courage to face the trouble head on. I'll leave that judgment to the historians."

Another question came from Chicago. "Isn't it true that one of the reasons these problems weren't addressed is because of the enormous holdings the political and industrial power structures had in those institutions, i.e. the East Coast establishment?

The barrage of questions continued for the next hour. The questions obviously reflected the nation's frustration.

From Nebraska: "If you were faced with the dilemma of feeding your family, or paying your taxes, which would you choose?"

From Texas: "With prisons already at full capacity across the country, did

Washington take into consideration the likely rise in crime rates in every state?"

From Florida: "With martial law in effect, what power – if any – do our elected members of congress have? Isn't it true that they are simply figure heads now?"

From Boston: "You know, in Monopoly, when the smart guys have all the money and control of the board, the game is over. How is that any different from what we've been seeing over the past 20 years where the middle class can't afford to do anything but make payments?"

It was a long morning for E. Fife Lindsey IV. Fifteen minutes into the conference he knew he had misjudged the passion across the nation. He was tucked safely inside the confines of the Washington beltway, like the rest of the governing class, and his vision of America was obviously distorted. Normally docile citizens, the kind who turned up for the marches carrying their American flags, were angry and frustrated, and looking for a way to vent their rage.

Finally, the conference was turned back to the local level and Colonel Jennings

Colton returned to the microphone. For 45 minutes, he, along with the governor, Albuquerque's mayor, and other elected officials, tried to answer questions and relieve fears. They, too, felt the intense frustration expressed in the pointed questions directed at them by those they were supposed to serve. Toward the end, the crime reporter for the daily newspaper asked about a subject with which the colonel was all too familiar. "Is it true that the murderers of the elderly Utah couple are still on the loose and have been seen in this state. Don't they represent a danger to the community?"

"I'm glad you asked me that," Colton began in a very secure, smug tone, "I have taken personal charge of the case. In the last few hours, I've directed units in such a way as to ensure capture, probably even as we speak. Such violence will not go unpunished and I guarantee that the citizens of this sector will be safe in their homes." As he finished, Colton noticed one of his female staffers trying to signal him frantically at the foot of the stage.

"If there are no further questions, we'll conclude this press conference," he said quickly.

As the people in the auditorium began to rise to their feet, and the noise of shuffling chairs filled the air, Colton nodded to the rest of the dignitaries and walked over to his aide.

"What is it Murphy?"

"I thought you might want to know, sir," the young woman began, "We've just received word that one of our choppers is missing and the fugitives have escaped. The report has it that one of our men is dead, the pilot was left behind, and Sergeant Anderson is nowhere to be found. I just thought because YOU have taken personal responsibility in this matter...."

Colton shot Murphy a cold look, stopping her in mid-sentence. Anger filled him.

"Son of a bitch!" he whispered. "I'm surrounded by incompetence! Goddamnit, I can see that I'm going to have to take care of this myself. If it's the last thing I do, I'll see those bastards in hell."

Unlike the smoke he'd been blowing up the media's ass for nearly an hour, this was a promise he intended to keep.

****

They had been in the air for almost two hours, except for a short stop at an isolated reservation town south of Gallop, where the startled Indians helped them remove the unconscious soldier from the back of the helicopter. Anderson was alive and would survive. Sullivan, enjoying the role of a soldier once again, promised medals for all those who took care of him.

The Australian was impressive as a chopper pilot, keeping the craft low to avoid radar. He was delighted with the fact that he could still remember how to fly it after so many years. Jim was even more grateful, marveling at Sullivan's simple-yet-complex make-up.

At times, the radio would crackle with a conversation that was indecipherable to anyone but a pilot. Sullivan monitored the channels, but showed no signs of concern.

They both knew that the aircraft was probably reported missing and that a search would be mounted. The hope was that they could cross the border before anyone had time to react.

"There," Jim said from the co-pilot's chair. "That's I-10. We don't have far to go now. How's the fuel?"

"If the bloody gauges are right, no worries, mate," Peter answered.

"You know, it might be best to go in for a while, then turn east. If word gets out about a hijacked helicopter, I'm sure most of the cops in the Southwest will be looking for us. Somehow, I don't think the Air Force is going to respect Mexican territory if they spot us flying around."

"Yeah, I'd say your right. There isn't much of anything you Yanks DO respect about Mexico, is there now?"

"The tequila and the water," Jim answered looking out the window, "Either one of them can kill you."

"Aw, you Yanks are bloody sissies. Never could hold your liquor. Now the 'stralians, that's the blokes who can drink.

There's not a drop in the world that worries a true blue 'stralian."

"It ain't the liquid, my friend," Jim retorted, speaking like a man with experience, "It's the little amoeba inside it that crawls up your ass and makes you wish you were dead!"

"Bring the bloody bastards on!" Sullivan shouted. "I need a cold beer so bad I could drink the sweat of the bloomin' town drunk, I could!"

Jim shook his head. "What are you going to do after we get to Juarez?" he asked.

"I think my best bet is to get to the coast, maybe crew a ship back home. Then I'll head for the Outback and do some jackerrooing. Been a long time since I've done that. I'm sure things will be as bloody useless there as they are here. We always did take after you Yanks, even to the point of following you down the toilet."

The tired American looked at him intensely. "I'll tell you what, if they should get me, don't worry. As far as I'm concerned, you are John Jones from England, heading for Brazil. You know, we've only known each other for a couple days, but I feel I could trust you more than anyone I know."

"I've found trouble brings that out in people. Now don't go bloody sentimental on me, mate. We both did what we had to do. Someday, we'll meet in a pub in 'stralia, have a few schooners of beer, and tell lies to our grandkids. That is, if I can ever figure out which ones are mine!"

"I hope you're right," Jim said, patting Peter's shoulder. "I really do."

It wasn't long before they found the border. In a rush of metal and air, they flew into Mexico. Jim had mixed emotions about leaving the United States. He was a Midwesterner and always believed his country would look after him in good times and bad. The past days had shaken his faith in many things he held sacred. That faith was being replaced by the hard edge of a hunted man.

The flight continued unabated for another hour as they flew into barren stretches of Mexico. The land below was harsh, dusty Sonora desert with few signs of life, where the mistake of not having enough food or water could be fatal. In the distance, small groups of mountain ranges loomed above the landscape. They were desolate and cold, beckoning an unwary traveler to trouble.

The contrast between Mexico and the United States was that of the bumpy dirt road beside the paved super highway. It was a land of limited promise, but unlimited riches. Tucked away in the northern territories of the country were some of the largest deposits of oil and gas, as well as gold and silver, found anywhere in the world. Yet the cultural calamity guarantied its people would never benefit from that wealth. In a country where five percent of the population controlled 95 percent of the money, it was not surprising that a futile resignation descended on the Mexicans. They were born, they lived and they died, with very little change in between.

By now, as the world was spinning in turmoil, the Mexican government had taken to controlling damage where it could. Some parts of the country – primarily in the north – were essentially lawless. Powerful men, gaining their strength from the drug money pouring in from the north, ruled. The

Federales in Mexico City simply did not have resources to deal with it.

The calm of the flight was broken by a loud sputtering noise, followed by a backfire from the engine. The two men shot each other a worried glance. Quickly, the Australian's hands went to flipping switches and pulling levers. At the same time, he was also looking for a place to set the copter down. The large green machine gave out with one final dying cough.

"BLOODY HELL!" shouted Peter, "The bastard's out of petrol. Never did know these bloomin gauges to be right!"

"SON OF A BITCH!" Jim screamed. "What do we do?"

"Grab your knickers and hang on, mate, we're going down! And these bloody things don't glide very well. HERE WE GO!"

The forward motion of the craft stopped and it seemed to hang in the air for a moment. Then it fell. Luckily, Sullivan had kept the helicopter low, but both men knew the landing wouldn't be smooth.

Jim braced himself. If only I'd listened more closely to those flight attendant speeches, he thought.

The ground came up quickly. The shock of metal striking rock reverberated through the cabin. The landing runners smashed outward and the main hulk crumbled down in a heap. The large rotor blade, still whirling from centrifugal motion, slashed into the ground, and then bent upward. Dust and dirt flew up in all directions and then silence filled the air.

Sullivan, still clutching the control stick, his face brown from dirt and smoke, looked over at Jim. "Trade you pants, mate."

Jim's lifted his head from between his knees. "It wouldn't do you any good."

"Let's get out of this bloody heap, Jimmy. I was tired of flying, anyway."

The American didn't answer. It had not been a good day. The two men began crawling out of the wreckage, climbing over jagged, bent metal and pieces of shattered plexi-glass. Once outside, they turned and looked back at the metal beast. It had seen better days, too.

Jim walked over to a grouping of rocks. Standing on an elevated plain, he could see for miles over the desolate country. Small lizards scurried about and tiny birds jumped from one cactus to the other. Other than that, there was no sign of life. I've finally arrived at the bottom of the barrel, he told himself. His long, downhill spiral seemed to reach its logical conclusion. Dead men, crashes, murder; what could possibly come next? A slow, agonizing death in the desert, why not?

Sullivan, seemingly sensing his partner's despair, flopped on the ground beside him. "So what'll it be, mate, you going to quit?"

"The thought has crossed my mind."

"Well, I've been this way before and I can tell you, sure as bloody death and taxes, it'll only get better."

"Yeah. Maybe some soldier will put a bullet in my head."

Peter smiled. "I saw a dirt road a couple of miles back. Even in Mexico, it should lead somewhere."

"I suppose so," Jim replied simply.

The Aussie jumped up and went over to the copter. He rummaged around and emerged triumphantly hoisting a green canteen of water.

"Just as I thought," he laughed, "Even you Yanks wouldn't be flying around without something to wet your whistle."

Jim watched him closely; amazed that he still had the spark of life when despair was so near.

Again, Sullivan's zest pulled Jim from the edge. He remembered the promise he made to himself. He'd fight to the end.

Jim stood. "What do you say we get the hell out of here?"

"Now that's the spirit, Jimmy me boy. Blimey. I can smell cold beer just the other side of those mountains. Tell you what, I'll shout the first round."

"You'll shout ALL the rounds. I haven't got a damn dime on me. No, wait, I've still got a few bucks in my shoe."

"Hang on to your quid, mate. Consider it foreign aide. We Australians would be bloody well pleased to pull your arse out of the fire once again!"

Peter retrieved the automatic and Jim put on an army jacket he'd found in the chopper. His Levi's were dirty and his Reeboks scrapped, but he was alive and determined to stay that way.

CHAPTER 8

Across the country, in a middle class suburb of Detroit, Linda Barnes went about the business of trying to hold her life together. A few scraps of paper strewn about reminded her of the day's must-dos, though, like the dirty dishes piled in the sink, most would remain undone. The chores of daily life took a backseat to the current emergency. Her husband of 17 years had not contacted her in over two days. Jim Barnes wouldn't do that. Something, she knew, was seriously wrong.

Linda's eyes fell on her cell phone sitting in front of her. She reached out for it, stopped, then reached again. She dialed Jim's number, hoping against hope. And like the dozens of previous attempts, reached nothing but a message that "this customer is unavailable or no longer in the service area."

The winter wind rattled the glass of the sliding door leading to the backyard. Outside, snowflakes swirled, before landing on the once-green grass. The snow wasn't enough to stick, just a harbinger of things to come. Already, most of her neighbors had sequestered themselves for the cold months to follow, choosing to stay inside and wrap themselves in the security of their homes. Linda Barnes, though, shivered with uncertainty. Uneasy sense of impending doom gripped her; she couldn't shake it. At no time in their married life had her husband acted irresponsibly. If anything, he was overly cautious, always protecting their best interests.

A pang of guilt tightened her throat as she remembered his last phone call home. She wasn't there. Another missed opportunity in life; one she prayed she wouldn't regret.

Linda stood and walked to the desk in the small room off the kitchen. Once again, she checked her email, hoping for good news. Once again, she was disappointed.

Linda Barnes was in shape and still a good-looking woman, aging gracefully, if reluctantly. During the months Jim was in California, she'd had some laser surgery done on her face. It wasn't a major overhaul, but it removed some of the small lines and wrinkles that had crept up on her. She was happy with her look and anticipated the day the new "younger woman" would seduce her husband upon their reunion.

She preferred wearing tracksuits around the house, like the red one she had on, especially when the cold of winter neared. Besides, the house could be kept at a lower temperature, contributing in a small way to solving the energy crisis they faced. In a way, that spoke volumes about her life. She had always been socially conscious. An activist in college organizing sit-ins and marches, Linda bridled at unchecked power and authority exhibited by politicians who were supposed to be servants of the people.

Over the years, she watched and dreaded the gradual encirclement of all aspects of the citizen's lives by the monolith of bureaucracy everyone helped create. Few seemed to notice or care and that angered her. But she was a patient woman – a fighter – and she believed the time would come when people like her would be called on to right the wrongs.

The sound of a car pulling into the garage broke the spell of her quiet moment. Kelley Barnes, followed closely by her boyfriend, Billy Watson, bounded through the backdoor.

"Hi, Mom. Any word from Dad?"

"Nothing," she answered, and the same chill she felt every time the subject was broached, raced up her spine.

"What are you going to do?" asked Billy, an athletic looking young man with a broad face, and short cropped brown hair. He began to take off his letterman's jacket and set it on the chair.

"I'm going to have to get the police involved. He should have called or emailed by now. I swear, when he shows up, I'll strangle him!"

"Mom," Kelley began hesitantly, "Have you looked out front lately?"

"No, why?"

"I don't know. There's a car, ah, a brown car with two men sitting inside, just across the street. They look like they're watching our house. I thought maybe you had called the cops."

Linda Barnes looked at her carefully. She started for the front windows with her daughter and friend in tow. Slowly she pulled back the sheer curtains. Across the street, a dark haired man in an overcoat was looking back at her. He did not attempt to conceal himself, but instead, began speaking into a device attached to his wrist. Linda dropped the curtain and turned toward her daughter.

"I'm going out there to see what's going on. You two stay here, I'll be right back." She grabbed her jacket on the living room chair, and marched toward the door. "If anything happens to me, call the police."

With a turn of the knob the door burst open, helped by a gust of cold wind. She pulled the jacket close around her neck and began walking briskly toward the brown sedan. Inside, she could see a surprised look come over the driver's face, and he seemed to fumble around for a moment, not knowing how to react. By the time the determined woman reached the car door, the dark haired man had rolled down the window.

"Can I help you with something?" she asked in clear, controlled voice, not betraying her jangled nerves.

"Are you Mrs. James Barnes?" he said. Linda's heart sunk to the pit of her stomach.

"Yes, what is it?"

"I'm Lieutenant Mike Dunn of the 12th Military Command district. We've been asked to take you down to our headquarters. It seems there are some people who have a few questions for you." He opened a handheld computer. The screen showed his picture ID and credentials.

Panic swept over Linda, but she didn't show it on her face. Instead, she tried to collect herself. "If you've got something to say to me, why don't we just go inside and get it over with?" Her direct response surprised Lt. Dunn.

"No, ma'am. I'm afraid it's more complicated than that. Frankly, I'm not even sure what's going on. We were told to come out here and pick you up. No more, no less. I'm just following orders."

"I see," she answered. "Well, do you want me to follow you in my car?"

"No, you can ride with us. We'll see that you get home all right."

"All right then," she continued warily, "let me get my things, and I'll be right out."

"Sergeant Steadman here will help you," he cut in quickly, more of as an order than an offer. The other officer pushed opened the door and walked around the car.

Linda Barnes looked at them both and said nothing. Something was strange, she knew. If Jim were hurt, or dead, they would have said so by now.

She turned and shuffled back to the front door, followed closely by the sergeant. Kelley opened it as they approached.

"What is it, mom? What's going on? Is it daddy?" she asked.

"I don't know, honey," she replied. "These men want me to come with them. They're with the Military District. I've got to go now, but I'll be back soon."

Kelley didn't hesitate a moment. "We'll go with you. Billy can drive."

For the first time, Sgt. Steadman spoke up. "No, I'm afraid our orders are to bring your mother downtown alone. She'll be all right. It'll only take a couple of hours."

"Go and get my purse, will you, Kelley?" Linda asked.

"Sure, just a second." She turned and walked into the kitchen.

Billy had been watching the scene closely. For a young man, he carried himself with a certain amount of strength, which drew others to him.

"Mind if I take a digital picture of you, just to be on the safe side?" he said to the older man directly, looking him straight in the eye.

"I don't think that's necessary," he answered.

"Hey, what's the harm?" said Billy, holding his cell phone-digital camera. "You guys are on the up-and-up, right?"

"Sure, kid. Take the picture."

Billy snapped one.

"So we'll see you in a couple of hours, then," Billy said to Linda. "If you need anything, just call. We'll be right down." His words were measured and reassuring.

Linda appreciated the concern. Kelley walked up and handed the purse to her mother. She gave her a kiss on the cheek.

"Take care of her, would you Billy? I think we're going to need your help."

"Sure, Mrs. Barnes," he answered with pride, "don't worry about a thing."

She turned and walked back out the open door with the officer. Then the mother and wife stopped, and looked back over her shoulder. She had a sense that the world as she knew it was about to change.

She was right.

****

The direction the two weary men walked was not difficult to determine. The sun crested in the sky hours before, and was beginning to fall behind a range of gray mountains to the west. At best, only an hour of sunlight left remained. Both men knew that they had to cover as much ground as possible before darkness set in.

Walking down the dirt strip that passed for a road in Mexico was difficult. Rutted and rock strewn, it was probably just as easy to hike alongside it in the desert. Although the going was hard, their spirits were uplifted somewhat by the rich colors of the countryside which were beginning to burst out in all their painted glory. The greens and browns of the land met the mauves and purples of the dusky sky, as the last rays of the sun cast themselves across the mountains. It was a primitive country at its deadly best; a soft kiss betraying harsh reality ready to spring on the unsuspecting. At times, Peter and Jim felt like the only two people on the face of the Earth.

A chilly breeze picked up as night fell. The rich colors faded to gray, then black. Not having shelter might have invited loneliness, but the easy banter between them helped, and they drew strength from the company of the other. They continued on, walking into the Mexican night, not knowing what lay just beyond the next ridge.

Up ahead, a bright light drifted up over a hill. A car approached, but it was too far away to see anything else.

"Blimey, mate, I reckon our luck has changed," Sullivan said with the cockiness of one who knew it all along.

Jim hoped for the best. Maybe he wouldn't have to spend the night sleeping on rocks after all, he thought. The idea of snakes and scorpions crawling about all but guaranteed a sleepless night.

The car, an old Chevy low-rider, its rear end almost dragging along the road, finally picked them up in its headlights. It came to a stop about 20 feet away. Jim and Peter strained their eyes to see how many people were inside. The driver's door opened up, and a single, heavyset man stepped out. His hands were empty, which gave Jim some relief, and the thick, stocky form began walking toward them. As he came closer, the dark face with the deep-set black eyes broke out into a wide grin, with one gold tooth gleaming back at them in the half-light. After a murderous day, the two friends felt like a piano had been lifted off their backs.

Jim searched back for the high school Spanish that was a faded memory. He remembered seeing a handheld computer back in the copter that was programmed for every major language used on earth, but it was a mute point. The hell with it, he thought, let's try the direct approach.

"English? You speak any English?"

"Sí, senor, a little," said the man, smiling.

The Australian stepped forward and thrust his arm out. "Gidday, mate, Peter Sullivan's the name. Mighty glad to make your acquaintance. Wouldn't happen to have a cold bottle of beer, now would you mate?"

"Sí, senor. I just bought some Coronas. I was on my way out to shoot the deer."

"Bloody hell!" Sullivan shouted, looking up to the heavens. "Thank you, Lord! Thank you. I swear on me son's life I'll be at church at the drop of a hat."

"You got kids?" Jim asked, puzzled.

"SOMEWHERE, mate, I'm sure of it! Anyway, it's the bloody thought that counts. Could I buy a couple off you, err...?"

"Bernardo. Is no problem, senor. Help yourself. They are in the car behind the seat."

Sullivan slapped him on the back. "Good on you, mate, err, Bernardo, I'm forever in your debt." He set off with a hop toward the Chevy.

"Bernardo, maybe you can help us. Is there a town anywhere around here?"

"Si, senor…?"

"Jim."

"Jim. Is where I just came from." He turned, looking back up the road. "About 30 kilometers that way. Rielito. Is not much of a place by Gringo standards, but it is home."

Jim sighed.

"Bernardo, I know this is a lot to ask you, but could you give us a lift back to town? We will pay. I can't walk much further," Jim said.

The round-faced Mexican looked deeply into the tired eyes of the man standing before him. He had a quiet grace about him, and a bond seemed to be drawn immediately between the two strangers.

"Is no problem, senor Jim. The deer can wait for another night. Vamanos, I take you to mi amigo's place. He will give you a room for siesta. Hurry, we go! Before the strange one drinks all the Corona!"

The old, gray Chevy, with dents and scratches on the sides, bounced and swerved its way east, toward the small Mexican town. Jim sat in the front seat with Bernardo, sipping the best-tasting beer he had ever known. Peter was stretched out across the back, a cold Corona in his hand and a huge smile on his face, prattling on about Australian beer. The Mexican tried to understand what he was saying, but soon found it more convenient to simply say, "Si, senor."

Only when they reached the outskirts of the pueblo did they pass their first car. Bernardo happily pointed out highlights of the community, motioning in the direction of his home. He was a family man, with a wife and three children. His faced lit up as he talked about them. He explained that he was a simple peddler. His small shop in town was full of the clay pots, velvet paintings, and serapes seen all along the border.

His small town is a well-guarded secret to most Americans, but it does see its share of visitors. Decades of bartering with vacationers helped him learn English, he said. The bulk of his income came from Juarez. Once a month, Bernardo loaded his goods, drove the 200 miles to the city and sold to the shops that catered to the tourists. On his last trip, business was slow. It seemed to him that something was wrong with the Norte Americanos.

With a jolt, the old Chevy hit the pavement of the main road into town. Bernardo turned the car right and headed toward the center of Rielito. In the dark of night, the place seemed very small, with one or two gas stations, some liquor stores, a few shops, and a couple of restaurants lining the road. Everywhere, young men gathered on street corners, looking over each other's cars, watching the young women watch them. The mating ritual was just getting underway.

"Where'd you say we'd be going, mate?" Sullivan asked, leaning forward to talk over the back of the seat.

"Is an old hotel nobody uses no more. Raul, mi amigo, owns it. He still keeps one room there in case his Chiquita wants to play. That is, senor, if Juanita, his espousa, err, wife, as you say, is not looking." Bernardo's eyes lit up like a man who relished telling the secret.

The car rolled through the dusty town before coming to a stop at the far end. Jim looked up. Hanging above a padlocked door, an old wooden sign, swaying in the night breeze, proclaimed it the "El Grande Hotel." The three men stepped out of the car. Bernardo walked over to the padlock and pulled out a key.

"The missus know you got that key, old sport?" Sullivan asked with a grin.

Bernardo grinned back at him. "Is not what you think, amigo. I just look after the place for him. Besides, my wife would have my balls if she caught me fooling around. She's very good with a knife. Is not worth it."

The Aussie screwed up his face. "I'd have to say you made the right decision, mate. I've got no worries about boyfriends or husbands, but an angry woman? Well, there's just no telling what they might do. Bloody irrational, I'd say. Besides, you probably couldn't get her to sew your balls back on, either!"

Bernardo laughed loud, shaking his head.

Inside, Bernardo found a switch and turned on some lights leading down the lone hallway. They stood in a foyer that at one time was quite elegant. But on that night, it was littered with broken furniture and cobwebs. At the end of the room, an old counter stood, its wood dried and split. Torn purple curtains fell on each side of the boarded up windows, and a portrait of Coronado, with his gleaming helmet and lance, hung askance on the wall.

They walked down the hallway of two-story building, and Bernardo stopped to open the first door on the left. Once again, he turned on the switch, and the large room lit up. Jim and Peter were pleasantly surprised. Instead of the rat-infested hole they had imagined, the room had two beds and some nice furniture. The Mexican tile floor was clean, and there was a bathroom off to one end of the white painted room.

"Is not bad, hey senor?" Bernardo said, laughing. "I'll tell Raul you are friends of mine, so that he doesn't shoot you."

"Amigo, we definitely owe you one," Jim said with tired sincerity, "Someday, maybe we can return the favor."

"Is nothing, senor Jim. Americanos have been good to my family and me. I am not like the others, always bitter at the Gringos. You rest. I will come by in the morning and take you out to my hacienda. My wife makes the best eggs rancheros in all of Mexico."

With that, the kind man smiled and stepped out into the hall. Sullivan shut the door and looked around the room.

"Bloody lucky, I'd say, mate. Could have run into one of those banditos you see on the Westerns. Guns a blazing. Instead, he puts us up in a bloomin' love shack!" Peter continued, eyeing the two beds, one a single, the other a double. "Which bunk you reckon you want?"

Jim knew exactly what was going through Sullivan's mind. "Oh, I don't know. I'll let you have the big one. Probably a little softer from the use."

"That's what I was bloody well afraid of, you bastard!" Peter shot back, "All right, no worries. But if I come up with some venereal disease, I swear I'll haunt you till your dying day!"

"The way it's been going," Jim answered back, as he turned off the light and pulled his arms free of the army jacket, "we might not have enough time to catch a cold before that happens."

CHAPTER 9

Corporal Calhoun burst into Colonel Colton's office just as he finished his mid-morning videoconference with Washington. Jennings Colton was up to his eyeballs in meetings with civilian and military authorities trying to implement new policies in the military district. Making the transition from constitutional law to martial law was complex and taxing. Worse yet, as he was trying to change the world, a pair murderers remained at-large; a thorn in his side that wouldn't go away.

"They've found him, Colonel. They found Anderson."

"Dead?" Colton asked simply.

"No, but he's lost a lot of blood. Took one in the shoulder. The guys who stole the helicopter dropped him off at a reservation town south of Gallop."

"Hold it, hold it, Calhoun. No one 'stole' that Goddamned chopper. They overpowered our men. You got that? Some shithead leaks that story, and I've got a thousand reporters hounding me. Makes me look like a Goddamned incompetent. When I get through with Anderson, he'll wish they had finished him off!"

Calhoun looked intently at the Colonel and bit his tongue.

"EVAC says they can have another copter over there in a couple of hours. He'll be back here at Kirtland's infirmary this afternoon. We've also scrambled six Cobra gun ships looking for the perps. Satellites are locked on our sector, watching everything that moves."

"Good, corporal. I want you to get Orlowski in here. I need some damage control with the media. Those two bastards out there flying around in MY helicopter are reducing this command to the laughing stock of the whole Patriot operation. I've got two dead soldiers, a chopper pilot with his head stuck up his ass, and Anderson, the son of a bitch, bleeding all over the Navajo reservation! The last thing I need is CNN in here asking questions. I've got important policies to implement, and this chicken shit episode isn't helping!"

Calhoun shook his head in agreement.

"The wife of that Barnes fellow. I read the report faxed down yesterday. I want her ass picked up and brought down here. She's going to spend some time with us. Maybe we can flush them out when he knows we've got her."

"You know Colonel," Calhoun began quietly, "Something isn't making any sense. Here's an average guy: wife, kid, mortgage, dog, the whole suburbia thing. Now how is it that he goes off and whacks a bunch of people, right out of the blue? I don't get it."

"Who knows, Calhoun, maybe something snapped. They don't pay me to be a psychologist. All I know is I've got a bunch of dead bodies and my job is to stop him, once and for all. Did you see the sheet on his wife? Hell, she's been a rabble-rouser all her life. Probably part of some underground movement. Well, we don't have to pussyfoot around with that kind anymore. This is the day of the long knives, and I've got the biggest one in town."

"There are some reporters outside asking to speak with you. What do you want me to do, sir?"

"Throw their ass off the Goddamned base! I've had my fill of those bastards, too. No, don't do that. Make up some bullshit about how I am in staff meetings all day. We will prepare a statement to be released later today. Got that?"

"Yes, sir."

"And Calhoun. Leak word that I'm bringing the woman into custody. You know, big conspiracy thing, and all. At least we'll have a warm body to show some progress. That is, of course, if she doesn't hijack the Goddamned airplane on the way here!"

"I understand, sir. But I still think you might want to slow this snowball down, before it turns into an avalanche. There's something more here. I can feel it."

"Calhoun, I've got a lot on my plate right now, and I don't need this aggravation. I didn't start it. I didn't carve up gramps. I didn't even screw up, like Anderson. But I'll tell you this; it's going to come out MY way in the end. I guarantee you that. And I'll do whatever it takes to keep control."

'Whatever it takes' would have brought howls of protest from every civil libertarian in the country days before. But the law was under attack from all sides, and in the mayhem, it was difficult to separate the good guys from the bad. In many ways, the situation was similar to the old soldier's adage, "Kill 'em all, and let God sort 'em out later."

****

The plate was piled high with scrambled eggs. And the ranchero sauce, filled with peppers and spices, topped the dish in all its crowning glory. A steaming bowl of refried beans made its way around the simple oak table, followed closely by flour tortillas and more salsa. Jim Barnes had enjoyed similar meals in authentic Mexican restaurants, but the sheer delight of the food and the welcome surroundings made this one unforgettable. It was a small taste of home in a most unlikely place.

Peter Sullivan's eyes lit up as the feast came his way. Despite their guests' stubbled faces and well-worn clothes, Bernardo, his wife and their three children welcomed the visitors as though they were family.

"Senor Peter, after the meal, when your belly is full and your heart content, I will give you the best treat of all; my Maria will shave you with the razor and hot towel. As I told you before, she is very good with a knife." He winked at Jim, who smiled back.

"That would be wonderful, Bernardo. Yeah, I bloody well appreciate that. Have been looking a bit scruffy lately. Never can tell, I might find me future missus in your town."

Maria's face lit up in a huge grin. "Si, senor, I have someone you MUST meet. She is my best friend AND a very good cook."

Bernardo did not look up from his food, but quipped, "Si, to look at her is to be sure she can cook!"

His wife glared over at him in mock disapproval. "Hush, Bernardo. Remember, it is I who will hold the razor to YOUR throat again, too!"

Jim smiled as he took in the bantering. "You know something, Peter, you could do a lot worse. Senora Calrone, this is the best,

THE best. I was so hungry. When I get home, I'll tell my wife about this meal."

Bernardo looked up from his plate. "You know, Jim, you mentioned you were going to Juarez. I was going to go there at the end of the week, but it doesn't matter. We could leave tomorrow morning."

"Bernardo that would be great! I must start working my way back, and the sooner I get going the better."

"How about you, senor Peter? There is enough room in my car. I know you said you were going south, to the sea coast, but maybe you changed your mind?"

"No, mate, south it is. I think I can catch a ship out of Mazatlan. It's time I got my bloody rear end back to 'stralia. I've had too much excitement over here in the States. Bloody war zone, it is! Think I need to retire for a bit."

"Well, if you change your mind, I will be by to pick Jim up around seven. It will take us a day to drive that far. Our roads, they're not like the Gringos'."

Maria watched as the three men ate the hearty breakfast. When the children finished, she scrapped off their plates, and then waited for the men.

"How is it that you came to Mexico in the first place," she said to Jim.

"Oh, I guess you could call it a hunting trip. Our vehicle broke down some miles from where Bernardo found us. Except for the kindness of your family, it's been a disaster."

"There is much trouble up there, to the north, yes?" she asked.

"Yeah, I'm afraid so. A lot of people lost everything."

"In Mexico, we no have much to lose, so it's not so bad. We have our church, our familia, and our friends. The rest comes and goes. It does not matter," she said with a wave of the hand.

Jim nodded. "I think many Gringos are about to find that out the hard way. You begin to realize what's really important."

"Well, ladies and gents, I'm stuffed. Fine tucker, that was. Tell you what, Bernardo; let your wife go with me to Australia and I'll send her back a wealthy woman in six months. How bout it, mate?"

"I have a better idea for you, senor. Marry her friend, take her with you, and send me the money. I would never forget you for that favor!"

"Bernardo!" Maria said, waving her knife up and down.

The meal ended and the men retired to the front porch to rest and talk, in old world fashion. Jim looked around the dirt yard. Homemade toys were scattered about for the children. It was a far cry from some of the neighborhoods he saw in California. Somehow, he felt more joy, and saw more laughing faces on the children as they played with their sticks, old tires, and cans, then in any video arcade in Los Angeles. Gameboys, and new virtual reality toys had nothing on this simplicity.

Maria kept her promise of a shave for both men. Peter sat wide-eyed in the chair, lather covering his face, as the razor whisked his beard away. For Jim, it was a time to relax, enjoy the warmth of the towel and a sense of cleanliness for the first time in days. His mind returned to his college days when Linda did the same thing for him. He ached to return home.

"Bernardo, is there a land line phone, or even a cell phone in town that I can use to call the States?" Jim asked. "Better yet, a computer?"

"No, senor, I'm afraid not. Since the trouble began in the states, the government has shut down our lines. Nothing is working. It could be many days before it returns."

"No problem, " he assured him, "I'll try from El Paso tomorrow."

When they were done, the unlikely travelers thanked Maria, and bade farewell to all the family. Bernardo took them back into town and he dropped them off at a cantina Peter had spotted earlier that day.

"I will see you in the morning then, senors?" Bernardo said as the two men got out and closed the car door.

"Seven o'clock, sharp. I'll be there. Someday, I hope, I'll get the chance to repay you for all your kindness," Jim said.

"Is nothing, amigo. You would do the same, I'm sure." Bernardo waved his hand, and pulled away, the old car sputtering and blowing smoke out the tailpipe.

"Well, mate, I believe I'm getting a bit dry. How about a cold one to wet your whistle?"

"Sounds like a plan," Jim answered, and the two men entered the small cantina. Inside, a dozen or so metal tables and chairs were scattered around the dimly lit room. The whitewashed walls, covered with metal artworks and felt paintings, betrayed their age, as old bits of plaster crumbled to the floor. But it was clean and offered a good place to get out of the afternoon sun.

The two men sat at a table near the window. The cantina was half full, and a low murmur greeted them as they entered. There were no waitresses about, so Peter decided to take matters into his own hands.

"Hang on, mate. I'll see if I can't find out where they're hiding the beer." He got up and sauntered over to the long bar. A dark haired woman with fine features greeted him with a shy smile. They talked for a moment, Peter obviously enjoying the conversation with such an attractive female, and then she set two ice cold Coronas on the bar. The Aussie put some money down, winked, and returned to the table.

"The queen, mate. I've found the queen," he laughed.

Jim looked at him and shook his head. "What are you talking about, now?"

"As a traveling man, I can state from personal experience that every town has a queen. The object is to bloody well find her. Now, as luck would have it, where would she be but here, serving up my favorite liquid. Destiny, Jimmy me boy, that's what it is."

"Well, if you plan on sticking around here drinking beer all day, I hope your destiny finds a way to weasel some free drinks from her, 'cause we're getting a little low on funds."

"No worries, mate," Sullivan replied with a grin, "I'll give her a little time to cool off, and then work me magic."

"You better hope that one of these hombres in here doesn't already have a prior claim."

"No problem," Peter shot back, "I've got you to cover me backside, now don't I?"

Jim laughed. "I guess."

They drank for a while longer, and when their beers were gone, Peter looked back up at the bar.

"I might be a few minutes, mate. Just bear with me. Like it says in the Bible, all good things come to those who wait."

"Tell you what," Jim answered, "I'm going to wander around a little and check out the town. I'll see you back here in a few hours."

"Yeah," Peter replied, not taking his eyes off the woman across the room, "that'll do. Try not to get lost."

Jim got up and strolled outside. The afternoon sun bore down on the small town. Many of its residents were holed up in shady pockets near stores with merchandise for sale out on the street. They seemed resigned to the fact that business would be slow in the heat of the day, and content to simply watch life go by. It was interesting to Jim that a country so close to the most powerful, dominant economic force the world has ever known, would be willing simply to get by. Years before, he, like many others, would have written them off as lazy underachievers, waiting for things to happen. But on that day, as he looked into the brown, etched faces, Jim began to sense the rhythm of life around him. He was envious and calm at the same moment.

Jim walked up the main street, nodding and smiling at the merchants as they came up to him. When he told them "No dinero" to their offers of plates, jewelry, rugs and clothes, they accepted it with knowing grace, returning to find a cool spot to spend their time. Children followed him closely, watching for loose change, or a chance to perform some menial task and earn money. He tousled their hair as they pleaded and schemed. Finally, when all they're streetwise antics were unsuccessful, they fell away, melting into the crowds in search of another prospect.

Near the end of the town, as the shops began to dwindle, Jim noticed an old Ford Mustang with its front hood up, and a pair of legs dangling out the side of the engine compartment. The car was identical to the first one he owned out of high school and good memories flooded back. Haltingly, he walked over to the side of the faded red car, and looked down at the young man working on the engine.

"Hi, there," he began casually. "You speak English?"

"Sure, senor, they make us at school. We should talk like the Gringos, act like the Gringos, then, maybe make money like the Gringos!" he replied, grimacing as he tried to replace a spring on the carburetor.

"I'm Jim. What's your name?"

"Jorge Mendoza."

"What's the problem? I use to have one of these, and I think there isn't anything I haven't fixed once or twice."

"The engine is missing."

"Turn it on. Let's see what we've got."

Jorge ducked out from underneath the hood, and moved to the front seat. He twisted the key, and the engine started, sputtering and popping as it tried not to stall.

Jim moved in front of the Mustang, and began working with the carburetor. He relished the feel of the mechanical equipment he had grown up with. After a few twists and turns with some tools lying about, he stood up and motioned for Jorge to turn it off.

"Carburetor needs to be rebuilt," he said. "You got any place around here where we can get some parts?"

"My uncle. He has a junkyard not far from here."

"Good. Tell you what. I've got some time to kill, so we'll take it apart."

"But I have no money to pay you, senor?" Jorge said.

"Don't worry about it. I've got a friend here in town, Bernardo Calrone. Someday you do him a favor, and we'll call it even."

Jorge's face lit up, his brown eyes shining as he looked at the American. "Is a deal, senor!"

Jim took off his jacket and rolled up his sleeves. Hours passed as the two men laughed and cursed at the stubborn engine. The latest models in the states had computers that controlled every aspect of the vehicles performance, including trip directions and Internet communications. But in Mexico, the state of the art was years behind.

Fortunately, the young Mexican's uncle had some used parts that could be adapted to their cause. As the grease blackened his hands, and the sweat dripped from his brow, Jim lost himself in another world, another time. He was swept away from the chaos of the past days, secure in accomplishing something he could control. He felt as if someone had released a pressure valve and his body was finally allowed to relax.

At last, the moment of truth arrived, just as the sun was about to set on the western horizon.

"Fire her up, Jorge. Let's see how she runs."

The engine came to life with a strong burst of noise, and then settled down into a rhythmic purr. Jim smiled, and his arms shot up to the heavens above.

"The winner and still champion!" he shouted, remembering a line from an old movie years before.

"No shit, amigo. It does not sound like the same car that died here this morning!" Jorge shouted with excitement. "Come, let's go for a ride! You drive." He slammed the hood down, and they piled into the old Mustang.

Jim Barnes gripped the steering wheel and smiled.

"I used to have a lot of fun in one of these," he said.

With that, they roared off into the sunset, spraying rocks and scattering dust as the battered old pony came to life once again.

CHAPTER 10

The clear Mexican night began to give way to swirling clouds and the wind rose in a crescendo of blurring dust. Two hours passed since sunset and the tenor of the night had changed from one of peace to that of threat as the storm gathered. Merchants along the once-crowded streets had safely packed away their goods, aware that the calm of the Sonora desert could change quickly, catching the unwary in its fury.

Inside the old hotel room, two sweat-soaked bodies slammed together yet another time in sexual frenzy. The glass in the window rattled just above their heads, yet the lovers were oblivious. The lean, muscular body of the Australian grasped the naked woman below him, as her legs, entwined with his own, rose up with the intensity of his movements. Finally, at the peak of effort and passion, a guttural growl spilled out of his open mouth, and his head pulled back toward the ceiling. The dark-skinned Mexican woman, her body quivering and a soft whimper crossing her lips, also found that pleasure and release.

"Uhhhh...." Sullivan cried out, as his arms collapsed alongside her soft skin, and his head fell to her heaving breasts. They lay panting for endless minutes, their bodies welded together at the chest, until the sound of a door opening and footsteps approaching, broke the moment.

Jim Barnes walked toward the bedroom door completely unaware of the activity on the other side. He reached for the handle and threw open the carved wood frame.

"Whoa, there. Sorry. Sorry," he said upon spotting the two naked forms staring across the room at him. At the same time he pivoted on his right foot and began retracing his steps back into the hallway.

"Hang on just a minute, mate," Peter cried out, watching in the half-light of the room. "Let us tidy up in here a bit and we'll be right."

Jim's hand rose up and waved as he reentered the hallway. "No problem. Take all the time you need."

Bare feet padded across the plain wood floors and hastily discarded clothes were picked up and put on. Giggles met with giggles as the lovers stumbled, hurrying to get dressed.

"Now we're right, mate. Front and center. I want you to meet me new sheila. Don't be shy." Sullivan yelled through the open doorway.

Jim walked back and entered the room. Long ago, Jim had walked in on his college roommate in the throes of passion. He felt as sheepish now as he did then.

"Jimmy, meet Juanita, the queen of this small, but pleasant town," the Aussie said with a sarcastic smile.

The American recognized her from the bar and held out his hand.

"Mucho gusto," she said, smiling, meeting his eyes for only a minute. She was shy, it seemed.

"She doesn't speak much of the King's English, but in the language of love, she ranks right up there with bloody Chaucer and Shakespeare," Sullivan said, grinning widely.

"I'll take your word for it," Jim answered before changing the subject. "What happened? You drink the place dry? I went back. Thought you might need a little help finding your way home."

"No, Juanita was kind enough to do that for me. We decided she needed a break before getting back to pushing the suds on the night shift.

"I see," Jim said as he walked to the single bed and flopped his tall frame down on it.

"Listen here, Jimmy. Juanita was telling me about some bloke who's in town and looking for a good card game. Worst bloody poker player in Mexico, she says. Game's on for tonight. I figure it's God's way of telling me I'm not such a bastard after all!"

"Well, you two go ahead. I'm going to stretch out here. I'll come down a little later."

"Good on ya, mate. By the time you get there, I'll have made me bloody fortune, I reckon!"

"That's if you don't fold the first hand," Jim shot back, "I don't think our finances would sustain a losing streak."

"Not bloody likely, mate. You're talking to Peter Sullivan, the man who single handedly cleaned out the bloody Yank 82nd Airborne in Vietnam. Sent those Cub Scouts home with their tails tucked 'tween their legs, I did. Prepare yourself for the best meal in all of Mexico, mate. I'll be buying."

Sullivan laughed, and threw his arm around the small shoulders of his new love. Together they walked out into the darkened hallway and disappeared from view.

Jim brought his hands up behind his head. He stared at the cracked ceiling and listened as the wind picked up outside. He thought to himself that it wouldn't be long before he, too, touched the smooth skin of his wife, whom he missed so much.

As the wind swirled outside, and the room darkened, he slowly closed his eyes and faded off to sleep.

****

For Linda Barnes, the 'West' had always been the stuff of fiction; gunfights, cattle rustlers, and good guys wearing white hats. Her world was Middle America, with paved streets, PTA, and bridge club on Thursday. Little in her experience could have prepared her for that first journey to New Mexico.

She arrived by plane the day before, escorted at every moment by two armed agents of the government. She wasn't sure whether she was a prisoner or simply another innocent victim of some horror that had befallen her husband. The burly men answered next to nothing, offering only information they were authorized to give. Her journey was in fear. Her mind raced in the silence. Her confusion and dread matched the political climate. Once on the ground, other men put her through a barrage of procedures; from finger printing to retinal eye scans to DNA analysis. Authorities had every molecule of Linda's identifying characteristics tucked safely away in a data bank, but not one of them would answer the simplest question: "Where is my husband?"

Now in a small room in the barracks-like complex on the military base, Linda paced. The anxiety of waiting for what was to come, was taking its toll on the slim woman. Someone, she promised herself, was going to pay for the way she had been treated.

Just then, she heard footsteps approaching on the colorless linoleum of the hallway. She turned to face the door that opened, as expected, without the courtesy of a knock.

"Please come with us now, Ma'am," came the emotionless request of a young soldier dressed in his green fatigues, and spit-shined black boots.

"Don't you people ever knock when you're entering a woman's room?" she asked with an acid stare.

"We do as we're told. This ain't no country club," came the reply from the other soldier, dressed in a dark Ninja like outfit, and still in the hallway holding his laser sited M-16.

"That's the first intelligent thing I've heard since I got here. This sure as hell is no country club," she shot back.

Quickly she gathered herself and started off down the hall, the two men in tow. Passing through the entrance doors of the gray building, the group walked out into the early evening. The chill in the air struck Linda. A sudden loneliness descended upon her, miles from home, in a place that was large, looming and frightening. She quickened her pace.

Finally, they came to what looked to be the headquarters building. The three climbed the stairs and entered. The place was a beehive of activity, with staffers rushing about. The technology mesmerized her. A wall of screens showed ever-changing views of highways and buildings, moving cars and pedestrians walking the streets. Where two or three gathered at a street corner, there was the camera in their midst, zooming in nice and tight. The pictures, it seemed came from cameras planted on the streets to those rotating miles above. Occasionally the shot would zoom in on a license plate number before blinking off to find another.

In the office itself, thin computer monitors buzzed and gave off an eerie light reflecting on the tired faces of the men and woman who sat before them. It was the nerve center for a controlled area of the southwest part of the country, and it was intimidating.

Sergeant Calhoun stepped forward from behind an office partition. "Mrs. Barnes?" he asked pleasantly.

"That's right," she replied, sizing up the tall black man with a wary look in her eye.

"Please come with me. Colonel Colton will be meeting you in the conference room."

She nodded and followed him through a maze of desks until they came to a room with a large, mahogany table toward the back of the building. Once inside, she sat in a padded chair and looked around at the walls filled with pictures of various Air Force jets in flight. Calhoun followed her in and sat down.

"Can't someone please tell me what's going on?" she pleaded. Calhoun seemed to Linda to be the first rational person she had met.

The sergeant shook his head and returned her gaze. "It won't be long now. The colonel will be here in a moment."

"Is he alive? Is Jim still alive?"

"As far as we know, yes. I can't get into it any more than that."

At once immense relief and bitter anger swept over her.

"Who do you people...." She wasn't able to finish, as the commanding presence of Colonel Jennings Colton appeared in the doorway.

"You WILL speak only when spoken to!" he yelled. "You are a detainee of the United States Government. Do you understand that, Mrs. Barnes?"

Linda momentarily lost her breath. She looked up at the dark man as his eyes narrowed in on hers.

Colton didn't wait for her reply. "My name is Colonel Jennings Colton, commander of this Sector. We believe your husband is a murderer and a fugitive from justice. You may, or may not, be involved. THAT, we will ascertain later."

Linda Barnes stared blankly back at him, shaking her head once or twice to see if she was truly awake. Finally she was able to formulate words.

"Is this some kind of joke? I mean, you've got to be kidding."

"It's certainly no joke to the people who are dead and I can assure you I haven't been laughing these last few days. Your husband has caused me a good deal of grief, and I mean to catch him, whatever the cost."

Linda began to stand up, a rage burning in the pit of her stomach.

"A lawyer. Get me a fucking lawyer, NOW!" she screamed in a cathartic release.

"Afraid not, lady," Colton answered, with the sureness of one who held all the cards, "In case you weren't aware, we have martial law in effect, and I repeat, I call all the shots."

Linda Barnes looked over at Sergeant Calhoun, who turned away from her glance.

"What's going on here, sergeant? Would you please tell me?" she begged, her life unraveling at the seams.

"Ma'am, there's been a lot of trouble and your husband is right in the middle of it. Some of our people are dead, as well as a couple up in Utah. We're not sure how it all comes together, so we need to get some answers. That's where you come in."

"Now," Colton continued as he walked the room, "my people are going to spend the next few hours, or days, or weeks, if necessary, going over everything you know, until we get what we want. In the end, what we want is your husband."

"MY HUSBAND is an executive with an internet firm," she answered defiantly, "MY HUSBAND is the father of our child, and has never done anything more than double park in his entire life! MY HUSBAND is NOT the kind of man who would do the things you're accusing him of. Now, I don't know what kind of bureaucratic rock you just crawled out from under, nor do I care, but I WILL tell you this: You are making a big mistake, and by God, I will NOT let you destroy our lives without a fight!"

Colton stopped, smiled, and looked back at her. She was tough, he knew, but he could crack her.

"Well, now that we've both stated our positions, I suggest we begin what is obviously going to be a long process in determining the truth."

"As long as that's what you're looking for," Linda said.

"Oh, that's what I'm looking for, Mrs. Barnes, and I'm prepared to take as much time as necessary in finding it. By the way, to help motivate you, you should know that the government has seized your house, your belongings, and all your bank accounts - just in case your husband eludes us."

Linda bolted out of her chair, pointing at the colonel. "You can't do this!" she screamed, "I haven't been charged! This is still America, isn't it? What about my daughter? What will she do?"

"Until we settle this matter, once and for all, she is being looked after," Colton said. "Times are tough, Mrs. Barnes. Things have changed. Order is paramount, and I am in charge of maintaining that order. Frankly, I have much more important things on my plate, but I have taken a special interest because this was the first such incident under my watch. I mean to set an example."

Linda Barnes' world was crashing down around her. Before her stood a man who she judged not only responsible for that, but psychotic to boot. Not without a fight, she promised herself through her anger and terror, not without one helluva battle.

****

A sudden crash ripped Jim Barnes from his slumber. He sat upright and his eyes, filled with sleep, searched the dark room in momentary horror at the prospect of a sudden, surprise attack. But quickly, the feeling passed as he began to realize where he was. He took comfort in the four secure walls surrounding him.

Outside, the windstorm continued unabated. A crumpled metal awning had rolled down the street and hit the small hotel.

He climbed from the bed, his clothes still on, and stumbled over to the window. The wind swirled dirt in the darkness. Jim turned and looked around the small room. Sullivan was gone, he remembered. Probably broke, by now. He shrugged, and decided to track down his friend, even though his body yearned for more sleep. Jim promised himself he would return shortly.

The cantina was close by and the American reached it intact, although the surging wind had twice tried to knock him off his feet. Once inside the door, he dusted himself off and looked around the crowded room. Many men stood at the bar, mingling with some of the finer ladies in town. The tequila and beer flowed and the loud din of animated Spanish mingled with clinking glass and laughter.

Over in a corner, Jim saw a hand waving across a sea of bodies and the smiling face of Peter Sullivan bobbing up and down between shoulders. Jim smiled, waved back and started toward his traveling companion.

"Sleeping-bloody-Beauty finally arises, mates! Just in time to check out me winnings, I reckon," Peter said, addressing the men at the card table.

"Well, I just wanted to see if we were going to have to rob a store to eat tomorrow," Jim shot back.

"No worries mate. I've had what one might call an unusual streak of luck, I have. The boys here, who, by the way, don't speak much English, have been good to this wayward traveler."

"I can see that," replied Jim, as he eyed the dollar bills accumulated in front of the Australian. "Are those things still good?"

"Well, they work real well here, I can tell you. Juanita," Peter said as he picked up two fives, "how bout being a good sheila and getting us all another round? Keep the change for yourself."

The dark eyed Mexican girl smiled and weaved her way toward the bar.

"Now, Jimmy, mate. I'd like you to meet a friend of mine, who, unfortunately, is the source of some of my good fortune. Emilio Chaca, meet Jim Barnes.

The man was sitting directly in front of Peter with his back to Jim. Slowly, he rose to his full six-foot height. He turned. The man's penetrating black eyes bore into Jim. His brown face, sharp and angular, looked as if it had been sculptured from stone. His jet black hair was combed straight back, held in place by grease. He stared intensely at Jim, as if in search of some telltale weakness.

Emilio Chaca was an awesome, brooding presence by any standards. He was the personification of danger.

"Ah, Gringo," he said in a quiet baritone, offering his strong hand to Jim.

The American just nodded his greeting, unable to find the words to reply. It was as if he were standing before some dark unknown.

Peter Sullivan broke the moment with his half-drunken banter as he gathered about him more winnings on the table.

"Emilio, here, has offered to give me a lift down to Hermosillo in the morning. Says he has to check on some property he owns down there. Bloody nice of him, I reckon."

The Mexican turned away from Jim and sat back down at the table, lighting up a long, Cuban cigar.

Jim Barnes didn't answer for a moment. His silence would have been deafening had it not been for the drunken state of the men around the table.

"Yeah," he said slowly, "Real nice. When are you going?"

"First light. I'll wake you up before I go. Now a true mate would spend his last night with his cob bah, I reckon. But Juanita there has made me a better offer, so I'll be staying at her place. I want you to know, mate," he finished with grin on his face, and a gleam in his eye, "I had to think bloody long and hard on that decision."

"Three seconds?" Jim asked, smiling.

"Two," Sullivan replied without missing a beat.

"I'm honored. That's a second longer than it would have taken me."

Peter grinned up at his partner. "How about setting in on a hand? I'll shout you the money."

"No, that's OK. Got a big day tomorrow. I think I'll grab a bite and head on back across the street."

"Suit yourself, mate. Like I said, I'll be by to say our adi-bloody-oses in the morning."

Jim nodded and turned to walk toward the door. He stopped for a moment and glanced back at the affable Australian in all his glory – deep in money, beer and woman.

"Sullivan?" he called out, a sudden feeling of dread seizing him.

Peter looked up, but kept his hands moving dealing the cards. In front of him, the dark stranger raised his head slightly, as if to be in position to catch every word spoken.

Jim smiled. He made no further comment. He didn't know what to say, anyway.

CHAPTER 11

A hand came out of the darkness and lightly nudged Jim Barnes' shoulder. He jumped, shaken from a deep, but disturbing sleep. Slowly his eyes focused on the figure looming over his bed and he recognized the Australian. Peter stood quietly in the early morning hour. An association that had witnessed the full range of emotions, from life to death, fear to triumph, was coming to an end.

"What time is it?" Jim asked, his voice rough and gravelly.

"Near on six o'clock, mate. A bit early for the condition I find myself in, but bugger it."

Jim pulled himself up and swung around, sitting on the edge of the bed.

"So, this is it? You heading out?"

"Yeah, I'll be on me way now. Chaca is waiting downstairs in the car. Bloody nice ride, it is. A new Chevy. Could you guess?"

Barnes smiled. His head was beginning to clear, and he too was starting to feel some emotion as the idea of his friend's leaving took hold.

"You got all your stuff? I don't want to have to ship anything half way around the world trying to chase you down."

"I'm right, mate. After the last few days, I'm lucky to still have me hide. By the way, I left a hundred Yank dollars over there on the table. Half me winnings. I figure we were fifty-fifty partners in this whole mess, and we might as well finish up that way."

"Thanks a lot, Peter," Jim said. "You didn't have to do that. You know, I'll never forget you. You saved my life. Maybe some day I can make it up to you."

"Now, don't go getting all mushy on me, you bloody bastard. For all the shit, it was as exciting a time as I've ever known. When I get back to 'stralia, I'll have yet another adventure to tell me mates."

"Here," Jim said as he scribbled on a scrap of paper left on the nightstand. "This is where you can find me in Michigan. I'd write your address down, but it probably changes every week."

"No worries mate. Someday, when all this trouble blows over, I'll come looking for you again, dragging me missus and a brood of kids. Make you put us all up, I will. Pay back is a bitch!"

Jim thought to himself of how many times over the years he had promised to keep in touch with someone, only to let the opportunity escape. This one would be different, he vowed silently.

"See ya," he said quietly, holding his hand out.

Sullivan looked down at him and froze for a moment. Then, in a quick movement, he reached forward, locked hands, and pulled his friend to his feet. The two men embraced, slapping each other on the back. The Aussie pulled back slightly, looked directly into Jim's eyes, and with a wink and a grin, said, "Gidday, mate."

With that, Peter Sullivan spun on his heels and headed off down the hall; the hop in his walk still visible in the half-light.

Within the hour Jim, too, had gathered his things and had straightened up the small room. He left $20 on the table for the owner of the hotel as small payment for their accommodations. If Bernardo were true to his word, he would be there soon, so the American decided to wait outside.

Riellito was just beginning to stir from the long, windy night. Women made their way to the bakery for breads and sweets while many of the shop owners cleared up the debris and lifted their awnings to shade themselves from the sun's rays. It was business as usual.

Jim Barnes leaned back on an old wooden chair outside the hotel and surveyed the dusty street. In the distance, Bernardo's old car sputtered toward him. It was loaded with boxes of handmade trinkets, clothes and other traditional souvenirs he would take to his customers in El Paso.

"Hola!" said the smiling, round-faced man as he lurched to a halt a few feet away, "Is a wonderful day for a trip, no?"

"Sure is, Bernardo," Jim answered. "Good to see you again."

"My car is loaded down to the axles. Hopefully I can make lots of money this trip."

"How long does it take to get there?"

"We should make the drive to Juarez by early afternoon. That's if we have no problems."

Jim stood up, and walked around to the passenger side of the old auto. He reached through the open window, unlocked the door, pulled it open, and sat down inside.

"Where is your amigo, Peter? I should say adios to him. He is a good hombre," Bernardo asked.

"He's already gone," Jim replied casually. "About an hour ago. Told me to tell you thanks for everything."

Bernardo looked perplexed. "Where is he going? How will he get there?"

"He met a guy last night playing poker. Said he owned some property in Hermosillo and was going to check on it. It worked out perfect for Peter."

Bernardo's face lost all expression. "This man, what did he look like? Did you get his name?"

"I'll tell you, Bernardo, he was a strange looking son of a bitch. Dark and mean. The kind that makes your blood run cold. I think his last name was Chaca."

"Emilio Chaca?" Bernardo asked, now pale.

"Yeah, that's it. Emilio Chaca."

Bernardo turned, staring through the windshield into the distance. His eyes narrowed, and he took a deep breath.

"Senor, your friend, he is in danger. Grave danger. Chaca, he is an animal. It is said that he has a camp, to the south, in the mountains. There he keeps the Gringos to work his gold mines. No one comes out alive. People just disappear, like they never existed."

Now it was Jim's turn to go pale. A sudden adrenalin rush threatened his rationale. Then, his boyish face hardened and his eyes bore in on Bernardo. The decision came quick and easy.

"I've got to help him."

"Quickly, senor, help me put these boxes inside. There is only one road to the south. If we hurry, maybe we can catch them before they get to the mountains."

"This isn't your problem, Bernardo. Let me use your car and I'll do it myself," Jim shot back.

"No, senor. With Chaca, you will need my help. Hurry! We must go!"

The two men scrambled from the car and within minutes emptied everything into the hotel. Lighter and faster, Bernardo brought it back to life and slammed down the accelerator, fishtailing as he careened past pedestrians and shops.

The chase was on.

The two men spoke few words as the old Chevy sped down the bumpy asphalt road. Potholes littered both sides of the curving, uneven stretch of Mexican highway, and a small white cross marked the spot where an unlucky traveler met his end. As the morning sun rose to their left, Jim's eyes strained in the distance for a glimpse of the newer, faster vehicle that carried his friend to an uncertain fate. But all that could be seen were dust devils, cacti and tumbleweeds blowing across the parched land.

An hour passed. All Jim could do was hope he'd reach his friend in time.

Miles away, Emilio Chaca drove leisurely along the winding countryside. He was in no hurry as he drove his still ignorant captive to the place that would be his last home. The Gringos, he thought to himself, the sorry Gringos. So smart, and yet so stupid. Once again, a lowly Mexican had the better of one. He was a spider with a new fly in his web.

Years before, growing up in the border town of Nogales, Chaca had witnessed the contempt and cruelty the Norte Americanos had for his people. His mother served drinks in a small bar and the Gringos thought nothing of pinching her and humiliating her. They threw pennies in the dust and laughed as he and his small friends scrambled after them.

From a young age, Emilio Chaca took in the derisive laughter and vowed that one day he would make them pay. One day they would grovel. One day, they would fear him.

That time came when, on a drug running trip up from Hermosillo, he had wondered through the mountains south of

Riellito and found an abandoned gold mine tucked deep in the hills. It was sheltered perfectly on three sides, providing full view of the valley below and the only road leading to it. He had heard tales from the old timers that there was still plenty of gold to be found. But pulling whatever metal there might be from the earth was an expensive gamble the seemingly no one wanted to take.

His plan came together immediately. Emilio Chaca used his profits from the drug trade to buy the land and begin building a fortress in those mountains. He had the funds to recruit a small army of men to protect him and his land. His first kidnappings were remarkably easy. And as he held their lives in his hands, forcing the slaves to work the mines was even simpler.

As the years passed, gold poured out of the Mexican hills. Chaca became invincible. He took short trips to Juarez, Riellito and other towns near the border to lure gullible Yankees to his lair. He was choosy, though, picking candidates that seemed least likely to be missed – single men on the run who used Mexico as a protective blanket. More often than not, it was like taking candy from a baby, just as it had been the night before with the drunken one who spoke with a funny accent. Now, he sat beside him, with his head leaning back on the headrest, trying to nurse his throbbing skull back to life with a short nap.

Chaca's dark eyes rose to the rearview mirror where he spotted a cloud of swirling dust miles behind. It was a car, he knew, closing fast. He made a mental note to be aware. Bony hands gripped tighter around the steering wheel and he pressed down on the accelerator.

In the distance, the dust cloud drew closer. Chaca could make out two people in the front seat. By reflex, he reached to the revolver tucked into his belt behind his brown leather coat. His fingers touched the wood of the handle, and he was reassured. If trouble were to come, someone would die, he knew.

The road began winding more as it came up from the desert to meet the foothills. It was much more treacherous driving, with the dirt falling away at a steep angle from the shoulder.

Chaca's attention was divided between the road and the car in his rearview mirror. Next to him, Peter Sullivan slept peacefully.

Suddenly, the car carrying Jim and Bernardo lurched forward in an attempt to close the remaining distance between them. Bernardo leaned on the horn as the old engine screamed.

Shit! Chaca thought to himself, as Sullivan began stirring from the noise behind them. The Australian's eyes flickered open. He turned around and caught sight of his two friends in hot pursuit, waving frantically as they closed to within a few feet of Chaca's car.

"What the bloody hell...." were the only words he was able to speak, as Emilio Chaca, in one swift movement, brought his revolver slashing through the air, landing the barrel with full force on the back of the Australian's head. Blood spurted from the open gash. Peter sat stunned, looking straight ahead for a moment. Slowly, his eyes rolled upward, and he slumped down on the seat, a steady stream of red staining the cloth.

Chaca's eyes were wild with rage and excitement, and he let out a primeval scream.

Jim had seen the blow delivered. One thing was certain; the Aussie was out of commission.

"We've gotta watch it!" Jim yelled, straining to bring his voice above the noise. "He might have a gun! Have you got a knife, a revolver, ANYTHING?"

Bernardo's eyes stayed fixed on to the road. Sweat was dripping from his tanned brow.

"Here," he said, reaching into his back pocket and pulling out a six-inch switchblade. It had ivory sides and brass fittings – a thing of beauty, not a toy found in the tourist traps. With a flick of his thumb, the blade snapped open. It gleamed in the morning sun. "I hope you know how to use this, amigo."

Jim nodded, although it was a lie. He took the weapon from Bernardo and closed the blade. Jim knew he could use it, if it was necessary. Only days before he could not have been certain.

"We must get him off the road, into the desert. Hold tight!" Bernardo shouted

His old Chevy shot forward and crashed with a thud into the rear bumper of Chaca's car. It seemed to stun the driver in front, as he swerved sharply to the left, and then steadied the car. Bernardo smiled, as though enjoying this new excitement. His foot forced the pedal as far as it would go. Again, metals collided in a loud crash.

The two vehicles shadowed each other as they raced up the winding slopes. Dirt and gravel shot up in all directions, and rays of bright sunlight glanced off the glass and steel. Chaca maneuvered to the center of the road, using its full width.

"Uno mas!" Bernardo yelled. And again the engine roared, and the old Chevy slammed ahead.

But this time, Emilio Chaca was waiting for him. In the instant before impact, Chaca swerved violently to his right, nearly driving off the side of the road. As he did, his foot crammed down on the brake, and his car, nose down, skidding on the dirt.

Bernardo slammed down on the brakes. The cars threw a thick cloud of dust into the air as they halted side-by-side.

Jim turned and looked into Chaca's dark eyes. Horror gripped him the Mexican raised the barrel of his revolver and leveled it at his head. As if in slow motion, a smile crossed the thin lips of the man who dealt in death.

"GUN!" Jim screamed as he instinctively threw his head forward. The revolver erupted in a blast of fire and gunpowder.

The bullet from Chaca's gun seared the air just above Jim's neck, slicing full force into the head of the wide-eyed Mexican, just above his temple. Exiting out the other side, it left a huge jagged hole of blood, bone, and brain tissue dangling from the opening. Bernardo's hands tightened on the steering wheel in a death grip, as he slowly fell forward, his chin resting on the worn plastic and eyes wide with shock.

Despite the death scene before him, Jim's senses were sharp and keen, like a soldier in a firefight. Keeping his head down, he moved his foot across the floorboard and stomped on the accelerator. The car jumped forward, veering sharply to the left. Jim peeked above the dash just in time to see it hit the high embankment.

Then there was nothing. Jim heard only his breathing and the wind whistling through the open windows of the auto lost touch with the ground.

But the quiet ended quickly. A crashing roar erupted when the front of the old Chevy slammed down into the desert, and began rolling; once, twice, too many times to count. All went black for the American inside.

After what seemed like the longest, most peaceful sleep he had ever known, Jim's eyes flicked open. Instantly, he drew back in horror and fear. Inches from his face, the ghoulish death mask of Bernardo Calrone stared back at him, as the two lay crumpled on the driver's side door of the wreckage. He wanted to scream, but could find no voice. He wanted to run, but could barely move his legs. Cramps shot up from his wrist, and he looked down at his hand, which still held the knife, his knuckles white from the tension. Then, in a sudden burst of adrenaline, Jim began scrambling, crawling, pushing his way up and out of the car through the open window above him. As his body met the open air, relief swept over him and he scratched and clawed even harder to escape the stifling prison. He slid down the twisted metal into a heap on the ground.

The once youthful face of Jim Barnes stared upward, half conscious, into the bright sunlight. He was cut, bruised and battered.

Then, a dark shadow slowly enveloped him. Jim looked up, without recognition at first, at the brown, sweat soaked face, black pencil thin mustache, and sharp, protruding cheekbones Helplessly, he watched as the stranger's deep eyes narrowed and a thin smile crossed his lips. The man held up a gun, and the hammer cocked and ready to fire.

From some deep, forgotten instinct, the will to live rose up from his soul, and his eyes flared with fire. In his right hand, he could still feel the ivory and brass from before. His thumb twitched, and the razor sharp blade of Bernardo's weapon snapped open. With anger, disgust, and hatred, Jim swung his right arm up, and around, and buried the blade into the calf of the shocked Mexican standing above him.

"AAAHHH!" Emilio Chaca screamed, his contorted face rising to the heavens. Then he brought his eyes down, and they settled on the source of his pain. On reflex, the revolver in his hand came crashing down on the skull of Jim Barnes, and the American slammed into the dirt.

Chaca bent down, pain scorching through his bloodied leg. He grasped the handle of the knife, and pulled slowly, freeing the steel from his leg. The Mexican looked at the blood-covered blade. He pushed the knife forward, back toward the silent man who lay beneath him. It came to rest along side his exposed throat. With a twitch of a muscle, Jim's jugular vein would be ripped open, and his life would seep into the desert sand.

Instead, Chaca pulled the knife away and slowly closed the blade. Deliberately, he moved closer to his victim, as if to whisper in his ear.

"No, Gringo, not yet. There is plenty of time for you to die. First you must pay. When I am finished, you will beg me to kill you!"

CHAPTER 12   Part Two

For three-and-a-half years he could hear the night wind blow through the knothole in the rotted slat of wood behind his head. Chill and crisp in the winters that passed, the air was now hot and sultry as the summer day gave way to the darkness. As he stretched out his haggard form on the sweat soaked army blanket beneath his pale body, he was certain that another fitful sleep awaited. Slowly, he turned to his left, and as was his habit during the previous months, and tugged loose a small, sharp stone wedged between two boards. He scratched a faint "x" in the gray wood. Another day in the bowels of hell was over.

Jim Barnes lay naked in the stifling heat of the large, barracks-like room that housed the camp's prisoners. Crows feet etched in the hot sun framed his dark, tired eyes. Once again they took in the room. Crudely built bunk beds jutted out from all four walls, each with a makeshift mattress of old blankets and straw. The prisoners tossed about in their discomfort, and the room was filled with coughing and grating snores. Forty men occupied that space; 40 men who yearned for a way out, for some form of salvation.

He brought his hands up and cradled his graying head of hair. He once took pride in his thick, sandy brown locks but now his hair now was nearly shoulder length and stringy. Cut with an old, dull pair of scissors, the styling of the past was gone. So too were showers, replaced with baths in a nearby creek as the only answer to the smell of filthy flesh. His fingers bore the cuts and scrapes of years clawing at the earth, and bruises dotted his arms and legs. Yet, they had become powerful from the lifting and pulling, and his muscles bulged beneath the tight skin. His body, once destined to pass quietly into potbellied middle age, was lean and strong. It was a peculiar development from a time of pain. When all the structures of life he had relied on failed, his mind, his soul, and his body, rallied to protect him.

Above, on the boards that creaked and groaned, his friend Peter Sullivan struggled for sleep. As he turned, the rickety wood frame swayed, and threatened to collapse and deposit them on the dusty concrete floor. Rust covered nails pounded into gaping wooden joints gave out shrill squeaks.

As sleep approached, and his thoughts drifted, Jim wondered again what had become of the world he once knew. Somehow he felt that people such as his wife and daughter were paying a terrible toll. Before the fall, it was blow and go, take what you can get and to hell with the consequences. He could remember the feeling of drowning in an unending stream of trivia, as presented on television, radio and the Internet. Yet, he and his collection of "things" had gladly fallen in lockstep, not willing to take the time to think, reason and look ahead. The cold shower of reality singled him out with a vengeance. His only prayer was that his own misery canceled the debt of those who meant the most to him. It was a simple, sincere thought, but one that had little chance of reality.

Jim Barnes came from a world that had wrapped itself in the collective security blanket of delusion. It was a place where experts, commissions, studies and "smart guys" ruled. Even when they contradicted themselves, as was often the case, the discrepancies faded off into meaningless oblivion, never to be heard from again. All the "little engines that could" continued merrily down the track, grasping for the good life. Jim smiled to himself at the naivety of that thought.

He scratched his eyes, drifting away into unconsciousness, searching for a simple peace. Minutes became hours.

Suddenly, a hand reached out from the darkness and grabbed his genitals, pulling them up and back to the point of excruciating pain. He felt a cold steel blade press against his manhood, as another set of hands pinned his shoulders to the bottom bunk. Fear and panic rose up from every fiber of his body and his eyes searched the black room. Then, the grinning face of his attacker, eyes wide and insane, came into focus and a cold chill swept his shaking body. Emilio Chaca, his face inches from the American, his breath fowl, smelling of green chilies and peppers from an earlier meal, came into focus.

"Maybe it will be tonight, my friend," he hissed quietly, cherishing each word as he spoke, " that I cut off your balls and feed them to you for a last supper. What do you think, Gringo?"

Jim was petrified, but tried to not betray his emotions. Steadying his resolve, Jim glared back at Chaca.

"If it was just you and me, alone, maybe you'd be the one doing the dining," he said in a cold whisper.

Chaca's eyes grew wide with rage.

"I should kill you now," he whispered. "It would be easy for me to do. Maybe that's what you want, eh? No. Not tonight. I will slaughter you like a pig in front of everyone. But not before you spend more time in my mines, Gringo. One day you will beg me to kill you. Until then, sleep tight. Maybe I will come back another night and we talk again."

"Do that, Chaca," Jim shot back, cold sweat gathering on his forehead, "and next time leave your dogs behind."

Chaca smiled, and fell back into the darkness, followed by half a dozen of his armed men. The door to the outside closed quietly behind them. Jim took a deep breath, as though he'd been trapped beneath the water.

"Bloody hell, mate, that one almost cost you your knackers," came the twang of Peter Sullivan, as his faced appeared over the side of the bed.

"Yeah, well fuck HIM!" Jim retorted, defiant and angry at the helplessness he had felt.

"I told you, mate, we've got to pick our spot, and now...."

"Screw THAT, and everything else in this Goddamned place," Jim said, cutting Peter off, his voice rising, "I say let's have at it! If we die, we die! It'll probably be better than what we have now. I'm telling you, it's gotta end, Sully, its gotta end. I can't take it much longer."

"It's going to end, mate, but on our terms. You've got to keep that bloody temper under control, cause I can't get out of here without you."

Jim shook his head. Rage and helplessness overwhelmed him and his eyes began to water.

"I swear I'm going to rip that son of a bitch's head off with my bare hands someday. That miserable, sick, psychotic...." The words caught in his throat, and he could not finish.

"You'll be first in bloody line behind me, mate. Let's just make sure we stay alive long enough to get the bastard. Now get some sleep." Sullivan pulled himself up and settled back on his mattress.

"Hey, Yank," he said in a loud whisper.

"Yeah, what is it?" Jim answered.

"Just so you know, I was ready to jump the bastard if he started sawing on your privates. I figured you'd only loose one by the time I got to him." Peter grinned in the dark. "One other thing, mate, you might want to start sleeping in your bloody underwear."

Jim tried to hold back, but a smile cracked his face. "You Outback son of a bitch...." he said, letting the words drift off.

The quiet of the room returned, interrupted only by muffled noises of the night. If anyone else had heard, or seen, what happened, they were too smart to acknowledge it. Survival in Chaca's camp meant keeping a low profile and minding your business.

The men in the room had been hardened to their fate. Most were Americans, but there were a few Mexicans also who had the misfortune of crossing Emilio Chaca.

****

By the time the Sunday sun rose above the mountains that surrounded the compound, it was nearly seven o'clock. Normally, the men would have been up by five and walking the trail into the hills before six. But even the evil that was Chaca retreated on the holy day, and the men had that time to mend or rest for the grind to come. As light filtered into the room through the cloth-covered windows and the cracks in the dried out wood boards, the building came alive with half naked bodies shuffling about. Most tried to be first to the outhouses nearby. Others sat on the edge of their bunks and gathered their wits about them.

Peter Sullivan was already up, standing beside the bunks, as he pulled his tattered blue jeans up around his slim waist.

He hadn't changed much through his time in the camp. His long blond hair concealed any gray that might have surfaced and his face still had that ruddy, earthen look about it. Sullivan had known a hard life, and survived many uncomfortable situations. He was convinced that his time with Chaca was just a temporary inconvenience, and that sooner or later he would be on his way again. He pulled his navy blue t-shirt over the brown hair on his chest, and glanced down at Jim.

"Up and at 'em, mate. Tuckers on, and you wouldn't want to miss THAT, now would you? Let's see, what could be on the menu? Eggs bloody Benedict, hash browns, toast and Vegemite, and some tea."

"Corn gruel and water," Jim replied matter-of-factly.

"Hey, don't be messing with me food, Yank! Let me dream for just a little while longer, will ya?"

Jim sat up and swung his legs around to the floor. He slipped on his underwear and sat still for a moment, rubbing his face in his hands.

"When we get out of here, we're gonna eat, my friend. BIG time. I don't care whether we have to beg, borrow, or steal the money, or widgets, or whatever else their using these days."

"Sounds right by me. You know what I've got me heart set on, mate? A pie floater, that's what! I can taste it now."

"What the hell is a pie floater?"

Peter looked up, and moved his hands as if he was creating the dish right in front of them. "You get some bloody pea soup, put it in a bowl, sink a meat pie in the middle and cover the whole mess with tomato sauce. A bloody delicacy, it is!"

Jim showed no expression on his face, but sat silent, staring straight ahead. Then slowly, he turned to the Australian.

"We better make our move pretty soon, man. You've been in here too long."

"Don't knock it 'til you've tried it, you whack. I'll say nothing more," he shot back smiling. "Bloody hamburgers!"

Jim dressed quickly in the jeans and blue cotton shirt beside his bed. He began to pull on the boots he inherited from a dead prisoner a few months ago. He looked across two bunk beds and caught one of the Mexicans eyeing the pair enviously. Their eyes locked on to each other.

"You'll have to wait until I'm dead, Hector," he said in a strong, clear voice. "So don't even think about it."

The Mexican smiled, his gaping, rotten teeth flashing. "Ez no problem, Gringo. I can wait. I am a patient man." He picked up a sharpened wooden stick near his feet, and began flipping it in the air. "By the way, even Gringos can't live without balls!"

Jim stared back at him. He knew that sooner or later the time would come to deal with Hector Higura. It had happened a few times before. Fortunately, he had come out the winner of the battles. The prisoners, despite their common enemy in Chaca, tried to establish a pecking order. Sullivan knew this instinctively and let his wits get him out of most spots. On rare occasions, tough, it was kill or be killed. Jim's business "wars" of the past, the hostile takeovers, paled by comparison.

The two men stepped outside in the bright morning sunlight and took in the area around them. It was a relatively small compound, surrounded on four sides by a ten-foot wall of stone and mortar topped with broken glass and rows of razor wire. Beyond the wall was a 30-foot wide strip of no man's land, bordered by wood fencing. Two guard towers were constantly manned, the sentinels armed with machine guns. Jim and Peter knew that it was one thing to scale the wall, but a vastly different proposition to sprint across the strip of open land unnoticed.

Inside the walls, the only structures were the barracks, a makeshift ramada with wooden tables for meals, two outhouses and a rickety basketball hoop nailed precariously to a plywood backboard. Even at that early hour, a few prisoners played pickup games. Chaca had effectively created a place that was devoid of life, but just slightly better than the alternative.

Once a day, at a time determined by Chaca scanning his computer, the guards would roll out yards of camouflage netting to cover up anything that might be of interest to the spy satellites that routinely crossed overhead. It wasn't just men like Emilio Chaca that were being watched. Rather, it was a part of everyday life in the new world order.

To their right, the sound of metal banging drew their attention. It was two guards opening the "pit," a six-foot square hole dug four foot into the ground, lined with wood, and covered with a corrugated metal top. It was the last stop for anyone who dared to defy Emilio Chaca. No one could survive the heat of the high desert for more than a few days. Ghoulish curiosity accompanied each opening of the lid.

"Isn't that the Yank from New Mexico," Peter asked quietly, "Harry something. Maybe he died quickly."

"Yeah, if the scorpions got him before the heat. He was the guy running drugs across the border for Chaca. Bad choice of partners."

"How long has he been in there?" Sullivan asked.

"I think he made it four days. Not bad for a white guy. Seems like the Mexicans can last for weeks."

"Yeah, it probably isn't too bloody different from their homes, I'd say. Whew! Smell that, will you! Let's make sure we eat down wind, huh mate?"

Jim nodded and the two began walking across the dirt compound to the gate. An old pickup truck bed was backed into the opening with two barrels of gruel and buckets of water. Men were lining up to receive their meager rations on old tin pie plates.

As they moved forward in line, Jim could see beyond the trailer, past the strip of no man's land, and through the open gates of the wood fence. Emilio Chaca's house stood about 100 yards away, shaded by large gum trees at the base of the mountain behind it. It was single-story stucco house, painted white. Across the front was a long veranda, with tables and chairs and a white picket railing. To Jim, it looked like something out of a Tennessee William's play, set in the South.

Watching the men move forward to get their food, Emilio Chaca stood behind tinted glass windows. A slight smile crossed his lips as he saw Jim approach the wagon.

"Vamonos!" he ordered to the armed men in the room beside him. In a particularly pointed fashion, the group burst through his screen door, and marched out across the area toward the compound.

Instantly, the Aussie's eyes rose up and caught sight of the men drawing near. It was trouble, big trouble, and they had to be prepared.

"Here they bloody well come, mate! Now, don't go shooting off your mouth, will ya. I think you pissed the bastard off enough last night."

"He's the one who had ME by the balls, remember? If it ends here, so be it," Jim said calmly, his body tensing. "I know I'm going to try to take at least one with me."

Peter Sullivan's face flushed red with anger. He snapped around, and stood toe-to-toe with Jim.

"Listen carefully! You aren't going to say or do a bloody thing, UNDERSTAND? The bastard's a cold-blooded killer, but we can beat him if you'll just back off! If there's no other choice, then fine, we BOTH go down fighting. But you don't do a bloody thing until I make the first move, or by God I'll kill you myself. GOT THAT?"

Jim was startled by the fury of the Australians words. He was a patient man, maybe too patient, waiting for his opportunity to strike, and no one would get in his way. The two friends eyed each other carefully, and then Jim nodded.

"Good," Peter said simply.

Behind him, Chaca approached, gathering four more guards as they came up to group.

"What is this?" he called out mockingly. "The Gringo, he stands in line, waiting to eat the food of a simple Mexican! Is that what I heard from the Norte Americano? You have no pride, senor! You stoop so low as to take the meager offerings of Emilio Chaca?"

"Well, mate, if truth be known, I'm the bastard who talked him into swallowing his pride," Sullivan began, trying to deflect attention to himself. "Bloody unfortunate misunderstanding last night, I'd say. What say we forgive and forget?"

Chaca's head turned suddenly toward the Aussie. "Forget? Never, senor. I don't NEED to forget. I'm the one with the guns. Remember? I think it's time the Gringo puta pays a price. Take him!"

The two guards who had slipped behind Jim leaped forward and pinned his arms behind his back. A wild helplessness seized him and he struggled for his footing. Chaca slowly began unbuttoning his white cotton shirt, carefully removing it from his lean body. He handed it to the burly Mexican standing behind him, and then suddenly, violently, brought his boot up and slammed the toe into Jim's groin.

Jim screamed in agony, gasping for breath as the searing pain shot throughout his body. His legs gave out, and he crumpled to the ground. The guards supporting him let go. They were no longer needed.

Sullivan lurched forward, in an effort to help, when he felt the cold steel of two rifle barrels sticking in his back. There was nothing he could do.

Chaca began walking around the fallen man and talking as if giving a lecture on pain.

"You see, Gringo, the old days have gone. There are no 'spics' or 'wetbacks,' only those who have power, like me, and those who don't, like you!" With that, his foot shot around and smashed into Jim's ribs. Once again he cried out in agony.

"The Mexican people," he continued, "they used to suck up to the Americans. `Si, senor,' 'what can I do for you, senor?' But now, is no more. You have what they had all along, NOTHING! And now, you must learn the lessons of the jungle. I am here to teach you!" Once more he viciously kicked the fallen man in the head, nearly knocking him out.

Chaca knelt down beside Jim as he writhed on the dirt. He smiled through his gaping teeth. "First you must spend some time in the pit. Then, when you are begging to die, I, Emilio Chaca will personally take you out and gut you myself, no?"

Jim looked up at him through half closed eyes, pain tearing through his body.

He couldn't breathe, let alone talk, but his eyes, still defiant, spoke for him. In a grudging way, Emilio Chaca was impressed.

"Hold on there a minute, mate!" Sullivan cut in. "Where I come from, you give a man a sporting chance before you finish him!"

Chaca turned to look up at the Australian. His audacity was surprising, and it also intrigued him.

"What did you have in mind?" he asked cautiously.

"Well, it's obvious the Yank is out of bloody commission. Why don't we make it you and me? Let's see now. What can we do to break the blasted boredom around here? Cards! That's it! That's what got us into this bloody mess to begin with," Sullivan said, groping for time. "One hand, five card stud. If I win, he lives. If you win, have at it. If I remember right, you played the game pretty well back in Riellito."

"You want to play for the life of your amigo?" Chaca answered with a cocky self-assurance, "Si, why not? He will die here sooner or later, anyway. But there is just one thing. If I win, you go to the pit, too. Yes?"

"I deal?"

"Of course," Chaca said, smiling. "You are my guest!"

"Good on ya then, mate! Have Brutus here fetch us some playing cards, and let's have at it."

Chaca nodded toward the guard behind Sullivan, and he headed swiftly toward the house. Then he motioned for Peter to follow him to the ramada.

"Mighty white of you, mate," Peter said with a wide grin on his face, not betraying the loathing he felt, "I like a sporting man. Makes me homesick for 'stralia."

The guard returned and handed Peter a sealed deck of playing cards. Both the guards and prisoners began gathering around the players, drawn to the life-or-death contest. Jim was unconscious on the ground, with a young guard pointing a rifle down at him. They were the only people missing the action.

"Now then," the Aussie began, fumbling with the package and feigning nervousness as he shuffled the cards awkwardly, "Seems like the last time we played, you won the hand. Maybe my bloomin' luck has changed."

Chaca eyed him coldly. "It will be your ass if it hasn't."

"Seems like the only thing missing is a cold beer. Tell you what, mate, one minor wrinkle. If I win, I get an ice-cold Corona, too. If I don't, well, I won't need it anyway. Yes?"

Chaca was much more serious now. He didn't want to be made a fool of, but he nodded his agreement.

Sullivan smiled, and finished what he was doing. He set the cards down on the table with a loud smack. "Right then, cut?"

Chaca looked up at him and shook his head. If the Gringo was able to doctor the deck someway, he didn't want to play into his hands.

The Australian picked them up, and began his monologue. The men around them stood silently.

"One down for each of us," he said, sliding them in front of each man, "Now the fun begins." Sullivan was calm and cool, confidently eyeing the Mexican.

"We start out with the queen of hearts for the man, seven of clubs for me. Next card, a red duce, ten of spades for the good guys. Not showing much, so far. This should begin to tell the tale," he continued, looking directly into the dark eyes of the man in front of him.

"Now then, what have we here. Queen of spades for Mr. Chaca, a pair showing. Not bloody good. Four of clubs for young Peter. So far, a hand of trash. Last card we play down."

His life, and that of his friend, was out on the table for all to see. Except for the two down cards in front of both men, their fate was decided.

"Let's see what you've got, mate."

Chaca smiled confidently. Slowly, he reached out and flipped the first card over. Jack of spades. Then his bony fingers moved over for his final play, and upended the remaining card. A red four.

Peter watched with nerves of steel. If the third queen had come to the party, it would have been all she wrote.

"Well, now, I guess it's my turn. Let's see what the poker gods have in store for me." His hand moved forward, turning over the first card to reveal the four of hearts. Peter sat with a pair of fours with another showing in Chaca's hand.

Suddenly, Chaca looked up at Peter and spoke. "One moment, senor. I tell you what. I like your style. An hombre with big balls. You are a man, not like the rest of these Yankees. This is my offer; we stop here, and I kill your friend, just like I said before. But you live. Or we go on. It's up to you."

Chaca obviously loved toying with the men he controlled, watching carefully their expressions, their eyes, and the calculations that must have been going on behind them.

Peter Sullivan showed no emotion. He did not speak, and his eyes bore in on Chaca. Seconds that seemed like hours passed. The men standing around shuffled and stirred, waiting for the next move.

Without shifting his gaze from Emilio Chaca, Sullivan's right hand crept forward and grasped the corner of the last card facing down. He held it softly for a moment, and then turned it face up.

The four of spades.

The prisoners standing about erupted in a loud cheer, celebrating a small victory in a place where few existed. Chaca's once confident expression turned ice cold, his face frozen in a mask of hatred. Somehow he had been cheated, and made a fool of by the swaggering foreigner. Slowly, he gained his composure, and stood up.

"We will play another day, senor," he said, with short, clipped words. With that, he turned quickly and marched for the open gate, a dozen of his armed men in close pursuit. As he passed the prone figure of Jim Barnes sprawled out in the morning sun, he did not even look down.

Suddenly, Peter Sullivan was a hero to the men standing about with broad grins on their faces. He basked in that glory for a moment, and then looked over to where Chaca was disappearing from view.

"I'll bet the bloody bastard forgets me grog!" he snapped, shaking his head, "Ah, well. Wouldn't be the first time I was cheated out of me winnings."

Slowly he gathered up the cards on the table, and said to no one in particular, "Somebody give me mate a hand onto his bunk, would ya? A lucky bloke like that deserves a day off!"

Hector Higura walked close to Sullivan.

"Chaca thinks you cheated him, Gringo."

"Smart man," came the simple reply.

CHAPTER 13

A year earlier, on a bright June morning, the Governor's office of the State of New Mexico was expecting an important visitor. It was midweek and the city of Santa Fe was moving at its normal, laid-back pace. Traffic was light, as usual, in the once-bustling art galleries and shops. In its day, the town was a prime destination for the rich and famous from California and the East Coast, who flocked to the New Mexican capital to escape the frenzy of their own self-indulgent lives. But in the two-and-a-half years of military government, a gray pall had been cast upon the cultural frivolities that many once believed essential to the "good life." In Santa Fe, and everywhere else in the nation, the new reality returned people to the basics. Work, family, and a sense of balance with nature, which had long been lacking in the highflying days of the past, were now most important.

But a toll had to be paid for the transgressions and excesses of a society in which image, deception and illusion had become tools of the trade for government and industry. The toll taker was about to enter the elevator, along with four of his aides, and ascend six floors to the office of the highest ranking civilian authority in the State of New Mexico, second only in power to himself. Jennings Colton, recently promoted to general, stood motionless as the box lifted him to his destination. He was un-elected, unaccountable but to a select few in Washington, and undeniably in control. He called the shots.

In another time, the word 'dictator' would have fit Colton like a glove. With precision, he had restructured life in Sector 47. The trains certainly ran on time. Thanks to the brilliance of Operation Patriot, though, the general was a hidden puppet master and not a public tyrant pounding on a podium. The planners of Patriot were careful to leave in place, in appearance, thecivilian centers of government. When restructuring society, Colton and the other sector commanders around the country, merely 'consulted' with the powers that be. It worked like a charm.

In the beginning, the populous blamed every wrinkle on 'those damned politicians.'

Few knew who pulled the strings. And when unruly citizens gathered to protest, they were detained or dispersed harshly and quickly, all for the sake of order, and all at the supposed command of some figurehead who no longer had power. In time, people traded their individual rights for stability. They did so because they were weary. They did so because they didn't know who the enemy was.

Joe Public hoisted the white flag and said, "Make it work." Jennings Colton, and others of his pedigree, was happy to oblige.

The elevator doors opened on the sixth floor and the general was first to depart, walking briskly toward the security desk in the large foyer of the governor's office. The room was filled with the trappings of power. Artifacts and knickknacks adorned walls and shelves, each a piece of the culture and heritage of the New Mexican landscape. But also present were computer screens and surveillance cameras recording every movement, every sound. Sensors hidden in the walls could fortify the office in seconds if an emergency called for it. Public servants could be none too careful.

"Is he in?" Colton asked the female staffer sitting at the desk, declining any small talk with one so far below his station in life.

"Why yes, General, the governor has been expecting you. He asked if you could wait just a moment while he finishes an important telephone call."

The stone face of the regional commander looked down on the woman, and then, in an unusual twist, the corners of his mouth turned up in a smile. He turned around to glance at his aides, shook his head, and strode off for the large double doors that separated him from the governor. With a twist of the ornate doorknobs, General Colton had arrived at the theoretical seat of civilian power. He and his men burst into the room, and startled the balding, paunchy man sitting at his desk with his feet up, talking on the phone.

"Oh!" the governor exclaimed excitedly. "Got to go. I have important visitors."

He replaced the receiver and stood as the general approached his desk.

"Good to see you, Jennings, good to see you. Please come in and sit down. I hope you weren't inconvenienced."

Colton returned the smile, his strong jaw jutting forward.

"Not at all, Russell."

"Can I get you something? Let me see, I believe last month you preferred Kentucky bourbon. The same?"

"No, I'm afraid I have to cut our visit short. We have some major staff meetings to attend to in Albuquerque and I must get back. It looks like all the pieces are finally coming into place. It's only taken Washington better than two years to get its act together."

The governor looked at him and laughed. "As one who has devoted his life to public service and witnessed the movement of bureaucracy, I should think that the restructuring of our society in two years is tantamount to a miracle!"

"I could have taken care of it in six months," Jennings answered. "Anyway, as you are well aware, the hallmark, the focus of governmental functions, is control with a capital C. This society has grown so diverse, so unwieldy, that it was inevitable that it would begin to unravel.

For any of us to have any kind of future, control is needed. To achieve that, the computer models indicated that a vast accumulation of knowledge and information was paramount. It is now in place."

Russell Harris looked at the man sitting in front of him with mixed feelings of admiration, loathing and distrust. Only the admiration showed.

"The national currency cards. Are they ready to go on-line?"

"We are a couple of weeks away. It will be announced with great fanfare at the Fourth of July celebration in Washington."

Governor Harris paused. His next question wasn't going to be easy.

"General, what is the feeling in Washington about the computer chip program? How do they think the public will react when they're ordered to have them surgically implanted? I mean, my God, are they prepared for the worst?"

"I am prepared, governor," the general answered. "That's all you should concern yourself with. As for strategy, we simply convince the citizenry that this is necessary to forward the interests of the nation. And, to put it bluntly, they have no damn choice about it."

General Jennings Colton was right on all accounts. The new national program, requiring every man, woman and child to be fitted with an implanted computer chip, would be carried out in earnest. The technology would allow the government to monitor, store and analyze billions of bits of information on anyone and everyone. Synchronized with satellites and the ever-growing number of face-recognition cameras, the chips could record every movement of the day.

Colton, sensing the governor's anxiousness, continued.

"Think of the possibilities, governor. This technology will save our country. It is nothing short of a miracle. The government will know everything from where you've been, what you said, when you last ate and when you last moved your bowels. Everything except what you're thinking. At least not yet," he said, adding a quick chuckle. "If you have nothing to hide, this is harmless. Remember, governor: Control with a capital C."

Governor Harris nodded. A new day was dawning. Hopefully, a better one. But the sacrifices would be great. He wondered briefly if it would be worth it, but the old public servant in him quickly squelched the thought. His government wouldn't harm the people.

The two men spent the remainder of their time discussing policies to be instituted in the months to come. Control of every aspect of human life was the watchword for society.

As the general shuffled papers, preparing to put them back into his titanium briefcase, which would seal and lock if the wrong hand touched the handle, the governor remembered a past annoyance.

"By the way, General, I've received some more letters from that lady you have at the Women's Detention Center. Linda Barnes is her name. It seems she's contacted just about every state and local agency that exists."

"As well as the offices of congressmen and senators," Jennings continued, unamused.

"Well, she has certainly stirred up a few citizens' groups. I'm beginning to feel some political heat."

"Governor, I don't respond to heat. She has been held as a subversive these last few years and I suspect that her case will resolve itself shortly. As you know, it goes back to some unfinished business I must attend to before we can dispose of the situation. Just forward to my staff any letters or documents you might receive concerning Mrs. Barnes. We'll take care of the rest."

The two men stood up and parted with a handshake. With the new policies to be introduced in the coming months, their meetings would no longer be necessary. But they had served their purpose, which was the illusion of citizen involvement. It had bought time.

After General Colton settled down in his black limousine, facing the staff people in front, and beside him, he turned to look out the window at the passers-by who had no idea that they were in the presence of a man who had played a major part in reshaping the way they, and their children, and their children's children, would live. Whether it was for good, or for evil, was not the point. It was functional.

"Sergeant Calhoun," he said. "I want to make a short visit to the WDC when we get back. It's been a long time since I've had the pleasure of speaking to Mrs. Barnes."

The pale, handcuffed woman was brought into a holding room, led by two female prison staff. They took her to a chair beside a long table and pressed lightly on her shoulders, forcing her to sit. She looked up at one of the guards, a black woman, and for an instant, found a glimmer of empathy. But quickly, the guard averted her eyes. It was not her place to judge right or wrong. After all, she needed the job. She needed to take care of her family, too.

Linda Barnes took in the depressing surroundings. Her once bright, alert eyes were ringed from many sleepless nights and long hours crying in the privacy of her cell. She vowed never to show her tears to the men who imprisoned her beat her, and she kept that promise for two-and-a-half years. Defiantly, she had gone toe-to-toe with anyone in authority, anyone with even a hope of helping her. If just one person would listen to reason, she thought, her long nightmare would be over. But reason was in short supply. Everyone seemed to be preoccupied with his or her own place in the new order. No one was dumb enough to jeopardize his or her fate for the benefit of some forgettable woman. So the days dragged on, and every once in a while she found herself in a room like the one she was now sitting in, being questioned by a pompous military type, who neither cared, nor wanted, to find the truth.

She sat quietly, sometimes shifting about in the orange prison jumpsuit provided by the State. Her hair had turned gray, and she wore it pulled back. Her once soft facial features hardened, reflecting the strain of the life she had known for too long. Wrinkles, once the dreaded enemy of the modern woman of the past, lined the edges of her mouth, and the corners of her eyes.

Suddenly, there was noise coming down the hall, and she turned in time to see the man who had brought her to this madness entering the room.

"It's been a long time, Mrs. Barnes," General Colton began with a half smile on his thin lips.

"That it has, Colonel. Oh, my, I see you have more medals and ribbons. Have all the good old boys gotten together and promoted you for the many wonders you have accomplished out here?"

"It's General, now, Mrs. Barnes."

"Ah, yes, General. Victor in the battle of the Midwest housewife. I'm sure your name will go down with the Pattons, Macarthurs, and Custers of military history," Linda said. "What do you want? Don't tell me that you have decided to do the bimonthly interrogation? Why, I'd be honored!"

Three guards, standing a step behind the general, looked at their shoes, obviously trying to stifle laughter.

Jennings Colton was caught off guard by the venom of her comments. He wasn't accustomed to hearing any form of disrespect from anyone, let alone the frail women in front of him. His tone betrayed his anger.

"No, I'm afraid that's not it. It has come to my attention that you abused the privileges extended to you. Governor Harris has informed me that you have written quite a few letters. Frankly, I'm not sure that anyone cares about a former radical subversive brought to justice. After all, you are old news."

"Come on, General," she began, eyeing the tall man standing in front of her, "Have we been smoking some of the weed you use to think so terrible in years past? A 'subversive brought to justice'? What you really mean is a citizen plucked out of her world by some half-cocked lunatic in search of enemies. I'd have thought you would have had enough of that after the North Vietnamese kicked your ass in the war!"

Colton's eyes lit up like a flare. She had scored a direct hit on a very sore spot. "WE didn't loose that war, my dear, it was rabble like you who screwed everything up."

"Yeah, I'm sure we did. Plush Pentagon offices, an unlimited supply of weapons and money, and your own private country clubs in Vietnam. Oh, and a few annoying body bags, but what the hell; It was all part of the job."

Colton was flushed with anger, but he could see that it was useless to continue arguing with the woman.

"Let's get back to the matter at hand, Mrs. Barnes. It has been better than two years since your husband went berserk and shot up half of New Mexico. I suppose there's a good chance he's dead. Either that, or he decided to cut his losses and leave you here. I might have miscalculated that point. Anyway, I could arrange to let you go, but I think the timing is inappropriate. Maybe just a little while longer."

Linda replied, softening her tone, "I have a teenage daughter somewhere out there fending for herself. I am her mother and I want to be with my family. Now why don't we end this nonsense once and for all? There has been no trace of my husband in all this time. I can assure you that if he were alive, he would have been here by now. I want to go home and get on with my life."

"I'm sure you do, Mrs. Barnes, but there is such a thing as order to consider.

Turning you loose now, after I vowed to track down the killers, wouldn't look good. So I think we'll wait awhile longer."

Linda began to rise off the chair, but was forced back down by a guard.

"You miserable son of a bitch! If there is a God in heaven, I pray you get what's coming to you! You sociopath bastards cover your neuroses with words like 'order' and 'public good.' Well, bullshit! One day, General, one day you and your ribbons, and your medals, and your brass stars are going to meet reality, and it isn't going to be pleasant. You think you have everyone fooled? Well, you couldn't be more wrong! You don't have a clue as to the character of the people in this country. When they wake up and find everything gone, look out. I just want to be alive to see it."

"Be that as it may, Mrs. Barnes. We'll see who wins in the end. In any case, there will not be any more letters from your poison pen. I'm going to have you transferred to the federal correctional facility in Belen, with instructions to limit your outside access. You'll have to do your writing on the shithouse walls."

He began to walk to the open door, then stopped and turned around.

"You have no idea what your up against, lady. You either go along with the program, or you are set aside. Period. Discussion and debate are a thing of the past. I'd advise you to keep your mouth shut, and quite possibly you might see your daughter before she reaches middle age. You know why I do the things I do? Because I can!"

With that, General Jennings Colton walked briskly out the door, followed closely by the three soldiers.

As they reached the end of the hall, Sergeant Calhoun caught up with the man who issued orders. He stepped in front of Colton, blocking his path.

"General, you have to reconsider. Sending that woman to Belen is a big mistake. You know that prison is a no man's land. The guards are as bad as the inmates! I hear they sell the female prisoners to the men for booze and money. We're talking gang rape, and anything else you might think of. There's four reported cases of Hepatitis C Sir, whatever she's done, she doesn't deserve that!"

"Calhoun, you're compassion is touching. Now get the hell out of my way."

Calhoun looked at the general in amazement. Slowly, the sergeant fell back, allowing the general to stride ahead. He stayed in his spot, lost in thought.

"Sergeant!" yelled the general from down the hall. "Are you with us?"

CHAPTER 14

For his entire life he marched to the drumbeat of some authority, some system that defined and controlled his existence. It was the price of an orderly society. But on that muggy, monsoon day in August, high in the Sierra Madre Mountains of northern Mexico, Jim Barnes marched, along with all the other captives, at the point of a gun. Years into the hell that had become his life, the difference between the two escaped him.

Armed guards walked alongside the bedraggled group of men, sometimes coming up from behind and kicking them for no reason, other than they possessed the power to do so with impunity. Hatred filled the tired eyes of the victims, and silent prayers were lifted to the heavens for just one chance at revenge. But that hope dimmed after each hard day of toil in Emilio Chaca's gold mines.

The sound of a jeep rumbling up the narrow dirt road broke the monotony of the hike and the men lifted their heads to see who was coming. As the vehicle rounded a bend just below them, the unmistakably dark presence of Chaca came into view. He sat in the passenger's seat, accompanied by a driver and an armed guard. But, for once, the eyes of the prisoners looked beyond the master. Sitting in the back was a beautiful woman. It had been a long time since they had seen the female form so close. As the jeep rolled to a stop, Chaca turned around to speak to her. She looked to be in her late 30s, with dark black hair and high cheekbones. Her skin was richly tanned, but too light to be Hispanic. Her eyes were round and expressive, and they showed traces of the same fear that most of the men knew well. She had aged beyond her years, her face betraying some accumulated wisdom lines learned only in the school of life. As Chaca spoke to her, she shifted uncomfortably in the seat, her white, loose fitting cotton top and blue jeans rubbing against the torn vinyl. Her blouse obscured the well-proportioned figure below, but that mattered little to the men who had already undressed her in their minds.

Chaca jumped from the jeep and walked toward the men, holding up one hand as a command to the guards to get them to stop. Chaca was about to flaunt his power for the beautiful lady. His eyes scanned the long line for a victim he could torment.

"You there!" he barked, pointing to Peter Sullivan. "Don't you have no manners? Can't you even say hello to this beautiful woman who has come to see the men who work so hard for Emilio Chaca?"

Peter, realizing that the bait was set for him, decided to take the challenge.

"Well mate, it's like this," he said slowly. "I'm a bloke that's not much into words. I'm more a man of action. So, if it's action she wants, well, I volunteer. Mr. Excitement, that's me name!"

Chaca looked at him and grinned.

"Ah, Mr. Excitement, yes, I see. Unfortunately, she is not here for your enjoyment, but for mine." Jim glanced back at the young woman and saw her wince.

"In any case," he continued, " I was just telling my friend that there are two kinds of people; those who serve, and those who are born to be served. It gives me great pleasure to think that you have chosen to serve me in the dirt of my mines, and make me rich in the bargain. It is something I learned from the

Gringos. Now then, are we going to work hard today, and find lots of gold?"

Sullivan met his stare without blinking.

"Oh, you bet Emilio. I'm going to see if I can find you a big nugget," he said, pausing for effect. "I'll bet you'd like a big one, now wouldn't you?"

The men broke out in muffled laughter. Chaca's eyes darted around the small group and silence followed. Then he returned his gaze to Peter, and the corners of his mouth rose up in an evil grin. The game continued and he intended to end it on his terms.

"You have been here a long time, amigo," he began slowly. "Maybe you are growing tired and would like to stop this hard work. How do you Gringos say, 'retire?' I am sure I could arrange that for you."

Sullivan took a step toward Chaca. The game was getting dangerous, but he wouldn't back down.

"Not bloody likely, mate, I hear the benefits aren't too good. Besides, I live for the day when I can service you REAL good, if you get me drift."

"Yes, senor, I understand." He paused for a moment, looking up and down the line at all the men. His eyes set on Jim briefly and then moved on.

"I'd like to give you a token of my appreciation for all the hard work you have done for me. I know it's small, but on such short notice, what do you expect?"

Chaca turned around and began walking back toward the jeep. He looked directly at the armed guard who had accompanied him, and raised his head slightly. The man stood up, fixed his gaze on Sullivan, and smiled as he walked toward him. When he was within arm's reach, he lashed out with the butt of his rifle, and slammed it across the forehead of the Australian. A loud thud echoed in the thick air. Peter staggered back, but did not fall. Instead, he folded his arms as he stepped up again.

"You still owe me a bloody cold beer, mate," he said with all the control he could muster. Then, under his breath he finished with, "You bastard."

Emilio Chaca grew rich by instilling fear in his prisoners. This one called Peter Sullivan wasn't living by those rules. He would have to die, someday, if only to set a stern example to the others.

The tension in the air was stifling. Jim Barnes focused in on Chaca, waiting for any movement to signal trouble. None came. He was standing closer to the jeep then the rest of the men, and had made up his mind to move on Chaca and kill him with his bare hands if at all possible.

His thoughts must have been transparent, for when the moment passed, he glanced back at the woman. Her eyes were transfixed on him. The two locked on to each other, neither showing emotion, watching each movement, each expression, searching for some subtle hint as to the character behind the face. Then, the engine roared, and the jeep began rolling down the hill. Her head turned slightly, briefly, catching one last glimpse before returning forward. Was it a signal of some interest, he wondered, or just another lonely soul looking for a way out?

He could not think in terms of his physical presence, although his body was finely chiseled and lean from the backbreaking work. Jim watched as the jeep disappeared around a bend. He shook his head and began walking up the incline of the road, questions racing through his mind.

But somehow, someway, the walk seemed easier and lighter. It was as if a new chapter was to be written in his ordeal, and with it brought new possibilities and the chance for change. His step quickened as he moved toward the Australian.

****

That night, as darkness fell after the evening meal of corn gruel and tortillas, a group of the men gathered around a small wooden table outside the bunkhouse. Some pulled up crude, handmade stools, while others sprawled on the board deck, staring off into the dark mountains. Overhead, monsoon clouds gathered.

Peter Sullivan reclined on the rear legs of his stool and braced himself with his foot against a support post that held up the roof overhang. He casually shuffled the deck of cards won earlier from Chaca, and then silently began flipping them toward a worn leather cowboy hat upturned a few feet away. Jim Barnes sat on the floor nearby and stared across the compound at the lights from Chaca's house.

Eduardo Conasto, a whiskered Mexican with rough hands and a wide grin, looked down at the American.

"I think your friend Pablo longs for what he cannot have, no?" he said toward the Australian.

Peter smiled. "You might be right, mate. Looks like a bloody lovesick teenager to me.

"More like 'lust-sick,' you dipshits. Hell, we've all been walking around with poles stuck down our legs," threw in Max Fisher, a long lanky Texan sitting across the table.

"No, no, senor," shot back Eduardo, "I took good care of mine." He held up five fingers and wiggled them in the breeze.

Jim's face broke out in a grin, but his gaze stayed on the house in the distance.

"I'm surprised any of you could even remember what a hard-on is, let alone do something about it."

"Well, I for bloody one, took a vow of celibacy when I entered this establishment. Thought it would be good for me character."

Max spoke in his slow Texas drawl. "Well pardner, I wish you had told me that three years ago. I've been sleeping with one eye open and my cheeks slammed shut all this time."

They all broke out in laughter, a luxury that rarely happened.

"What have we here?" Jim asked out loud, as he watched the gate open and a group of armed men come toward them.

"Maybe they've come to tuck us in the bloomin' sack," Peter said casually, but his voice held an edge to it.

"Oh, shit," Eduardo spat, shaking his head. "Look there, its that puta Chaca coming to fuck with us! I tell you, I've had all I can take. He never quits. Maybe I can kill him before they get me. What do you think?"

"Too bloody right, mate! Go for it! Five quid says they let you strangle the slimy bastard before they kill you!"

"Everybody just shut up. I don't feel like dying tonight," Jim said sharply.

Chaca walked toward the men sitting on the porch, but motioned for his men to bring over four others near the ramada. When they were all gathered, he looked down at Jim and spoke.

"You, and this one here," he said pointing at Eduardo, "along with those four. Tomorrow you go for a little ride."

Jim was suspicious. "Where to?"

Chaca snapped, "Ez none of your fucking bizness, Gringo, but I will tell you anyway. I have a large farm near Hermosillo. There I grow the weed that you Yankees like so much. Ez time for to harvest my crop, but I am short-handed. Some of my workers decided to strike out on their own, and I was forced to kill them. Now you will go in their place to bring in the marijuana."

"Wait a bloody minute, mate!" Peter exclaimed, falling forward in his chair, "How did I get left out of this detail?"

"Oh, you, Mr. Excitement. We need you here to liven up the place!" Chaca said, laughing.

"Listen, mate, forget the beer, forget everything I've said or ever thought of saying. You happen to be talking to an expert in this field. Nobody could touch me bloomin' stuff in Vietnam. You need me to oversee this operation. Quality bloody control!"

Chaca was amused, but he refused to budge. "Sorry, Gringo, not this time. Your friend there can tell you all about it if he survives the work."

Jim looked at him coldly. "I'll survive. Count on it."

"Yes, I'm sure. You leave at first light. If you try to escape, you die. If you don't do enough work, you die. If you even look at the woman, you die. Do you understand?"

"The woman?" Jim asked, "What's she got to do with it?"

Chaca's gaping teeth showed in the darkness.

"Why she is my partner! She looks after my interests."

Jim Barnes watched him closely, but said nothing.

"First light, amigos. Be ready or we'll shoot you. Oh, and work quickly so you can return to my mines. There still is much gold for you to dig!" He spun on his heels and walked back toward the gate.

"Bloody hell, you lucky bastard! You're heading for nirvana and my bloody ass is stuck here!"

"This might be it, Sully. This might be our chance. If I can get away from there, I swear to God I'll bring a Goddamned tank column back here and blow that son of a bitch to hell!" Jim nearly shouted.

"If you get away, I want you to bring back three things, beside the tanks. One, a meat pie, two, some samples of his crop, and three, the sharpest bloody filleting knife you can find cause I'm going to skin that bastard and make a bloody wallet out of him!"

Crickets sang their night songs and a coyote howled at the moon in the desert. Otherwise, the men fell silent. For the first time in two years, Jim's body tingled with excitement. Tomorrow would be an opportunity – in some way.

Sullivan broke the silence.

"Two wallets mate. One for you and one for me!"

****

"Apurate, Gringo," hissed the foul-smelling, whiskered guard as he pointed his rifle at Jim and the other men, motioning them to get into the back of an old pickup truck. Large parts of the dilapidated vehicle were either rusted or torn away, including the metal bed they would sit on for many miles to Hermisillo.

"Shove it up your ass, you miserable fucking pig," Jim replied with a wide grin on his face, knowing that the man in front of him spoke no English. The guard smiled in return and said nothing.

The six men piled into the back of the truck, trying in vain to find a comfortable spot. But it was difficult maneuvering around the old Corona bottles, car parts and rotting food.

Eduardo sat down beside Jim with his back to the passenger side of the truck and looked around.

"If these two pigs are the only ones making the trip," he said in a whisper, motioning toward the driver and the guard with the rifle, "I think this is our lucky day."

"Let's hope so," Jim answered, also surveying the scene, "But I can't believe Chaca would be that stupid. Two of them to guard six of us? I could kill those two myself."

Jim sat quietly for a moment, thinking about the statement he just made. It rolled off his tongue as nonchalantly as talking about a baseball score. It struck him how far he had fallen from the civilized world he once knew and the assumptions that were the bedrock of his life.

It chilled him to think how fast and furious the descent had been. But there was no disputing the fact that he was at the bottom of the pit. If he was able to claw, and scrap, and kill his way out of it, the haunting thought remained that the Jim Barnes who once existed would never be found again. Soldiers could fight in the hell that was war, but they did so in a system, and they returned to a civilized society. It was clear to the middle-aged man riding in the back of the old truck, like so much garbage, that he would never look at life in the same way again. Reality, not illusion, was the only thing that mattered to him now.

The pickup lurched forward as the gates to Chaca's prison opened. Jim and Eduardo looked ahead hopefully. But as dawn's light spread over the roof of Chaca's house, they saw another jeep carrying three more guards. It was parked in front, waiting while the woman from the day before walked toward them with the dark man at her side.

"Son of a bitch!" Jim muttered under his breath. "I knew he wouldn't screw up. Goddamit."

"Who knows, amigo," Eduardo said quietly, "maybe we will still get a chance. Just be ready. You must be ready at all times."

Chaca bent down and gave the young woman a long farewell kiss, to which she seemed to respond, and then helped her get into the passenger side of the vehicle. She wore the same clothes from before, but thanks to the rising sun, it was easier to see the slim outlines of her body.

Then the pickup's engine roared, and again lurched forward as the near clutchless pile of junk strained to move. The jeep fell in behind them as they began down the winding road. In the half morning light, through the cloud of dust kicked up behind them, Jim looked back through the windshield of the old Willys, and once again his eyes locked on to the fine features of the woman's face. She returned his stare, not looking away, and then slowly, deliberately, brought her hand up and wiped it across her lips.

His mind raced in all directions, startled and confused in a way only a female could accomplish. Was she toying with him? Was it a setup, a trap? Or was it a signal, a calculated gesture to convey a message? Only time would tell. His body tensed with excitement.

By midmorning, they were over halfway on their journey across the Sonora desert. When possible, they stayed on the main road. But more often than not, they cut off into the brown and green countryside with its bumpy, twisting roads, to skirt small towns. Though no one in authority would have noticed, or cared, Chaca's men never took chances. Anarchy was all around, and it was better to bypass any confrontations than risk trouble.

Finally, they came upon an old white board, painted with the words "Ciudad de Kennedy." The pickup veered off in that direction, and soon came upon a group of small shacks. Near one were old cars in various stages of disrepair. Greasy parts, oil pans and rusted mufflers were strewn about. At another, children played in filthy conditions in front of what must have been their home. To the left of that stood the largest structure, with faded white paint on the wooden walls, broken clay tiles dangling from the roof and an old Coke machine standing guard by the entrance. Chairs were scattered about both on the porch and inside the old walls. It was the nearest thing to a cantina in that part of a forgotten world.

The vehicles pulled up and stopped with a squeal of the brakes. The men in the back of the truck, hot, tired, and thirsty, slowly climbed out. Jim Barnes looked around and took in the splendor of Kennedy City, then jumped to the ground with everyone else, all under the watchful eye of the grizzled Mexican with the carbine.

"Nice place," Eduardo mocked.

"You got it, amigo," Jim replied.

Children from the house began to gather near the captive men, staring in wonder at the ragged group, but keeping a safe distance.

"Get these men some water," came a woman's voice, as she jumped down from the jeep and began walking toward the cantina.

"Ez not necessary, senorita," came the retort of the tall, thin guard nearest her. "They will survive for one more hour."

The woman stopped and spun around, casting a menacing gaze at the guard.

"You heard what I said, now DO IT! They aren't animals and neither am I." She glanced back over at the six, shook her head, and then walked into the old building.

"She's American," Jim whispered to Eduardo.

"Yes, and she's Chaca's woman. Do not make the mistake of trusting her," he shot back quickly.

"I won't," he answered, but something inside told him there was a possibility.

They gathered around the hand pump of a well, and drank the lukewarm liquid as though it was a gift from heaven. Jim splashed water on his face and hair, and pushed it back, looking up into the scorching sun. Then, he slowly walked away from the other men, under the watchful eye of the guards and moved close to the wood railing surrounding the old porch. He leaned back against it, hearing it give way slightly, and looked out across the desolate place. Tumbleweeds, cactus and sagebrush as far as the eye could see.

"Hard to believe anyone could live here," came the soft tones of a woman's voice a few feet behind him. He turned slightly to see her standing in the doorway, running her fingers through her long, black, straight hair. He cracked off a splinter of wood from one of the wood pickets and put it in his mouth. Then he turned back around nonchalantly, but his heart was pounding.

"I'd say so," he said simply.

"It's not far now," she continued, "maybe an hour."

He shrugged. "An hour, a day, it doesn't really matter."

She stayed quiet for a moment, looking around the hot, dusty scene.

"It's better at the ranch. You'll see. It's in a valley, with a stream. Miles of green."

"I'm not looking for a vacation spot," he replied sharply, "I'm looking for a way out. Feel free to tell your boyfriend."

"He already knows."

"That's good, because if I get half the chance, I'm coming for him, too."

She pulled her cotton blouse down against her firm breasts, dusted off her jeans, and began walking toward the jeep. A few steps from Jim, she stopped, and turned to look him directly in the eye without flinching.

"We're all looking for a way out. Who knows, maybe lightning will strike and we'll all live happily ever after. Could happen."

With that, she turned and walked away.

Jim watched her move toward the jeep. It was nice to talk to someone other than a man after all those years, but he wasn't sure about her. A black widow spider enticing her victim before the strike?

The barking Spanish of the guard near the pickup broke his train of thought. Jim moved back to the other men, climbed back in and found his seat. As the engines came to life, he tilted his tan face toward the clear blue sky, and then rolled it back in the direction of the woman behind him.

Once again, her dark eyes bore down on him with a penetrating stare.

CHAPTER 15

The old pickup bounced along a rutted dirt drive past large, ornate steel gates, held open by two men carrying Uzi submachine guns, and rolled toward a sprawling one-story ranch house. As they approached the white stucco hacienda, Jim began to see the extent of Chaca's ranch. Behind and to the left of the tree-shaded house were large barns and horse corrals. Nearby were a tack room and quarters for the guards. About two 200 yards away, standing unprotected in the scorching sun, was a long, narrow wood building with a tarpaper roof. Slated wood vents along each side stood propped open by boards, and there was a single door in one end. Surrounding the bleak structure on all four sides was an electrified, barbwire fence.

As the truck continued on in the direction of the compound, the jeep carrying Chaca's girlfriend continued on and stopped in front of the house. The woman got out, dusted herself off, and started for the long veranda that covered the doorway. She glanced one last time in the direction of the pickup and then turned away.

The old truck slowed to a stop and Jim saw their welcoming committee. Standing with his arms crossed over a hairy chest covered only by a leather vest stood a hulk of a man. Well over six feet, with broad shoulders and powerful arms, the bearded man watched impassively as the new arrivals approached. He stood defiantly with his legs open. A coiled bullwhip hung from a leather strap at his side.

The armed Mexican guards began to spread out and trained their rifle barrels on the six arrivals, motioning for them to get out. Without speaking, each jumped to the ground and stood, waiting like kids about to be punished by a stern father.

"I am Barot," the large man said in a rough, gravelly baritone voice, "While you are here, you will work for me. You will do as you are told, WHEN you are told, with no questions, Si?"

The six shifted uncomfortably on their feet, but did not answer.

"Out there, in the valley," he continued, sweeping his hand in the direction of the green fields in the distance, "we grow the marijuana. You are here to harvest it. If you try to escape, the dogs will hunt you down, and I, personally, will kill you. I have done this many times before, and I do it well. Now, you will all turn around and face the house."

The men did what they were told, looking at each other with fearful glances.

Barot lifted his right hand and unhooked the bullwhip from his side. He let it open out on the ground, like a long, deadly snake waiting to strike.

"I have found that it is best for you to understand what happens if you decide not to cooperate, so there is no misunderstanding."

With that, his huge arm snapped the bullwhip back and then sent it slashing forward, striking the first man across the back in the blink of an eye. Before he had time to cry out in pain, the whip ripped the man standing next to him. Jim was second from the end and he braced himself for the white-hot pain to follow. He was not disappointed.

As the leather cracked across his skin, Jim believed his back would explode. He clenched his teeth hard and closed his eyes, but he made no sound. He was the only man to stay silent. Beads of sweat rose up on his brow and his fists tightened. He lifted his head slowly and looked toward the house, where he could just make out the shape of a woman standing beside an open window taking in the scene. His eyes narrowed with hatred and he fought to control himse.

"Ah, Gringo," Barot said to Jim when he finished, "You say nothing. You take the pain like a man! This is good. Maybe you are a tough hombre, eh?"

Jim Barnes slowly turned his six-foot frame around and faced the large man. He glared at him defiantly, not caring what happened.

"Put that whip down, and let's see who's tough," he spoke slowly, deliberately.

A large grin broke out on the chubby face of the Mexican. His eyes lit up in a psychotic stare and laughter rose up from his round belly.

"This whip, amigo, it is a part of me. I eat with it, I sleep with it, and I make LOVE with it! I cannot let it go so easy!" With that, his arm snapped back once again, and sent the lash careening toward Jim. It struck him at the top of the shoulder, and drove him down to his knees. A second assault struck him in the lower back, partially ripping his blue cotton shirt. Blood rose up from his wounds and he slumped down, gasping for air. Barot pulled the whip back again and used all his strength to send it slashing forward. But just as it was about to land on his exposed back, Jim spun around and grabbed it about a foot from its pointed end just before it struck. With perfect timing, he jerked back, pulling the carved wood handle out of the startled Barot's hands. For a moment, it was nothing but dead silence.

Then, instantly, the guards began ratcheting shells into rifle chambers. Jim Barnes looked around at the men who could take his life if commanded. He turned again, staring up at Barot, who was walking toward him. The huge man stopped just a few feet away, his cowboy boots within easy reach. He bent down slowly, picked up the handle of the whip and began coiling it up. At the same time, he spoke to Jim.

"Yes, you are tough, senor. You will make a good worker. This time I will let you live. But next time, it will not be so good," he said, spitting tobacco juice on Jim's leg. "Now, Gringo, get your ass up and through the gate. Work begins in two hours."

Barot stood, spun on his heels and strode away, leaving the guards to take care of the rest. Eduardo rushed over to Jim, and helped him to his feet.

"You crazy bastard, that man's a killer. You must be smart, senor. Do you want to die?"

Jim was in too much pain to answer. He grunted, and hooked his arm around Eduardo's shoulder. Together, they limped toward the long building that would serve as shelter while they picked the crop.

Unnoticed in the distance, the curtains of the tall window in the house fell back softly, shading the room from the sun's light. The shadow of the young woman disappeared into the darkened place.

****

Two weeks passed. The six men from the mines joined others whose bad luck brought them to the ranch to work as slaves. Work started early and ended late, filled with hours of chopping the tall plants with machetes, and loading them into wooden carts. They made a sizable impact on the many acres of marijuana and it was clear that in a few days, their work would be done.

Jim Barnes recovered from his wounds. He accepted his stay at the ranch with the same hatred he reserved for Chaca's mines. Most of the time, Jim was thinking, looking for a way out. But even with machetes in hand, the workers were no match for the dozens of armed guards watching over them. Barot's hulking presence stood over everything and everyone. He was the master of this place. At times, he would strike out with his whip, just to remind someone who was boss.

That afternoon, hours after the sun had crested in the sky, the men lined up for one last pass through the green plants. They stood close together, like a line of human combines, hacking and sawing at the crop that would increase Chaca's profits.   Steel blades swished through the air, leaving the fallen plants for the men behind them to gather.

Jim had switched off his mind, numbing himself to his circumstances, flailing away at the gangly weeds, when suddenly a searing burst of pain shot out from his upper left arm, momentarily taking his breath away. At first, he thought it was Barot's whip. But then, looking down, he was shocked to see a huge, six inch gash shaped like a half moon gushing blood just below his shoulder.

"Ahhh!" he cried out, dropping his machete and bringing his other hand up to cover the gash. The cut was deep, almost to the bone, and he needed medical attention, fast.

"I am sorry, amigo!" cried out a Mexican worker by the name of Raul, as he too dropped his machete to the ground, its blade covered with thick, red blood.

"I did not mean to do it!" He reached over to try to help Jim.

Jim gritted his teeth, trying to control the pain, but he was losing the battle.

Raul quickly ripped a piece of cloth from his shirt and began wrapping it around Jim's arm. Barot strolled up to see what was happening.

"Get back to work!" he shouted at Raul, his right hand fingering the bullwhip at his side. The young Mexican didn't need to be told twice.

"What is this? The tough Gringo bleeds all over my crops!"

"My arm's ripped open. I'm loosing a lot of blood. I need some help," Jim said quietly through clenched teeth. His head was light. He was losing consciousness.

"Bullshit, amigo!" Barot shot back, "You will be fine. I've had bigger scratches from mosquitoes! Just let me tie this cloth a little tighter, and you can get back to work."

He grabbed the loose ends of the torn shirt, and pulled hard, sending a wave of white-hot pain through Jim's arm.

From behind, the clopping of horse's hoofs drew nearer. They stopped close by the American.

"Barot, STOP!" came the angry voice of a woman, as she quickly dismounted. "Can't you see that this man is in agony?" She marched over to Jim with all the authority she could muster and examined his bleeding arm.

"Ez nothing but a small cut. He will be all right, senorita." Barot answered arrogantly.

She looked up at him and snapped, "A small cut my ass! Help me get him on the horse. I want him back at the house so I can try to sew him up. NOW!"

Barot was a man unfamiliar with taking orders from anyone, let alone a woman. He eyed her closely and knew she meant business. He knew his years of loyalty to Chaca would not hold up to the hours this woman had shared his bed.

"If that's want you want, senorita, OK by me. But I tell you; it's not worth it. A Gringo dead, a Gringo alive, what's the difference?"

"You forget," she said icily, staring into his black eyes, "I am a Gringo, too!"

They walked the half conscious man to the horse. Barot reached over with his two huge hands, and took Jim by the waist, hoisting him effortlessly onto the leather saddle. Once on top, he leaned over, clutching the horn, trying to hang on.

"You two!" Barot cried out at the nearest of his men, "You go with them. Kill the Gringo if he tries anything."

"That won't be necessary!" she answered, again thrusting her jaw forward, "I can handle this. He's not in any shape to do anything."

"But..." he tried to argue.

"You heard me!" came the retort.

She walked around to the front of the horse, and picked up the dangling reins. Slowly, she led the large animal out onto the trail leading back to the white hacienda. Behind them, the booming voice of Barot could be heard, along with the crack of his whip.

"Get back to work, putas! We have much to do!"

The men didn't argue. But Eduardo, his body tense, and tired, looked over at the man with the whip. His lip curled up in anger.

"One day soon you will eat that whip, amigo," he muttered. "This I promise on the grave of my mother!"

****

The late afternoon air flowed through the open windows of the small bedroom. The sheer white curtains danced in the slow breeze and rays of light flickered, and then grew dim, as the sun set beyond the valley.

Jim Barnes lay sleeping on the single bed, his wounded arm resting in the lap of the woman who sat beside him on a chair. She had long since been able to control the bleeding and was preparing to stitch up the gaping flesh. His eyes twitched open, searching the room in panic.

"Be still," the dark haired beauty ordered, but with no trace of malice in her voice, "This is going to hurt."

She picked up a hooked needle, and threaded a small piece of line through the end.

"I use to do this for my brothers in El Paso after their fights. They didn't like it, but it had to be done. I'm going to put some alcohol on it to try to numb the skin a little. Grit your teeth."

Jim looked over at her. The liquid hit his open flesh, stinging. His arm shot out in reflex and he gave a low groan. Then, the pain seemed to ease, and the woman prepared to sew the skin.

"Where are the guards?" he asked quietly.

"They aren't necessary. Besides, we need each other," she said, concentrating on her work.

Jim eyed the fine features of her face carefully. He gazed at her small, upturned nose, smooth, tanned skin and full, perfectly shaped lips.

"Just how do you need me?" he asked cautiously.

She said nothing for a long moment and then slowly lifted her eyes from the stitches, gazing into his.

"You are strong. You watch, and listen, and calculate. I knew from the first moment that you would be the one to help me escape from this place."

Jim Barnes appraised her carefully, studying the face for the smallest sign of betrayal. But she met his gaze and held it.

"Chaca's woman wants to escape? From what? It looks to me like you have it pretty good here."

"For starters, I am not Chaca's woman. I am a survivor. Call me what you will, a whore, a prostitute, whatever. I am alive. Many before me can't say that."

Jim was caught off guard by the sudden turn of events. He wanted desperately to believe the woman, but he wouldn't allow it – yet.

"What's your name?" he asked.

"Maggie Stanton," she said quietly, "Well, Marguerite, but I hate that. You?"

"Jim. Jim Barnes."

She smiled through her perfectly white teeth and nodded.

"You're American?" Jim asked.

"My father is American, an oil engineer from Texas. He met my mother in Juarez. I guess you could say I grew up around oil rigs and taco stands," she said with a self-mocking smile.

"What happened? How did you end up here?" he said, then noticed her wince from the pain of reliving past events.

"I'm sorry, I didn't..."

"No, it's all right," she answered quietly. "It's just that sometimes when I think about how stupid I was, it really hurts."

She did not look up, but skillfully continued with the needle.

"I got real tired watching other people make lots of money. You know Texas – big cars, big houses, big deals. I had some friends who were running a little dope up from Hermosillo and they were making a killing. It seemed so easy. They asked me if I wanted in, and I said sure, why not. We made a couple of trips. It was a joke. When we'd cross the border, I'd unhook a couple of buttons on my blouse and the border patrol would spend more time looking at my boobs than what was in the car. It was clockwork. That is, until one night we got ripped off by our contact in Mexico. There was a big fight. The Federales showed up. The last time I saw my friends...." she paused, and drew a deep breath, "they got their brains blown out along a back road. Nice way to die, huh?"

Jim didn't answer. He watched her talk, sensing that she had never told the story before. He waited for tears. They didn't come.

"I spent the next couple of months in a private jail. They did things to me that little Maggie Stanton never dreamed existed. One day, Chaca showed up and bought me. He brought me here. That was a decade ago."

"You've been here 10 years and you haven't been able to escape?"

"Chaca's influence goes well beyond this ranch. He has people in every town between here and the border. I wouldn't get five miles by myself."

She finished the last stitch, knotted the thread, and cut it.

"What about you? What's your story?"

Jim turned his head and looked back up at the ceiling. "I'm not sure I remember, it's been so long."

"Well, you have a wife, or girlfriend named Linda. That I know. You mumbled the name while you were sleeping."

"Wife," he said, thinking how strange the word sounded after all the years that passed.

In the next few minutes, he briefly filled her in on the whirlwind that was his recent past. When he finished, she drew in a soft breath. "And I thought I had it bad."

"You do," Jim said quickly.

Just then, they heard footsteps approaching the kitchen door near the bedroom.

"Keep quiet," she whispered. "Pretend you're asleep. We have a lot to talk about."

With that she got up and exited the room to meet the visitor. Standing outside the door was one of the Mexican guards. Maggie opened the door and stared at him with her most intimidating gaze.

"What is it?" she said sharply.

"Barot wants the Gringo," said the guard.

"He is asleep. He lost too much blood to be moved. I have him tied to the bed. He won't be going anywhere."

"But senorita..." the old man began.

"You heard me," Maggie snapped, "He'll stay here for the night. Tell Barot to post a guard in a couple of hours when I go to bed."

She watched the man shrug with resignation and turn to do what he was told. When he was a safe distance away, she returned to the room.

"We don't have too much time," she said to Jim.

"You sound like you've thought about this quite a bit," he answered.

"I have. Every day, and every time he touches me. I'm sure this will be the only chance for both of us."

Jim looked at her through the darkness. Her large, brown eyes glistened with sincerity.

"I have some weapons hidden under the floorboards in the back storeroom. You will be leaving in a few days. I will get them to you. Barot must die, and two or three of his men. The others will give up with little struggle. That will give us time to make a run for the border."

"There's only one problem," Jim said. "The guy on the path by the mine? He's a friend of mine. If I go, he goes. I won't leave him behind. Chaca would kill him sure as hell when he found out we escaped."

Maggie looked at the American closely.

"OK, let's try Plan B. You go back to the mines with the others. Chaca is going on his trip to Texas to buy guns. That usually lasts two weeks. I'll follow you there in a couple of days, making up some excuse. You get your friend ready. When the time is right, I'll get some guns to you. It will be tougher, but with Chaca gone, it might work. Besides, we'll be closer to the border."

Jim watched her face closely as she spoke. There was no doubt in his mind that it was now or never for the young woman.

"I knew when I looked at you there was something going on behind those dark eyes," he said softly.

"Let's hope Chaca didn't see the same thing," she countered.

They talked and planned for three more hours. Then, to deflect suspicion, she left him alone in the room and called the guard to come in and watch him.

Jim barely noticed the man. He closed his eyes and sighed, confident that the end of the nightmare was approaching.

At the other end of the house, lying across the large double bed, Maggie looked up at the ceiling fan as it slowly traced circles on the stucco walls. For the first time in years, she was excited, not only at the prospect of leaving, but also for the man who would help her.

CHAPTER 16

The end of the harvest neared and the machete-wielding men bore down on the marijuana crops still standing. The monsoon of August blew with full force and the air was heavy with humidity. But the valley around them was green from the night rains, and it was a pleasant diversion from the barren desert to the north. Except for dealing with Barot, some of the six men from the mines wished they could remain.

Jim Barnes wasn't one of them. With his arm tightly bandaged, he stood up among the tall green crops, his strong upper body glistening with sweat. He had a new lease on life and, for the first time in around four years, hope for the future. His mind fixated on the plan he and Maggie Stanton had so carefully conceived a few days before. The risks were grave, but it was a chance.

Jim checked his wound. The stitches were beginning to itch, and there was general discomfort from the healing process, but he was past the risk of infection thanks to the woman. She not only saved his life, but his spirit. She seemed a kindred soul. Her beauty also enraptured him, but he pushed those thoughts aside, keeping his focus on escape.

The guards watching the work crews had relaxed considerably since the first few days, as no one dared to start any trouble. Barot made his point, and by now, only a fool would challenge him. So the guards talked among themselves, not paying as much attention to the workers chopping the marijuana, and the days drifted along.

Only one man failed to fall into the routine. Eduardo Conasto, Jim knew, was close to the breaking point. The heat, the humidity and the work were taking a heavy toll on him. And like so many others, he had nothing left to lose. It was a dangerous combination.

Time after time, Eduardo raised the machete and chopped down on the base of the plants, but constantly watched the guards. Physically, he was taller and stockier than most of his countryman. Muscles rippled from his wide shoulders from years in the mines. He moved away from Jim, nearer to the edge of the uncut plants, where the swaying green would swallow him up.

Jim noticed Eduardo inching away. He knew Barot's whipping had triggered a primal hate in his fellow prisoner.

For a second, Jim and Eduardo locked eyes. The American, without speaking, tried to dissuade the suicidal escape attempt.

It was futile. As the men nearest Eduardo were distracted by the noise of a truck approaching, he slipped into the green plants, and disappeared, almost unnoticed.

Jim watched in horror as his friend stole away, wanting desperately to tell him to wait, to have patience, for escape was only days away. Jim's mind whirled, trying to decide what to do. He turned quickly, waiting for someone to sound an alarm, but it did not come. No one had seen anything.

Just then, the sound of a whip whistling through the air caught Jim's attention, seconds before it struck him across the back. Once again he felt the ripping pain, and he grunted as his body shook from the blow.

"What are you looking at, Gringo?" Barot cried out, "You have work to do! This time the woman is not here to help you. It is only you and me. And my whip!"

He broke out in an evil grin and pulled his arm back to strike again, but he stopped abruptly, looking around studying the faces of the men he tormented. They watched him in silent fascination, waiting for his next move. But Barot knew that one face was missing, the one of the large Mexican.

"Andele, muchachos!" he shouted out to the guards, motioning them to gather. "One is missing. The big man. Who has seen this?"

Each of the men quaked in fear, not daring to answer.

"All right then, I will deal with you later! Where was he working? Quickly, show me the place!"

One man pointed to the last spot Eduardo was standing. Barot stomped over and searched the area for a trail. Clearly visible in the tall plants were broken branches and trampled leaves where the fleeing Mexican had run.

Barot stood up and smiled again, then his lip turned down in a sneer.

"I will take care of this," he said, looping the bullwhip in a circle and strapping it to his side.

"Watch these men carefully until I come back. I will show them what happens to a fool who dares run from Barot!"

He started off through the tall weeds, arrogantly stalking his prey. A hundred yards ahead, the desperate man slowed and listened. Cracking twigs and the swish of branches told him someone followed. His dark eyes turned around and flashed in a demonic glance and he began setting his trap. The hunted was truly the hunter.

Minutes passed. The guards and workers all halted, expecting to hear Eduardo's screams. Barot marched on through the plants while Eduardo waited.

Finally, Barot closed the distance between the two to less than 50 feet. On instinct, he slowed, his eyes scanning the weeds for sign of his prey. His forehead held beads of sweat and his fingers loosened the strap on the bullwhip. He stepped carefully, slowly, deliberately, like a hunter nearing his kill.

He stopped. Ahead, the tall plants grew untouched and untrammeled. The trail was at an end. He looked at them for a moment.

Then with a roar, Eduardo sprung up from the covering that concealed him, his machete rising high in the thick air.

Lunging forward, with steel cutting through the air, Eduardo drove the gleaming blade down across Barot's back, striking just above the shoulder blade, and slicing effortlessly through the thick muscle.

"Agggghhh!" screamed the huge man, his eyes and veins on his face bulging.

He turned around slowly to face his attacker, as if someone had just tapped him on the shoulder. He struck out with a vicious backhand, hitting Eduardo with the force of a heavy log and knocking him to the ground.

Barot stood and glared silently at the man at his feet. Then he took his hand and felt over his shoulder to the wound on his back. His huge, brown, calloused hand came back covered in his own red blood.

"You die NOW" he screeched, lost in an uncontrollable urge to kill.

He snapped the bullwhip back and sent it slashing forward, striking the still-dazed Eduardo on the right wrist. The bloodied machete flew in the air, landing about 10 feet away. Barot jerked back the whip, to land another blow, but by that time, Eduardo had recovered.

In a quick movement, Eduardo leap to his feet, and dove, shoulder first, into the midsection of the man with the whip. A huge rush of air escaped his lungs, and the two combatants tumbled to the ground. They kicked and clawed at each other, gouging at eyes, pulling hair, until their fingers were covered with the bloody flesh of the other. They rolled, over and over, smashing the plants, each screaming and grunting with the fury of hell.

Finally, they rolled back near the bullwhip lying on the ground. Barot felt it first and grabbed it. In one deft movement, he brought it across the neck of the man beneath him. With blind rage in his eye, he began to press down, choking off life.

But Eduardo summoned every bit of strength left to reach out, and snatched the bullwhip a little further up toward the handle. With a huge adrenalin rush, he wrapped it around Barot's neck, and brought his other hand up to help apply the pressure. Life for the two had come down to which man could survive the longest.

Seconds seemed like hours as their eyes bulged out at each other, fierce hatred raging unspoken. The tan muscles on their arms rose up, and large blue veins burst to the surface of the taut brown skin. Their fingers screamed out with cramps, the nails white from the pressure, but each refused to let go.

Finally, for just a brief second, Eduardo felt the tension on his neck ease. He looked at the man above him, and saw his large eyes begin to cloud.

It was the beginning of his march toward death.

With all the strength left in him, he tightened the whip one last time and he felt a noticeable release on his throat. Barot's eyes fluttered and then they rolled back into his head. The blood streaming from his back had sapped the rest of his energy and he was beaten.

Eduardo jerked the ends of the whip in his hands, and at the same time rolled the huge man over, as close to death as he could possibly be without the final, involuntary release.

Slowly, painfully, he rose up, stretching his full length to the blue sky above him, gasping for air. He turned, and looked down on the ground. A few feet away lay the machete covered in dirt and blood. He walked to it deliberately grasped the rough wooden handle. Then, with the

look of an executioner in his eye, he walked back to where Barot lay semiconscious, choking for air.

"Ez time for YOU to die, you bastard!" Eduardo hissed through clenched teeth, saliva and blood dripping from the corner of his mouth.

His right hand rose up quickly, hesitated for an instant, then lashed downward, the bloody blade striking Barot just below the tangle of leather around his throat. It continued cleanly on to the dirt below, severing the head of the dark man whose eyes looked up perplexed. Then slowly they rolled back upward, into their sockets. The huge body, no longer attached to the head, twitched, and then fell deathly still.

Back in the clearing, the men stood about, waiting. As expected, they heard Eduardo's screams in the distance and they knew that Eduardo was paying a horrible price. The guards were certain that Barot would finish the foolish man the way he had so many others.

Time passed slowly and the tension mounted.

Then, from up the road, the sound of a horse trotting broke the silence. In seconds the tall animal rounded the last bend, and came into view. Maggie Stanton, her long black hair flying out, was sitting high in the saddle. She came up to the group of men and stopped, taking in the scene, but not understanding what was going on. She looked from face to face, waiting for an answer, then turned to the sound of mayhem approaching from the green plants.

Tramping out of the bushes, screaming at the top of his lungs, Eduardo staggered and stopped, holding the dripping machete in his right and, and the severed head of Barot by the hair in the other. Blood and gore dripped to his feet.

"PUTAS!" he bellowed, his eyes raising up and rolling back, whiskered face gleaming with sweat, "Here is your feared Barot! Take him and go to hell!"

He swung his left arm back, and flung the lifeless pale head with a mighty toss toward the Mexican guards who were too stunned to react. They screamed in horror, and fell back, as the head hit the ground at their feet, and rolled toward them. It seemed guided by some unseen hand. It came to rest with the woeful eyes staring up.

Eduardo cackled, well beyond the reach of sanity, "He's not so tough now! We can play football with the bastard!"

Jim froze. Every muscle in his body tensed, waiting for anything to happen. He couldn't move. He couldn't think. His brain refused to believe what his eyes had taken in.

Then, after what seemed like an eternity, Jim watched Eduardo turn, and settle his gaze nearby on the woman. Once again he screamed out in laughter, brought the machete up, and charged the place where she waited, too numb to speak or move.

In that instant, Jim's mind cleared, and he dashed forward in a race for Maggie Stanton. His legs churned through the cut plants, rising and falling as fast as his sore muscles would allow.

Then, just before Eduardo arrived, readying the machete for its fatal strike, Jim leapt through the air and tackled the hopeless woman, both falling headlong to the ground on the other side of the frightened horse.

The tall, chestnut mare Maggie rode reared up and moved back out of harm's way. Jim and Maggie lay on the ground, wrapped in each other's arms, gasping for air. Above them, the insane face of Eduardo cast his shadow down on the helpless victims. Slowly, he brought the machete up with both hands, to finish the job on the woman.

Jim screamed, but to no avail. Silence seemed to engulf the clearing, and everything settled into slow motion; the wind, the leaves, the swirling dust and the machete.

The crack of a single explosion broke the silence and Eduardo's chest burst in a spray of blood and bone. Jagged edges of his torn tissue flew in all directions. He crumbled to the ground, dead before he landed on the two huddling bodies below him.

Jim and Maggie could not move trapped below the lifeless body of a man he once called a friend. A warm liquid spread out on his exposed skin, and Jim wanted to scream, but he could not find his voice. They lay there, locked in an embrace with a corpse.

Finally, Jim used what was left of his strength to roll Eduardo over on his side, and the two sat up, staring into the depths of each other's eyes, still numb from shock. Men rushed up around them, but they did not notice.

Without speaking, Maggie acknowledged a debt owed.

CHAPTER 17

In the late afternoon three days later, the small convoy arrived back at the mine camp. Six prisoners left, but only five returned – exhausted, beaten, and still shocked by what they had seen. Their condition didn't go unnoticed by the rest of the men as they gathered around the old pickup inside the gates.

Peter Sullivan heard the vehicle drive up and he raced outside to greet his friend, leaving behind a card game. As he trotted toward the truck with his distinctive hop, he could see Jim in the distance. One look told him that the time away had been eventful.

"I was hoping for a bloody tank," he began, not sure that his humor would go over too well.

"That comes later," Jim, answered quickly, looking around to see if any guards were within earshot.

Sullivan stopped abruptly, and looked carefully at him.

"You're serious"

"Very. We have to talk."

"Jimmy me boy, you bloody beaut Yank!" he said under his breath, "It was the sheila. You got to the sheila. I was betting on you, mate."

"Well, it ain't over yet, but if all goes well, we'll be out of here in a couple of days," Jim said as the two walked toward the bunkhouse.

"That bastard Chaca's not here. I heard he left for Texas. Too bad he won't be around for our departure. I'd like to give him something to remember me by."

"Some day we'll come back in a plane and nuke this damn place! But for now, all I care about is getting the hell out of here."

"Just you and me?" Sullivan questioned. Jim knew the wheels were turning in his head. There were some people that neither one of them wanted to leave behind.

"When the shit hits the fan, everyone will have their chance. Anyway, what are you doing now?"

"I was getting ready to add to me winnings. Had a hot game going. But stuff that! Let's go sit down under the ramada and you can fill me in on the plan."

They walked to the shaded area and found a spot away from most of the other men. Jim began to tell Peter the story of his trip to the ranch. The Aussie listened silently, shaking his head once in a while in disbelief, while absorbing every fact, every nuance of what had taken place. He watched his friend carefully as he told of the excitement brought on by the woman, and the terror that ended the harvest.

When he finished, Peter shook his head and whistled.

"Bloody Eduardo. I'd never have guessed the bloke had it in him. Always seemed like all the other Mexicans, resigned to his fate. I saw men go off like that in Vietnam. You didn't know whether to hug the bastards, or shoot them. Foaming at the mouth and carrying on. Whew! It gives me the creeps."

Jim looked toward the dark mountains as the sun fell behind the peaks. "He picked a good guy to take with him. Second only to Chaca."

"So when does the sheila, Maggie, get here?"

"Soon. We have to be prepared to move quickly. Surprise is our only chance. Don't say a Goddamned word to anyone. I didn't come all the way back here to screw things up."

"By the way, mate, if I forget to tell you, thanks for remembering old Sully. Given the same circumstances, what with the girl, and a handful of weed, I might not have been so bloody true blue, if you get me drift."

Jim smiled at his friend.

"Yes you would. Besides, I'd have haunted you for the rest of your days. You'd be looking down at my face every time you got ready to eat a meat pie."

"Come to think of it, Jimmy, I have seen some strange things in those pies back home. I might not have noticed!"

They punched each other playfully on the arm and talked for a while longer. It was good to see hope in the Peter's eyes once again, Jim thought. Somehow, someway, they would not be defeated. And they'd do it together, the same way it had always been.

Three more days passed, and life returned to the routine Jim had grown so accustomed to over the years.

Something about Mexico, something grinding and monotonous, tended to beat a person down. Centuries had come and gone. Rulers had governed and fallen. Yet the land and the people remained constant, locked in time, dry, dusty, and poor. If it hadn't been for the knowledge that escape was near, Jim might have surrendered to the time warp that surrounded him.

It was midmorning, with the sun at its apex. Jim's blue cotton shirt was soaked through with sweat, as he struggled to push the wobbling wheelbarrow out of the mine's entrance and down to the wooden trough. There, water would carry the dirt and ore to the sifters below.

The mining operation was something straight out of the old west, with little or no mechanical equipment to improve production. With all Chaca's money, he still relied on slave labor. Maybe, Jim thought, that was the point of the whole place. The evils that drove the man went beyond the accumulation of riches. The man was as close to inhuman as one could get and still walk upright.

Two separate mine shafts on the plateau high in the mountains waited like open mouths. Between them stood a clearing about a hundred yards in diameter. Both mines emptied tons and tons of dirt and rock into the trough, and at the bottom, a great distance away, small specks of gold were the reward for all the human suffering. Guards manned both sides of the high wood-sided contraption, trained to watch for the yellow coloring that had bewitched men for centuries. Chaca had no fear that they would help themselves, for each knew that a horrible death would be their punishment. Many eyes watched carefully as the muddy water worked its way down the mountain.

The cart Jim pushed had two wheels and high sides, designed not for comfort or safety, but for carrying the maximum amount of ore. It was heavy, and when loaded, was all one many could handle. Once the entrance of the mine was passed, and the blue sky opened up from the darkness, there was a slight grade down to the dumping point. It helped to make the work a little easier. But like a double-edged sword, it cut both ways, as the return trip empty was very difficult.

Although the air was hot and humid, it was still refreshing compared to the thick dust and dirt the men breathed inside. The more the picks and shovels flew, the worse it got. At least hauling the wheelbarrow out was a small relief. Jim and Peter switched wheelbarrow duty each day. That day, it was the American's turn.

Jim dug in his heels as the cart picked up momentum heading down the slope. His arm muscles tensed and his neck veins bulged as he fought to control it. Oddly enough, he was in the best shape of his life. His legs and thighs were powerful, and his chest pushed out. The cut on his left arm had heeled nicely.

He guided the cart to a stop and released the latches that hinged the door in front. The ore tumbled out on the splintered wooden slide, mixed with the water and began its journey downhill.

Jim stood a second, as he always did, to bend down and dip his hand into the rushing water. He splashed some on his forehead, and felt momentary relief from the heat. As he crouched at the knees, he saw two guards across the clearing watch him closely. That was not unusual, but something seemed different in their expressions. Jim stared at them, not fully comprehending, until he heard the roar of an onrushing object over his shoulder. As his head spun around, he had just enough time to see the second mine cart, loaded to the brim, about to crash on top of him. His arms rose up in defense, but it was of little use.

The impact crunched him back into the trough. The runaway cart veered sideways and rolled over on top of him. The weight was enormous, and he was pinned helplessly against the wood. Barely conscious, he was aware of a tremendous pressure forcing his head into the water.

"Help me," he muttered, his strength fading fast. "Please, someone."

How, what, and why no longer mattered. His head split with the ringing of bells in his ears, and his eyes went in and out of focus. Panic seized him, yet movement was impossible.

The bright day grew dark. Jim was vaguely aware of the many hands pawing at the dirt and stone, and wood crushing him. Most of the men had seen what happened and raced to help. Sullivan heard the shouting and emerged on the run from the mineshaft. He stopped for a second, adjusted his eyesight, and took in the scene. Down below him, men frantically pulled at the debris where two legs dangled over the edge of the trough.

The Aussie knew immediately it was Jim. His eyes darted from right to left for an explanation. Standing off to the side was Hector, from the bunkhouse, who stood with his arms crossed, and unmistakable joy on his face. Sullivan went cold with anger, but he had to get to Jim first. He jumped forward, half-running and half-tumbling down the hill.

As he got to the edge of the crowd, he looked down, and his worst fears were realized. There, amidst the chaos, lay his friend, unconscious. He jumped down into the melee and reached for Jim's soaking head. His fingers searched for the jugular on his neck, and he found a pulse. Sullivan heaved a small sigh of relief; it was bad, but not fatal, yet.

"Hang on, Jimmy!" he screamed. "Don't go and die on me now. Not now!"

Then, as an afterthought, he shouted, "Faster! Get this shit off him!"

Just then, a group of guards raced up and waded into the people helping Jim, shoving some of them aside. One grabbed Peter by the shoulder and jerked him back.

In a heartbeat he sprang up, and snatched the startled man by the throat. He looked into his frightened eyes, and was very close to ending his life. Then he heard the sound of a rifle cocking. Slowly, he released his grip, and stepped back.

Peter watched as they lifted Jim's limp body from the rubble.

"Go easy with him, ya bastards!" he yelled, damning the consequences.

At that moment, the Australian made up his mind to kill if they hurt him anymore. But even they had some decency left in their souls, and their movements were gentle, lifting him onto some planks someone had brought from the top of the hill.

The guards carried Jim down the hill.

Peter glanced about with a wild look in his eye. He caught sight of Hector at the top of the hill. He was about to re-enter the mine. Sullivan's blood ran cold. He had released the second cart.

Sullivan slowly began to circle the crowd, moving up toward the entrance like a cat on the hunt. His pace was measured, so as not to draw attention, but it was relentless.

With all the excitement, no one noticed the lanky man slip into the dark tunnel and disappear into the musty air.

Minutes later, a terror-filled cry from the depths of the mineshaft went unnoticed, also.

****

Maggie Stanton defiantly stood her ground, shoulders squared, with the look of authority in her eye. Her gaze froze the two men who carried Jim, seemingly dangling to life. They were headed for the guarded bunkhouse, but she would have none of it.

"I said put him in THERE!" she screeched in Spanish, pointing to a small servant's quarters near the main house.

Emilio Chaca was gone and the two Mexicans weren't sure just what to do with the injured man. If he had been there, the orders would have been to bury him, and get it over with. But he was away, and his wild-eyed woman, issuing orders, confronted them.

Maggie sensed they were wavering and went for the close.

"I will have your balls handed to you on a platter! DO AS I SAY!"

That was all they needed to hear. Turning in unison, they carried the stretcher toward the small stucco building. She raced ahead of them, and held open the door. When they entered, she motioned for them to set him on an old, single bed in the corner.

"Put him down gently."

They set the stretcher on the floor, seized both ends of the unconscious man, and with a grunt, lifted his dead weight onto the old mattress.

Her voice went cold as ice as she spoke again in Spanish.

"Now, get out! Don't come back until I tell you!"

They left the room, relieved to be away.

Maggie walked to the small window in the kitchen area, and pulled the curtains aside, letting in some sunlight.

She examined his body. He had chest injuries, for a start, and possible broken bones. He was likely bleeding internally. Maggie fought the urge to cry and panic. She was strong beyond her years, and she took control. She picked up a pan and pumped water in it, soaking a piece of white cloth at the same time. At the bed, she knelt down, looking at Jim's face.

Carefully, she began to unbutton his torn shirt, and noticed the cuts and scrapes on his chest. The blacks and blues of his skin were deep and rich. He was in trouble.

"We were made for each other, Jim Barnes," she said. "You get hurt, and I clean up the mess."

Then she whispered, "Please God, don't let him die."

****

Peter Sullivan paced like an agitated animal in front of the metal gates. He had no information on his injured friend, and his patience was wearing thin. The guards mostly ignored his shouts, and the ones who answered did so in Spanish, increasing his frustration. The sun was setting and darkness was falling all around.

Peter knew that Jim's hopes for survival rested on a spark of human kindness. The trouble was, in all his years there, he had never seen it. Life meant little or nothing in Emilio Chaca's world. It was easiest for someone to ignore the suffering, or dispose of them altogether.

The time had come to rattle a few cages.

"You bloody bastards, ANSWER ME!!!" he screamed at the three closest men on the other side.

Peter could take no more. He looked around on the ground for something to get their attention. A few feet away, a jagged rock lay half buried in the ground. He knelt and clawed at it until it came loose. He turned to face the Mexicans. With rage in his eye, he reared back, and fired it at the three men.

THUD! The stone hit one of them in the head, and he crumpled to the ground. His two partners stared at the fallen form in stunned silence. Both looked up to where Sullivan stood, braced for a fight. At first, they raised their rifles. But when they saw the challenge he was throwing down, they began walking toward the gate.

"Ez your ass, now, Gringo, you here me, YOUR ASS!" sputtered the tall man in broken English.

Sullivan smiled. He was more than ready.

"Well, well, so you bloody bastards DO speak something other than pig latin! You want a piece of me, mate, have at it!"

When Peter didn't show the expected fear, the smile on the guard's face quickly disappeared, and his jaw set. His eyes shifted nervously, looking for reinforcements. By the time the gate was partially open, Sullivan struck.

He shot his foot out, slamming the metal back into the two men, sending them backwards. Instantly, he moved forward, kicking the nearest man square in the mouth. The air erupted with blood and broken teeth. Stunned, the Mexican looked up at years of pent-up rage intent on killing.

The Australian walked over to the injured man, ready to finish him, when from behind a guard struck the back of his skull with the butt of a rifle, knocking Sullivan to his knees. He had time to shake his head just once, trying to regain his senses, before the other man's boot crashed up and into his chest. Air burst out of his lungs, and he fell forward. As he lay with his face resting on its side in the dirt, he could see the Mexican readying for the final blow with the rifle.

With all the strength he could muster, Peter spun around, and drove his fist into the man's groin. A look of utter disbelief came across his pained face, and he went down, clutching his crotch.

Sullivan drew himself up to his knees and stared at the stricken guard with hatred. It was time for him to die. His fist came together, knuckles first, as he was trained in the army, and he pulled back to deliver the fatal blow.

Suddenly, half dozen men jumped on him, pinning his arms and legs against the ground. Fists and legs lashed out as they flailed away at his body.

As Peter was about to pass out, he could smell the warm, foul breath of the first man he attacked, trying to talk through a bloody mouth.

"Don't worry, Gringo, we're not going to kill you yet! First I want to cook you like a tortilla in the pit! After that, we will cut your fucking balls off and feed them to you as a last supper."

In the moment before the pain closed his eyes, Sullivan turned, and looked at the face of his enemy.

His gaze hardened, and as a last act of defiance, he whispered, "Get stuffed, you bastard!"

Then, the blue eyes shut, and he passed out.

CHAPTER 18

By two the next morning, Jim began to regain consciousness. His eyelids flickered and he looked straight up at the cracked stucco ceiling. He was disoriented. For a moment, the injured man thought he was finally waking up from the long nightmare. But the smell of mildew from the old wool blankets and the dust-filled room brought him back to reality.

With a grunt, he tried to lift his head to look around. The pain shot through him like electricity. His wide eyes, watery from the suffering, seemed to be the only part of him not in pain. He caught site of movement in the dark room. He stiffened to protect himself from attack.

"So," Maggie began softly, as she moved to the chair beside him, "you've rejoined the living. I'd just about given up on you."

He tried to speak, but his lips and throat were dry, and he could only make rasping sounds. She held up her hand to give him pause and brought a cup of water to his mouth. The cold metal touched his lips, and the cool liquid tasted wonderful.

"Take it easy," she admonished. "Not too much. Not yet."

"Here we go again," he whispered, noticing the irony, "How did I get here? Where am I?"

"You're in the servant's quarters near the main house. You got here because I persuaded two of those idiots they would die if they didn't do as I asked."

Jim tried to look around the dimly lit room.

"I don't remember much. Sullivan, where's he?"

"The English guy?"

"Australian."

"He's got problems, too. I saw them haul him away to the pit. He put up quite a fight."

Jim shook his head. "Damn," he muttered.

"For now, Jim, you'd better worry about yourself. You need to heal. It looks like you were hit by a truck."

"Close," he said.

"The best thing to do is just lie back and get some rest. Don't move around too much, or you'll bleed all over this nice clean bed," she said, adding a nurturing smile.

Maggie stood up and walked toward the door.

"You're leaving?"

She opened it and the bright stars lit up the night over her shoulder. Her long black hair danced around her face in the gentle wind.

"I'll be back. I've got to keep you alive, remember? We've got to get each other out of here."

"And Sullivan," he said firmly.

"Him, too. Now, go back to sleep. No one will bother you."

Jim closed his eyes and tried to relax, but the pain was a constant reminder that escape would be much more difficult.

Across the compound, Peter Sullivan leaned against the dirt wall of the pit and cupped a hand on his rib cage below the heart. He was tender there, as well as many others places. Part of him was angry for letting his temper get the best of his good sense. But it felt so good to beat on the bastards; he would have done it all over again.

The corrugated metal roof over the pit rattled as the wind blew across the compound. It was locked in place to a wood frame, and only allowed a small amount of light to get in around the edges. The hole was designed solely for punishment and it handled that task well. The days, he knew, would be unbearable, with stifling heat; the nights cold and lonely. Once a day, the guards propped open the lid long enough to toss down food and some water; but just enough to prolong the suffering. Other than that, his only company would be ants, spiders and scorpions.

Sullivan poked around the ground with a stick that he found in the pit. In the distance, he heard a noise, and then some pebbles hit the top of the metal lid.

"Who's there?" he whispered loudly.

"It's me, Nikki Morales. I've come to tell you something."

It was one of the young Mexicans who bunked near Peter.

"What's up, mate?"

"I heard news about senor Jim. He is alive, but hurt badly. Chaca's woman takes care of him. He is in the small hut by the house."

Peter sighed with relief. Thank God she showed up. They both still had a chance.

"Rikki, lad, listen to me carefully. Get word to him that my bloody ass is in this hole. Find out how bad he is. Tell him I haven't got much time."

"I'll try, senor Peter. For you, I'll do my best."

Sullivan could hear gravel crunch as Rikki walked away. They had a chance, he thought, and smiled.

"Jimbo," the Aussie said, "what we need is a miracle recovery. You can do it, Yank. You can bloody well do it."

Sullivan rolled over on his stomach. Through intense pain, he pushed his body up.

"One," he grunted. They would have one chance, he knew, and they both had to be physically and mentally ready. His body screamed. Sullivan ignored it. "Two…"

****

Five days and nights went by and Jim Barnes' body was healing well. He sat up in bed, stretched his arms and grimaced slightly from the pain. Things could have been much worse, he knew, especially without the help of Maggie Stanton. She spent as much time as possible bathing his wounds and lifting his spirits. She nursed him in order to make him well enough for their plan, Jim knew, but at times, when her mood was reflective, she became the soft woman behind the hard exterior and he believed that they were more than just tools for the other's use. He tried to ignore that, for the focus of their partnership was unchanged, and it had to remain that way.

At midmorning, Jim decided to test his legs for the first time. Because the men were at the mines, he decided to risk it. He kept alert for the approach of a guard. They had to believe he was too sick to be moved.

Jim swung his legs over the side of the mattress and groaned as he stood. The pain was dull and throbbing. He steadied himself for a moment and then began walking toward the opposite wall. As he turned back to the bed, he heard the sound of footsteps in the gravel outside. He froze, knowing that he wouldn't have enough time to get back if it was a guard about to enter. His heart raced.

Maggie twisted the old doorknob and walked inside. She glanced at the empty bed, then quickly looked around the room, a trace of panic on her face. She sighed when she spotted Jim behind the door.

"I thought they might have taken you away," she said, closing the door behind her. She stepped toward him, as though to embrace him, but stopped herself.

"And what if they had?" Jim asked.

Maggie looked at him and playfully arched an eyebrow. "I guess I'd have to find someone else to get me out of here."

"I guess so," he answered.

"Come over here and let me see how you're doing," she said, changing the subject.

Jim moved to her slowly, their eyes locked on each other. She lifted the dressings on his chest. Her hands moved efficiently, pulling the cloth away, lightly touching the skin around the bruises and gashes.

"There's no sign of infection. No broken bones, either. I can't believe it," she said, shaking her head.

"I must have flinched at the right time," Jim replied.

"Like you're doing now?"

An awkward silence fell between them.

For the first time, Jim allowed himself to search his emotions. He could love this woman, he finally admitted. But not now. He was a married man, for one, although for all he knew, Linda had declared him dead and moved on with her life. And he wouldn't blame her for that.

More importantly, too much was at stake. They needed each other to escape.

Falling for each other would help nothing. He was sure she thought the same.

"It's a good self-defense mechanism," Jim said. "My flinching, I mean."

"I think you must be feeling better," she said watching his face redden.

"I'll be ready when the bell sounds."

"Good. Sit down; I've got some news about your friend. He's still in the pit, alive, but it's getting bad. The guards say they won't let him die until Chaca gets back."

Jim got up off the bed and started pacing the room, his aches forgotten totally.

"He'll be here Saturday. We've got to get out early that morning. Can you do it?"

Jim stopped and turned. He looked down at her resolutely. He did not speak.

Maggie had her answer.

"We've got to figure out a way of opening the gate."

His eyes bore in on her, looking for a sign that she was thinking about abandoning Peter. There was none.

"I've found some keys in his desk drawer. I don't know if they fit the lock or not, but it's worth a try. There was a gun in there too. I'll get it all here Friday night."

Jim turned and resumed pacing. Years ago, he would pace his office before important meetings. If he'd only known how inconsequential those 'life-or-death' deals really were.

"I'll need a knife, too. Get that here as soon as possible."

"OK."

"What about transportation? Is there anything around here?"

"They keep a jeep by the guard tower. We'll have to use that."

"Yeah," he said, lost in his thoughts, "I hope like hell they keep the keys in it."

"I'll check it out later, and if they aren't there, I'll figure something out."

"All right then, we'll do it about three in the morning, just after the guards change shifts. We'll give them a little time to get back to sleep and then make our move."

"That gives us just three days to get you healthy."

"I'll be ready. I've been waiting for nearly four years. I'll be VERY ready."

Then, as an afterthought, he said, "If you see anything else in the house we could use, bring it along. We'll need all the help we can get."

"There's a storage room in the back of the house. It's full of all kinds of weapons – some pretty high-tech. He's a freak about weapons. He's on one of his shopping trips now."

"Just be careful. We can't make a mistake."

Maggie shot him a hard look.

"I might have been stupid enough to get into this mess, but I've gotten quite an education since then."

Jim knew better than to answer.

He walked over to the window, and pulled the curtain aside just enough to see out. He stared at the view for a long time, taking in the whole scene. Maggie walked over behind him.

"The clouds are getting darker. It might storm," she mused.

"It's time we all got the hell out of here," he said. "Or die trying."

****

Over the next two days, their planning seemed to come together. As promised, Maggie delivered a large butcher knife. With a weapon, Jim felt much better about their chances of success.

Ironically, few years ago, the idea of plunging a knife into someone was revolting and unthinkable; the thought of it enough to send him dashing for the nearest anger-management class. Today, Jim relished the opportunity.

Both of them were satisfied that he had recovered enough to make the try, but in reality, they had little choice. If he had to crawl and scratch his way out, it would be worth the gamble.

Across the compound, Peter Sullivan slouched underground, wondering if he was going to take up permanent residence in similar surroundings. Darkness enveloped him physically and emotionally. He hadn't heard from Rikki Morales, and the thought crossed his mind that he had misjudged the young Mexican. Sullivan knew his time was growing short.

As he sat leaning against the dirt wall, lazily throwing pebbles across the dark hole, the Australian thought about Jim. He wondered if he was still alive, or so injured that he would be no help in escaping. But after spending many years with the man, and becoming closer than most brothers, Sullivan's strongest sense was that he was all right, and that he would find a way to prevail. The two men had learned to think alike to survive. Peter told himself to remain positive, and prepare to act when the time was right.

****

It was early Friday morning, a few hours before the sun would rise and twenty-four hours before the escape attempt. The sounds of the camp were muted and faint.

Coyotes crying out in the surrounding mountains broke the silence at times, then quiet would return. But few would hear, for most of the men slipped into the deepest part of their sleep, to tumble through the darkness for a little while longer.

Inside the small hut bathed in black, Jim Barnes slept quietly, his body finally released from the fitful hours earlier when sleep was difficult. His mind refused to calm down, wired to the excitement that would take place soon.

As Jim lay on his back, breathing in and out in a slow, rhythmic cadence, the handle of the door turned, and opened inches at a time, bringing moonlight into the darkened room. Quickly, silently, the young woman slipped inside, and closed the door behind her. She stood motionless, as if debating what to do next. Then, she crossed the room to the bed in the corner.

Maggie stopped there and looked down on his face. Again she saw the mixture of cold strength and warm kindness. For the first time in more than a decade, she let her heart feel for another, something she vowed would never happen again. But that night, she needed to be held, possibly for the last time, and together they could comfort each other.

Jim opened his eyes. He stared into the darkness, struggling to see. Oddly, he sensed her before he saw her. He smiled. He felt safe.

She held out her hand, and touched her index finger to his lips, as if to say I'm here now. Jim said nothing. Looking up into her deep-set eyes, he watched as she took a half step back and reach up to unhook the ribbon holding her covering. Noiselessly, the material fell to the floor and Maggie stood before him, naked and beautiful. He drank in her soft white skin, the fullness of her breasts and the gentle curves of her figure. She reached above her head and unfastened the comb that held her hair, and the dark strands fell over her delicate shoulders. It was a stunning vision, and Jim prayed he wasn't dreaming, and that if he were, he wouldn't wake up.

The reality of her presence was unmistakable. The air was laced with the scent of a woman. With his left hand, Jim pulled back the blanket that covered his naked body and moved over on the bed, offering a place for her. She lay down quickly, and then parted her legs slightly, allowing his to move into the soft moisture between her thighs. They held their bodies tightly together, never loosing eye contact, and Jim's hand came up and gently brushed some hair from her face. Then, an act long delayed began, as their lips met.

The next hour whirled by as the lovers devoured each other with unbridled passion. Their lovemaking combined raw power with lingering moments of gentleness that served to rally each other's strength for more of the same. Never before had the touch of a woman's body done so much to enliven him. It was if he was electrified after a long sleep. In the dark room, their two bodies melted together, time and again, searching for a way to make it last.

Finally, clinging tightly to each other, their hearts racing, they recognized the end was near as their collective strength ebbed away. With their faces only inches apart, a gentle haze came over the two lovers, and they drifted into sleep, fulfilled, satisfied, warm, and protected.

If life were just, the two would lay peacefully, savoring the touch of the other's skin. But harsh reality was brought home to Jim by the touch of cold steel on his arm. He woke up instantly, searching for the source of the intrusion. Standing above him was the guard Maggie had run off the day of the accident.

"Gringo, it looks like you are ready to go back to the mines, no?" the guard said with a satisfied smile.

Maggie was beginning to stir and Jim knew he had to act quickly. He had learned the secret of rhythm and how to strike when his natural body language did not betray what was about to happen. It was using the element of surprise when that was your only weapon. Jim dropped his eyes from the guard, as if to acknowledge defeat, and slowly turned toward the woman. But the instant before his gaze fell on her, his left hand came up swiftly and jerked the rifle barrel away.

The movement came so quickly that the Mexican tumbled down on the bed on top of the lovers. Already, Jim had gripped the handle of the butcher knife with his other hand. He drove the blade into the man's exposed throat. Blood erupted from the clean gash. The guard tried to

cry out, but only gurgles escaped. With one final thrust, Jim twisted the knife handle as he pulled it back, cutting the throat tissue even further. The dead man fell silently forward onto the wool blanket. It was a silent, efficient death.

Maggie had seen everything.

"Oh, my...." she began, trembling, just as Jim's hand came across her mouth. The blood of the corpse was spilling out onto her body.

"Don't move," he whispered, trying to gain composure. "There might be others."

Minutes passed but no one else raced in to help the guard. He must have acted alone, Jim thought.

Jim pulled his hand away from Maggie's mouth. She was shaking, but beginning to get control. He pulled the blankets back and quietly lifted himself out of bed. Jim felt around the floor for her robe, and placed it over her. Then, he put on his own clothes.

"Listen," he whispered again, "Don't talk. Get up and get dressed. Don't make a sound. You have to get back to the house without anyone seeing you. Can you do that?"

"I think so," she answered with a trembling voice.

"You must! I'll take care of this. It's going to be light in a little while, so we'll have to wait until tonight, like we planned. There's no turning back now, understand?"

She nodded. Jim locked onto her, trying to steel her with his eyes.

She got up and pulled the robe around her. Without looking at the man she had just made love to, Maggie walked to the door, then stopped. She turned suddenly and raced back across the room, throwing her arms around Jim's neck, kissing him. Tears rolled down her cheeks.

"It's going to be all right," he said. "We're going to make it. We're going to do this together, you'll see."

"I know that," she said. Then turning, she dashed back to the entrance. Quietly, she

opened the door and slipped out into the
night.

CHAPTER 19

A dead body leaves a miserable mess of blood, urine and excrement – nothing like the tidy scenes from movies and TV. But Jim took great care wrapping the corpse in the blood soaked blanket and he maneuvered him into a small closet behind the kitchen area. After he cleaned up the stains, his only fear was the smell that would soon waft out from the heat of the day. With luck, no one would miss him.

But if confronted, Jim now possessed the dead man's M-16 rifle, and that evened the odds. With the additional firepower, Jim believed luck was finally on his side.

The afternoon hours passed slowly, and he was very restless and impatient. It seemed to Jim that he'd spent a lifetime waiting for this moment. He wanted to get on with it, but he was too smart and calculating to hurry himself into a mistake. Years of living in the seamy underbelly of life had taught him cunning, and it served him well.

Once again, he heard the familiar steps coming near, and Maggie entered the small room. Her face betrayed the question that was on her mind.

"What did you do with him?" she finally asked.

Jim motioned with his thumb toward the closet.

"I'm afraid it's the best I could do."

"Here," she said, moving toward him, lifting the folds of her skirt to reveal a gun tucked into her panties. It was the same automatic they brought to Mexico years before.

Jim smiled. "For a minute, I thought...."

"No, no. Business first. I made sure the clip was loaded," she also gave him a set of keys. "I found these in the desk. What happens if none of them fit the locks?"

"One way or another, I'll get in," he said.

Maggie watched him closely and nodded. She knew he was ready.

"I took a walk over by the jeep. The keys are in it. You know, when we start that thing up, half the camp will come alive."

"Once I get Sullivan out, and give him the rifle, I won't be too worried. He has a lot of experience."

"What do you want me to do?"

"You'll stay here with the .45 and cover me. When you see us coming toward the gate, make your way over to the jeep and get ready to drive. All hell's gonna break loose and we'll have to get out of here quick."

Maggie nodded. "OK. Just don't take too long in there. I don't think my nerves can take it."

"Now, like we planned, try to be here about three, just after the guards rotate. If the sky stays cloudy like it is now, we'll have a decent chance of keeping out of sight. By the way, wear long pants. I don't know what we'll run into once we leave here."

Maggie looked at him with her large brown eyes and smiled.

"Thanks for the concern. I'll bring you some of Chaca's clothes for the trip. That ought to piss him off."

Jim began walking across the room. He stopped and turned.

"Um, Maggie, about last night.... It was unbelievable."

She walked over to him and put her soft hand on his cheek. His eyes likely gave away the struggle in his heart, but he needed to say something. "Thank you. I...."

"See you tonight," the young woman said softly, stopping him. She leaned forward and kissed him.

When they finished, Jim tried to speak.

"Maggie, you know...."

Tears formed in her eyes but her voice did not break.

"I know."

****

The roar of an engine broke the still night air. It was approaching 10 o'clock. "What the hell?" Jim said as he moved over to the window and pulled the curtain back slightly. Arriving with a flourish, brakes locked, Emilio Chaca pulled up in front of his house. He was a day early. In the light coming from the stucco house, Jim could see Maggie as she passed through the front door. With arms wide open, she greeted Chaca at the top step, and they embraced in a passionate kiss. Her arm slid down to his waist, and the two walked inside, closing the door behind them.

Jim let the edge of the curtain fall, and slumped against the wall.

"Son of a bitch," he said, his voice trailing.

From that moment on, everything they had planned was up for grabs. Could she get out? Would she get out? The one thing Jim knew for sure was that he and Sullivan were dead men if they didn't make it that night.

Jim returned to his bed and sat with his back to the wall. He picked up the .45 in one hand and the butcher knife in the other, feeling like Jim Bowie at the Alamo. His eyes focused on the door in the darkness, watching and waiting for something to happen.

Jim Barnes paced. A mix of nervousness and determination built upon his already-high adrenalin. A light rain was beginning falling, tapping on the Spanish tile roof. If it continued, the rain would be helpful in covering their tracks. Anything positive was welcome at that point in his life.

His thoughts were clear. He blocked out emotions. This was a mission. Chances were good he would die within hours and he accepted that fate. He faced death several times before, but in each case, the threat came quickly and he survived each with fast reaction. But now, in the still hours of the cool night, he had the time to take an inventory of the man he used to be and the one he had become. It was a sobering experience, not filled with panic, but a resigned calm.

It struck him that his own life seemed to mirror the American experience in years past. His journey had begun as a gifted man, in an exciting, fascinating, complicated time, and in a bountiful place. But as the years passed, the edges of society began to fray and the foundation seemed to shift and break apart, much like the troubles that had cursed him. What was once certain became doubtful. The smug arrogance and belief in systems gave way to the knowledge that they offered little security, when taken beyond the capabilities of simple men and women. Jim Barnes flowed with the river and it had left him in a dangerous place.

He vowed it would never happen again, if he survived the night.

The sharp clanging of a gate closing and the muffled voices of men exchanging greetings in Spanish snapped Jim back to the present. He jumped off the bed and approached the window. The guard change was in progress and show time was near. When Maggie got there – if she got there – he would be ready to go. Hopefully, at that time of night, the new men would be weary and prone to mistakes. It was a small straw to grasp.

Jim walked back to the bed and picked up the rifle, caressing the stock. Years of frustration were about to end one way or another.

Ten minutes passed. Then 20, then 40, and still no sign of Maggie. The guns, the knife and the bullets were all in place, but not the person who made it all happen. Jim knew he couldn't wait any longer. He had to make his move and Sullivan was the first stop.

Jim cracked open the door an inch at a time and peered outside. The guards were 100 yards away and he saw nothing out of the ordinary. Jim took a deep breath and slipped out into the damp night air.

The light rain landed on his face as he crouched and ran to a small tool shed a short distance away, holding the M-16 low to the ground. He hid there, stopped, and took a breath. His heart pounded.

Up ahead, a lone guard patrolled the perimeter of the wall between Jim and the gate. Nearby, an old trailer sat. It would provide cover until the unlucky man walked past. He would be the first to die.

With teeth clenched, Jim raced across the clearing, trying to avoid splashing in puddles. Jim's legs churned the uneven ground, claiming distance, until finally, with one last leap, he slid under the trailer headfirst in his best baseball slide, and came to a stop behind a wheel. He strained to hear the sound of an alarm, but none came. He lay quiet and flat, his chest muscles punishing him with pain.

In the distance, he heard the guard approach, making his way along the circular path. Closer, closer, the steps drew near, and Jim's hand gripped the handle of the butcher knife he had strapped to his leg.

Just as the victim passed, Jim sprang, his left hand coming up to cover the man's mouth, his right already pressing the blade against the small of the back at the kidneys. With one lunge forward, Jim buried it to the handle.

The guard let out a weak, muffled cry before his legs gave way and he collapsed to the ground. His muscles twitched once involuntarily, then he fell silent. The men in the tower had already settled in for the night, and did not notice.

Jim dragged the dead man to the wagon. He checked his pockets for keys, but found none. Quickly, he moved back to the gate and pulled out the keys Maggie had given him. There were four on the chain and two were obviously door keys. A third looked like it could fit a padlock. Jim kissed it for luck, and slid it into the opening. His hands, caked with mud and blood, trembled. He waited for the telltale click.

Nothing.

He twisted his wrist, but the lock would not budge.

"Shit!" he said under his breath. The fourth key was too large for the lock, and he was about to give up, but decided to give it one more try. With fury and desperation, he rattled the reluctant metal, until finally – click – It opened! Jim's eyes rolled up in thanks. He took the lock from the hasp, and tossed it a few yards away.

Jim slowly pulled the heavy steel gate, until he had just enough room to slip by. He picked up the rifle, crouched low, and again made a dash for the safety of the bunkhouse.

Once there, Sullivan was within striking distance. With every sense in his body tingling, he moved out toward the metal cover, hoping desperately to remain unseen. In the darkest part of the yard, with the mountains looming up behind, he reached the pit, and knelt down beside it.

"Who's there?" came a whispered question in the distinctive Australian accent.

"Shut the fuck up!" Jim shot back, barely audible. "Or we'll both be in there!"

He began to try to pry up the edges of the metal, but the frame was strong and it resisted. His fingers slid across the slippery metal latch, and he quickly became even more frustrated.

Sullivan could see that he was making no progress.

"How'd you get in here?"

"Through the gate."

"What about the lock?"

"I had a key."

"Then TRY THE BLOODY KEY, MATE!"

Jim produced the key ring again, and pushed the small one into the opening. Click. With one easy turn, the latch released.

"I'll be damned."

He pulled the lock free and began lifting the metal. It creaked and groaned. The noise was too much.

"Mud! Throw mud on the hinges!" Peter ordered.

Jim did what he was told, working it into the rusted steel, and the noise stopped. He lifted the lid about 18 inches and Sullivan began scrambling up. His head appeared first, whiskered, cut, and bruised, but he had the biggest grin on his face Jim had ever seen. He looked at his friend and winked.

In one swift movement, he was free of the hole and both men scrambled back to the safety of the barracks. They stopped, tried to catch their breath, and looked around.

"Here," Jim said, thrusting the M-16 toward the Australian.

Another broad grin crossed his face as he eyed the weapon.

"Bloody beautiful, I reckon! Somebody's gonna get hurt tonight. No worries!"

Jim nodded and took the .45 from his waist. Once again, they broke for the open ground toward the gate. Peter reached it first and passed through the opening like a ghost. He spotted the old trailer, and slid underneath, startled for a moment by the dead body nearby. Jim slid in right beside him.

"Nice job, mate. This is the bloke who put me in that fucking hole. Saves me having to look for him!"

Jim Barnes minced no words. "We're not looking for anything but that Goddamned jeep over there. Maggie says the keys are in it. We've got to get to the tool shed and then the small shack. Let's go!"

They ran through the light rain, mud soaking their shoes and pants. They were side-by-side, stride for stride, like two old stallions out for one last run. Finally, they got to the shack that had been Jim's home, and they stood up, with their backs against the wet stucco wall.

"Maggie," Jim said through gasps, trying to get his wind, "I've got to get her!"

"Forget the bloody sheila, mate! There's no time!"

"I'll make time. She's the reason we're both standing here. You head for the jeep. Give me a few minutes, then start it up and swing by. If we're not back, keep going!"

"You dumb bloody Yank! You know I'm not going to do that! Just get crackin', mate. We've got no time to waste."

They were just about to go their separate ways, when suddenly, from around the corner, a tall, thin man stepped into view and leveled a revolver on the two startled men. They froze and stared at the sneering face of Emilio Chaca.

"I love to watch the rain at night," he said slowly, measuring his words. "It happens so rarely in this part of the country." Then he pulled the hammer back on the revolver.

Emilio Chaca was about to end their misery, and try for freedom, when out of the darkness, a board whistled through the air, and landed with a crack on the back of his skull. His hate filled eyes rolled upward and he collapsed to the ground in a heap.

Out from the shadows stepped Maggie Stanton, barefoot, wearing only a wet nightgown clinging to her body. Her face was grim as she stared down at Chaca.

"Good on ya, my dear! Just in the nick of time, I'd say. Peter Sullivan's me name.

Bloody glad to make your acquaintance!" he chirped as if meeting her at a local bar.

Jim's eyes never left the fallen Chaca. Slowly, his hand felt for the butcher knife and he moved over to where his enemy lay helpless on the ground. In a trance, his heart pounding and hands shaking, he lifted up Chaca's head by the hair, and was about to cut his throat, when he caught sight of Maggie.

"No, please! Don't! Let the others kill him. He's not worth it. You're not an animal like him. Please, Jim, let's just go!"

Somewhere from the past, a memory of the man Jim Barnes once was came forward and reminded him of his place in the human race. After all the years of praying for this moment, he saw himself release his grip on Chaca's head, and it fell back into the mud face-down.

"I'll be glad to dispatch the miserable bastard," Sullivan said with a deadly serious tone, moving forward.

"No, she's right. The Mexicans will do a better job than we ever could."

"Now, we have one last hurdle. We go for the jeep. I'll drive. Peter, you cover. Maggie, for God's sake, stay down! Let's go!"

Forty long yards away stood the vehicle that would take them to safety, but it seemed like miles. Jim was first, face grim, charging like a halfback eyeing the goal line. Maggie was

next, appearing childlike as her bare feet splashed through the mud. Sullivan followed in the rear, eyes intent, showing none of his usual cockiness. He had the look of the soldier he once was, ready to kill and even more, ready to survive.

CRACK! A loud shot rang out in the rainy night and all three flew head first into the mud. Jim was confused, as the shot came from behind. He strained to look ahead through the rain. Then he spotted the fallen body of a guard by the base of the tower, lying dead with his gun at his side. Jim turned quickly, glancing back over his left shoulder. There, standing by the gate, lowering a rifle was Rikki Morales. The young Mexican had saved their lives. They hadn't even seen the guard who would have shot them at point blank range.

Suddenly, it was war. Sullivan opened up on the guard tower, and bullets blasted off into the night. The startled guards scrambled for their guns, trying to return fire.

"GO JIMMY!" screamed Peter, his face taut with emotion. "Get the bloody thing started. MOVE YOUR ASS!"

Jim and Maggie rose up and sprinted for the jeep. With one final leap, Jim landed behind the wheel. Maggie ended up in the foot well of the rear seat.

"Here! Take this! Shoot anything that moves," he said to her, handing over the .45.

Lights were coming on in the buildings that housed the rest of the guards. The men began stumbling out of the doors. Peter aimed a few well place rounds at them, and the Mexicans scrambled back inside.

"Run you fucking BASTARDS!" he raged, "There's more where that came from!" He stood out in the open, spinning around, almost daring someone to shoot. The warrior was finally avenging himself.

Jim snapped the keys over in the ignition, and the engine roared to life. His right hand nearly bent the shift handle as he shoved it into gear and the jeep lurched forward.

Just then, a guard jumped down to the first landing of the stairs, and leveled his rifle on them. He got off three rounds that ricocheted on the front hood and windshield before Maggie, holding the automatic up with both hands, fired one blast, striking the startled man in the middle of the chest. She opened her eyes in time to see his corpse flying backwards to the ground.

"Oh, my God! Get me out of here, Jim!" she screamed.

Mud sprayed back from the rear tires as the small vehicle fishtailed forward, searching for traction. Bullets whistled through the air in all directions, some friendly, some not, as they closed to where the Australian stood, taking on all comers.

Over by the gate, Rikki Morales fired round after round at anything that moved. He kept the remaining guards in the tower pinned down, sending lead crashing into the wooden enclosure.

"Come on out and FIGHT, you BLOODY SISSIES!" Sullivan screamed, venting years of rage. "Show us all how tough you are!"

He danced around like a prizefighter, looking for something to shoot. By the guards' quarters, a brave soul raced out toward him, holding up a pistol. Peter stopped, eyed his target with no emotion, and then brought the M-16 up to his shoulder. Quickly he squeezed the trigger, sending one bullet tumbling across the distance, striking the man in the forehead, leaving a nice,

neat hole. But behind his head, the entire back of his skull exploded, sending brains flying through the air.

"Dumb bloody bastard," the Australian mumbled under his breath.

Over inside the walls, more prisoners raced out of the bunkhouse, making their own try for escape. They ran around panicked, searching for protection and a place to hide. Jim roared up to where Sullivan stood, and jammed on the brakes.

"LET'S GET THE HELL OUT OF HERE!" he cried, mud and sweat dripping down his wide-eyed face.

Maggie lifted her head up from the metal floor, still caressing the gun in both hands. She got up on her knees, scanning the area with a determined look on her face.

"I'll cover!" she yelled at Sullivan.

The Aussie didn't need to be asked twice. With the grace of a high jumper, he cleared the sides of the brown vehicle and landed with a thump beside her. Quickly, the rifle came up to his shoulder, and he searched the darkness for another target.

Jim buried his foot to the floorboard, and the engine roared in protest, until he released the clutch, sending the mass of steel shooting across the muddy clearing. Sullivan returned fire from the back seat as the remaining guards took a bead on them. Maggie cracked off a couple of rounds, too.

Just a few more feet, Jim thought. Come on baby! Then from over his shoulder, he heard Peter scream out.

"STOP!"

Running after the jeep at an angle from the side, was Rikki Morales, arms flying and legs pounding the muddy ground. He was desperately trying to catch them, knowing that failure meant death.

Jim slammed his foot on the brake. He jerked the gearshift into reverse, and spun the tires mercilessly, trying to close the distance between them. Weaving and sliding, they got to within 20 yards of where the man was, when suddenly he crashed down in a heap, holding his leg. Jim kept the jeep flying backward, steering with one hand, until finally he skidded to a halt beside the young Mexican.

"I'll get him!" yelled Peter.

In a flash he was over the side and had his big hands on Rikki's collar. With all the strength left in him, the Aussie sent the boy flying into the back area behind the rear seat. His legs dangled against the mud-spattered metal. Peter scooped them up and slammed them over the railing.

Then, just as he was about to jump back in, a loud CRACK echoed, a sound different from all the other explosions around them.

Jim sensed instantly that something was wrong, and he turned to see Peter's eyes bulge in agony as he slumped against the back of the vehicle.

Over his shoulder, in distance, Jim could see the hulking form of Emilio Chaca, standing where they had left him, his arm extended, clutching a pistol.

"NO!" Jim cried out.

Maggie dropped her gun and clawed her way over the back seat, over Rikki, and reached out to grasp the Australian by the shoulders. He looked up at her, his blue eyes shining from the hurt and the moisture dripping down from his forehead.

"Be off with you!" he managed to say between coughs, "I'm rat shit."

The man she stared at was a stranger, who hours before meant nothing to her. But during the course of their fight for freedom and survival, they were fellow soldiers in arms.

Maggie gritted her teeth and with a mighty grunt, she jerked the wounded man up off the ground.

"BULLSHIT!" she yelled, as her arms groped for his belt buckle, pulling him the final distance inside.

The three bodies were stacked in a heap, with Rikki on the bottom, Maggie in the middle, and Sullivan on top.

"GO JIM, GO!" she yelled.

Once again they shot forward, wheels spinning and mud flying, careening into the dark, as the terrified riders silently prayed to be delivered from harm's way.

CHAPTER 20

They drove north on rutted side roads, guided by Rikki Morales, who was familiar with the area. Thirty minutes passed with little talk among the passengers, who were reflecting on the chaos they had just survived. Finally, from the back, Maggie leaned forward.

"He's going to die, soon, if we don't get the bleeding stopped. I don't think he can make it much further. These roads are beating the life out of him."

"OK," Jim answered quietly, "We'll pull up into those foothills and make camp. They won't be looking for us tonight. The sun will be up soon, and we can figure out what to do then."

A few more miles down the road, Jim spotted what looked like a ravine cutting up into the hills. This is as good a place as any, he thought, and turned the steering wheel to the right, while at the same time shifting into four-wheel drive. From the far back of the jeep, he could hear the moans of his friend.

"Hold on, Peter," he said over his shoulder, "we'll be there in just a minute."

Maggie moved back beside the Australian, who was semiconscious, and held his head in her lap. She stroked his face, trying to give him as much comfort as possible. Earlier, she had used part of her nightgown to bandage his wound, but the bumping and jostling destroyed the effort.

Jim concentrated on the muddy path up into the hills, driving around rocks and bushes, while watching for washes that could flip the small vehicle. The light rain still fell, helping their escape, as all signs of tire tracks would be washed away by first light. A little further ahead, the top of the low hills opened up into a clearing, where they would have a good view of the valley below and the mountains that hid Chaca's camp.

"This looks good," Jim said to Rikki, who sat beside him. His wound was not serious, more of a grazing blow to the fat of his calf. The bleeding stopped and Jim knew he would be in good shape to help if they had to fight their way out.

He killed the engine and sat still for a moment, grateful for the quiet. His body ached from head to toe, and cried out for sleep, but he had work to do.

"Let's put him under the overhang by those rocks, out of the rain," he said to Rikki.

They got out of the vehicle and walked around to where Peter lay. When Jim saw his friend, a chill seized him. For the first time, he knew the Aussie was in real trouble. The ruddy complexion of the man he knew had taken on a pasty pallor, and his breathing was labored. He looked like a dying man.

At that moment, he made a silent vow that his friend would be avenged.

Sullivan was lying on his side, and Jim scooped him up in his arms, like a child, and carried him to the rocky overhang. Maggie used the plastic floor mats from the jeep and spread them out on the ground, to protect him from the chill.

"Don't be dropping me ass, mate," Peter whispered through dry, parched lips. He tried to smile, but the pain was too great.

"The next time we do this, I hope you loose some weight," Jim answered, trying to make light of their predicament. He gently set him down on the plastic, and knelt beside him.

"We're going to get a fire started. Maggie will get the bleeding stopped again and you're gonna be all right. Just hang in there, OK?"

Sullivan curled into the fetal position and nodded his head. His eyes closed, as his body searched for the sleep that would take him away from the waves of pain.

Rikki walked up with a slight limp and handed Jim some matches he had found in the glove compartment of the jeep. Then he took off his Levi jacket, and gently placed it over the Australian.

"He saved my life and it comes to this. I am very sorry, senor," he said looking at Jim.

"He's going to be all right," the American answered, trying desperately to convince himself. "He's GOT to be all right."

Maggie walked up with some more strips of cloth. "Let me take care of this. You two get some wood. We've got to get him warm."

"Please," Jim said slowly, his voice choked with emotion. "Help him. It can't end this way."

She looked closely at the tired man in front of her, with his broad shoulders stooped from exhaustion, his face streaked with mud, wincing from the pain he still felt in his chest muscles. He thought of nothing but his wounded friend.

"I'll do my best, I promise.

****

Dawn came and passed, and the sun rose high in the cloudless sky. The rain ended hours before and the dry heat was welcome by the four people who stretched out on the rocky ground, resting their weary bodies. Jim drifted in and out of sleep, his mind refusing to let him find peace. Finally, he gave up, and silently looked out over the valley below them, plotting their next move.

"OK," he said to the others, "we've got to get out of here, but we have a few problems. We've got to get him to a doctor, soon, but he can't make it in that jeep without something to kill the pain."

"There's morphine back at the house," Maggie said without thinking, "but that's out of the question."

"There ez not much gasoline in the jeep," Rikki threw in, "I checked it this morning. We cannot make the town closest to here."

There was a long pause in the conversation. Jim spoke up again.

"We can't get out of here on foot. There's no choice. I've got to go back."

"No, Jim!" Maggie shouted, the intensity of her anger stunning the other two men. "I've seen you. I've been watching. You've been working up to going back for that pig Chaca ever since we got here. What is it? Is it for me? Is it for your friend? Or is it for you? You're the one who needs to kill him. Admit it! Goddamit, just be honest."

Jim stared at her without answering, not wanting to acknowledge the truth. He knew Chaca had robbed him, and all the others, of good years, young years, that could never be recovered. He was a maggot that murdered innocent people and he deserved to die more than any human being Jim had ever known. And the thought persisted that when he had the chance, he let her talk him out of it. Peter would be unharmed and joking right now had he not made that mistake.

"That way" he snapped, pointing in the direction of the mines, "has everything we need: drugs, gas and life for my friend. The other way is iffy, at best. I've got no choice."

She could see his mind was made up. Her flushed face softened and tears streamed down her cheeks.

"We made it out of there," Maggie sobbed. "We're safe now. Somebody can go ahead and get help. Please, don't go back. I ... I don't want to lose you. We can figure something out. Anything is better than going back to that place."

Jim turned from her. His own emotions overtook him but he couldn't allow her to see it. Hate, anger, love, and fear filled him.

Then quietly, in a hoarse voice, Peter Sullivan spoke up.

"Listen, mate," he began weakly, "seeing as though it's me we're talking about, I'm going to tell you what I want."

He paused to catch his breath, his pale blue eyes falling on each of the others for a moment.

"I know bloody well where I stand. I've seen it before. You can make some good time without my carcass dragging you down. I want you to give me the automatic, and be off with you. I'll take care of the rest."

As he finished, silence fell.

That was all Jim needed to hear. At that moment, his decision was made.

"Yeah? Well to HELL with THAT! As long as you've got a breath in that scrawny body of yours, there's a chance, and by God I'm going to see to it that you get that chance. We're not leaving you here now, or ever! Understand? That's out!"

He turned to Maggie and put both hands on her shoulders.

"Listen to me. I'll make it. I'll be back, I promise. We'll get out of here – ALL of us. There's no way they will be expecting me to come back. It'll be over before they know what hit them."

Maggie locked her jaw, and again showed the anger she felt inside. "If you die on me, I swear ... "

"I'll go tonight, after dark, and we'll be out of this country by morning. I can do this."

They spent the rest of the daylight hours covering all the details. Jim grilled Maggie on the layout of the house, Chaca's habits, the location of the drugs and weapons, everything that might help him survive. Nothing was considered trivial. If all went well, they would have the morphine, the gas, and water, to get them out of Mexico.

The time passed quickly, and darkness fell. Jim rested until nine o'clock, and then began to prepare to leave. Rikki Morales started another fire, near Sullivan. Earlier, Jim gave Maggie his blue cotton shirt to ward off the cold, leaving only a dirty T-shirt to protect him from the crisp night air.

Rikki came up and held out the rifle he had been cleaning for hours.

"There is a lot of life and bullets left in this gun. Use them well."

Jim looked at the young man and smiled.

"No, you keep it. You'll stay with the jeep at the base of the mountain and I want you to have something besides your pecker to hold on to if someone shows up. I'll use the automatic."

"What ever you say, senor. I'll start the jeep."

Maggie purposely avoided him, picking up sticks to show her displeasure with his decision. She was still angry, but resigned to his will.

Shivers ran through Jim and he knew it was not from the air alone. Slowly, he walked over to where Peter lay, and bent down to say good-bye. He was slipping in and out of consciousness, and his face showed the strain of the hurt shooting through his body. Jim lifted his hand, and stroked the Aussie's forehead, pulling the strands of dirty blond hair back, away from his eyes.

"Watch it, mate," Sullivan said, coughing between words, "People will talk."

"I just wanted to make sure you could see real well, 'cause when you see my headlights coming, we're getting out of here. For good."

"You're a bloody fool, Yank. There's no need to go back. I don't have to tell you that."

Jim ignored him. "I'll bring you back some warm cloths for the ride north. It's fall now. Anything else you can think of?"

"Yeah, a cold beer. The bastard owes me. That would lift me spirits."

Jim nodded his head and smiled. His words choked him.

"Just hang in there a little while longer. Maybe two hours, max. You'll be on cruise control when we pump that dope in you."

Peter grinned. "Just like 'Nam. You Yanks always were a bit partial to the stuff."

Jim Barnes stroked his forehead once again, expressing in touch what he was feeling in his heart. They had traveled many miles together, soul mates joined by war, brothers sharing a bond and a love that most would never know. He wanted the Australian to know.

Slowly he stood, still looking down at his fallen comrade. Then, he turned and began to walk away.

Behind him, Peter struggled to prop himself up on his elbows.

"I love you, mate," he said clearly. Jim turned, meeting Peter's gaze straight on without blinking. A sparkle of a tear formed in the corner of Peter's eye and he winked it away.

"Me, too," Jim said.

"One more thing, Jimmy. Just before you kill the bastard, tell him Peter Sullivan says "G'day."

"Count on it," Jim said. He turned, and walked down to where Rikki sat in the jeep.

Maggie was still some distance away, making herself busy, when she realized that Jim was going to leave without saying good-bye. She began to walk slowly towards him at first, and then broke out into a run, finally flinging herself into his waiting arms.

"If there was any other way," he stammered

"You'd better quit while you're ahead," she replied.

"Take good care of him, OK? Don't leave him alone. I don't want him to be alone."

She nodded, and rested her face against his chest, listening to his pounding heart. Jim took his two hands and gently pushed her back, their eyes meeting in the moonlight.

Tears streamed down her cheeks, as he bent forward and kissed her lips. When they separated, no words were spoken. None were needed.

The two men started back down the ravine toward a final rendezvous with the hell that had been their life and with the evil man who controlled it.

CHAPTER 21

Rikki Morales did the driving and most of the talking as they covered the distance back to Chaca's mines. The young man maneuvered the jeep with the lights off and Jim would have preferred he paid more attention to the road, but he spoke of his brothers and sisters in a small town to the north and how happy they would be to know he was still alive. Jim looked at him a several times during the ride, thinking how kind most of the Mexican people had been to him. Most just wanted to get by, nothing more. Even when speaking of Chaca, Rikki showed no bitterness, as though his evil was a natural disaster. Jim Barnes wasn't as charitable.

When they came to the base of the mountain road, Jim motioned for him to pull off to the left.

Rikki shifted back into four-wheel drive and drove into the high desert, finally coming to a stop in the protection of some cacti and bushes. He looked at Jim and waited for instruction.

"All right, wait here and keep that rifle handy. When you hear the shit hit the fan, give me 10 minutes, no more. If I'm not back by then, take off without me. You've got enough gas to get back, and a little bit further. I'm counting on you to get them out of here if I don't make it."

"I'll do it, senor."

"One more thing. I just might borrow Chaca's Blazer. If you see someone coming down the mountain, listen for a single gunshot. That will be me. Hold your fire."

"No problem. Take good care of yourself, Jim. You have been a good friend."

The American offered his hand, and Rikki took it. Jim jumped out and began the long climb up the mountain. Monsoon clouds were moving in, making the night was very dark. It afforded him cover.

His climb was slow and his footing was unsteady. At times, it seemed he slipped and fell backward more than he moved forward. Jim breathed hard. His body still ached from the accident. Finally, he made it to the top of the hill. Chaca's compound opened to full view. Jim ducked in behind a boulder and surveyed the scene.

More lights lit up the large area and he could clearly see the guards patrolling. Two guards walked the perimeter of the wall. Beyond that, everything else remained the same. Emilio Chaca had reasserted control. The others had not been able to take advantage of the confusion to escape.

He looked to the white stucco house, with its red tile roof protected under the blanket of the trees. The lights were still on and he noticed Chaca's Blazer parked around back. That was a break. It would be the first thing he would check out.

Jim rubbed his cold hands together and took the automatic out of his waistband. Surprisingly, he was not nervous. He was a man who focused on a job and was determined to see it through. Just the thought of ending this chapter in his life, one way or another, brought on a satisfying calm.

Jim drew in a deep breath, as though he was about to jump into a cold pool. He crouched and began moving to his right, still behind the cover of the rocks, skirting the open area until he was at a point closest to the house. Finally, he stopped about 50 yards from the pale green Chevy. Cautiously, he took in the whole scene, like a hunter stalking prey. There could be no mistakes, no slip-ups. The penalty was death.

Then, after satisfying himself that the time was right, he bolted from the cover and began rushing across the open ground. He had never in his life run so fast, or for a better reason. His legs erased the distance until he finally reached the safety of the old vehicle, and brought himself to a stop, as noiselessly as possible. Too excited to breath, his head spun around in all directions, searching out trouble. But there was no alarm.

Quietly and slowly, he lifted up and looked inside the Blazer. On a rack behind the front seat rested a short-barrel 12-gauge shotgun. Two blankets sat on the back seat, some empty beer bottles were scattered on the floor. Luckily, two gasoline cans were strapped to the sides of the rear bed. Jim had counted on the fact that most everyone carried spare gas, as running out of fuel in the Sonora desert could be a fatal mistake. The only thing missing were the keys, but Jim was sure he knew where to find them.

In another quick burst, he sprinted to the rear of the house by the storage room window. Maggie had unbolted the window the night before in case escape through the front door was impossible. Softly and gently, he pushed the splintered and cracked wooden frame. It moved, swinging up on its hinges.

Jim lifted his eyes over the sill and looked into the darkened room. It was empty. He pushed open the glass, lifted himself up and slid inside head first, gliding to the floor.

Silently he sat, and looked around in amazement at all the hardware. Emilio Chaca was truly a weapon freak, as Maggie had described. Rifles were scattered about, as well as pistols and boxes of ammunition. Army ordinance of all kinds, from mines to grenades, bayonets to smoke bombs, rested in boxes on the shelves.

The sound of a chair sliding across the tile floor in another part of the house broke the stillness. He held his breath and waited for the door to open, but he could hear no footsteps. A small hallway ran between his location and the main living area. Jim opened the door a crack, peeked out and saw no movement. He moved out, clutching the .45 in his right hand. Maggie said Chaca usually sat behind a desk at the far end of that room. It had to be him. It was time.

A step at a time, cautiously, measured, he inched forward toward the light. He could see the room was as Maggie described it; spartan, with minimal furniture and clutter in the corners. The walls were in need of paint and the beamed ceilings were covered with dust and cobwebs. Cheap Mexican art hung haphazardly about. Two velvet pictures of women on either side of a coat of arms, complete with swords, were the first to come into view. Chaca did not spend his wealth on the creature comforts of life.

Slowly, Jim continued forward, finally stopping in the shadows just past the arched entrance. Across the room, Emilio Chaca sat unaware of his presence, moving small leather bags away from the metal scales that stood in front of him. He was absorbed in his work, like a monk worshipping at the altar.

Jim Barnes leveled the .45 on Chaca's head and pulled back the hammer.

Only then did Emilio Chaca turn away from his bags of gold, lifting his head up, searching the room for the source of the metallic click. On seeing the American, the narrow slits that surrounded his dark eyes grew wide, and his mouth dropped open, stunned. The two men looked like statues, frozen in time, without even a breath to betray the life that beat inside their chests. An old clock on the wall ticked off the seconds in the still room.

Jim Barnes broke the silence.

"The keys to the Blazer," he said with a cold, commanding tone. "Now!"

Chaca watched him carefully, calculating if and when he would use the gun. There was no question he was capable, after the shoot-out from the night before. He inched his right hand

across the desk, and picked up a small key ring, holding them up for Jim to see. With the flick of his wrist, Chaca sent them flying. Jim snatched them in midair.

"If you shoot, gringo, my men will be in here within minutes, and you, too, will die."

Jim smiled. "I've been dead for some time now, thanks to you. It doesn't matter."

Chaca's experience told him that a man unafraid of death was a force to be reckoned with. But he had never met a man without a price.

"You know, there is enough gold on this table to make you a very wealthy man. I tell you what. You take it and go, now, and we will call it even. You will have been well paid for your years in my mines."

"And whose going to pay for the family you stole from me? Or the brains of my friend you blew out? Or the hole in the back of the Australian? There isn't enough gold in this world to cover all your bets, Chaca, you miserable bastard. If there's a Hell, you're about to find out, right NOW!"

Just then, a man stepped up on the porch outside, unaware of what was going on, and walked over to the screen door.

"Jesus!" he managed to say, just as Jim Barnes turned and pulled the trigger of the automatic, touching off a loud explosion. The bullet ripped through the screen and hit the Mexican in mid-chest, and he was swept backward, thrown to the ground by the force.

Jim's arm swung back around to finish Chaca, just in time to see the desk, and all its contents, come flying toward him. The gangly Mexican was right behind, reaching out for the man who wanted to kill him.

The two bodies met in the middle of the room, and the impact knocked the .45 out of Jim's hand before he had time to squeeze off another round. With ferocious savagery, they kicked and clawed at each other, gouging eyes, and ripping hair. Rolling and twisting, arms and legs flailing away, the two enemies fought to kill. No quarter was given, no rules observed. It was mankind acting out the simplest, most basic instincts.

Finally, Chaca managed to roll on top, his bony hands squeezing down on the American's throat, trying desperately to crush the life out of him. Jim's eyes bulged in his head and he gasped for air, holding the man back with his arms extended.

Sweat and blood dripped down from Chaca's forehead. Jim was close to the edge. The muscles in his arms began to cramp and his head spun from the lack of oxygen. He knew he was fading.

From somewhere deep inside, one last surge of strength rose up, and he brought his fist back, looking through clouded vision at the hated face of Chaca. The Mexican knew he was close to finishing him, and he smiled...

With a violent thrust forward, he caught Chaca flush on the jaw.

Crack! The impact sent him backwards, tumbling toward the place where he sat minutes before. Stunned, his head rested on the cold tile floor. Chaca sat up, preparing to defend another attack. He searched the room for a weapon. Lying a few feet away, just out of reach, was the automatic, cocked and loaded.

Jim was also up, with his back against the wall. Debris was scattered everywhere around the overturned desk and tables. Beside him the Coat of Arms had crashed to the floor, knocked off the wall. Inches from his fingers, lay the gleaming, stainless steel blade of one of the swords. Jim grabbed it.

He watched as Chaca made his move for the gun. The evil man's trembling fingers gripped the handle and he turned to finish his adversary.

Jim snapped his right arm forward, sending the sword flying through the air like a spear. It struck Emilio Chaca just below the breastbone, slicing through the soft belly like butter, finally coming to a stop as it exited his back. The gun in is hand fell to the floor, and he stared down at the blade in shock. He slumped back against the desk and watched as his red blood poured out on the floor, soaking some nearby bags of gold.

Jim Barnes pulled himself to his feet and staggered to the bleeding man, never taking his hate-filled eyes from him. He bent down slowly, and picked up one of the bags of gold, red and sticky from the oozing liquid. Then he gripped Chacas black hair and jerked his head back, pushing the leather into his open mouth. He moved his face closer to the dying man, while at the same time his hand gripped the scabbard of the sword.

With a chilling, icy, tone, he whispered softly, "Peter Sullivan says G'day!"

Jim Barnes twisted the handle, turning the blade, and with a violent thrust, he ripped it up, toward the heart, slicing through bone and tissue. The Mexican's chest erupted in gore.

Emilio Chaca's eyes rose up, and a gurgling sound spilled from his bloody mouth stuffed with the pouch of gold. He looked at the man who had killed him, still wanting to strike out. Then his body shuddered, his muscles tensed and released.

The struggle that seemed to last for hours had only taken a few minutes, and Jim Barnes quickly realized his fight wasn't over. Men shouting in Spanish were running toward the house, and he had seconds to act.

As the first man reached the porch, staring in disbelief at his fallen master, Jim snatched the pistol up, and sent a blast through the opening. It struck him in the shoulder, sending the stunned man spinning to the ground. Two others, following behind, turned, and scrambled for cover, giving Jim a few seconds.

With his mind racing, he fled into the storeroom. His eye caught sight of the box of hand grenades, and within seconds, he had one in each hand, and a third in his pocket.

As he raced back into the outer room, he caught sight of some guards squatting behind wooden boxes for cover. With one motion, he pulled the pin on the first grenade and threw it sidearm out the open window. It landed in the dust, skipped a few feet to the boxes and then exploded with a roar that sent wood and bodies flying through the air.

Next, he turned his attention to the tall tower across the yard. Once again, he lobbed another grenade. This time it landed at the base of one of the legs. It sat there before exploding just long enough for the men up above to know they were in big trouble.

KABOOM! The blast obliterated one of the tower's legs and then it came crashing down, along with flailing bodies, in a massive cloud of dust.

After that, the mayhem seemed to quiet, as the shooting slowed. Jim pulled the last grenade out of his pocket, and looked over at the gate closing off the compound. As he was about to pull the pin, he noticed some of the prisoners moving too close, waiting for something to happen.

"WATCH OUT!" he screamed. The men saw what he was about to do and scrambled for cover, nearly trampling each other in their panic to get away. He drew back and tossed the small metal bomb toward the steel gate. It exploded, sending metal spiraling into the air, twisted and mangled. A large opening in the wall that had kept them from freedom was now agape. Inside, the men screamed and shouted at the opportunity to live again and raced toward the fleeing guards, bent on revenge.

Jim turned back into the room and tried to get his bearings. Morphine. I've got to get the morphine, he thought. He started to run for the bathroom, but stumbled over Chaca's outstretched legs, crashing to the floor. There he saw some small bags of gold and he scooped them up and jammed them in his pockets.

Jumping back up, Jim raced to the bathroom, to the spot where Maggie said the morphine was stored. Quickly, he snatched it from the shelf, and dashed back into the storage room. With two long strides and a leap, he scrambled back through the open window, tumbling to the ground, and then rolling back up. At the Blazer, Jim grabbed Chaca's keys and brought the beast to life. His heart pounded and his spirit was alive with excitement. He slammed the automatic into reverse, spun his tires, and brought the machine around, facing the road down the mountain. The engine roared as he fishtailed forward, weaving through the dirt and dust, past the inferno he had created. Men were scattering in all directions. Chaca's reign of terror was over.

Rikki Morales was all ears and eyes as he heard the explosions from the bottom of the mountain. The night sky was lit up like a Christmas tree, as the flames swept higher and higher. He wondered if Jim survived. His got his answer when he heard the roar of an engine coming down the hill. He held his breath, waiting for the signal they had worked out.

Seconds passed.

Finally, a single gunshot exploded into the night. Rikki Morales smiled.

CHAPTER 22

Maggie Stanton dropped her head and closed her eyes when she saw the headlights of two vehicles coming across the valley. There was no way of telling whether it was Jim, or Chaca's men coming to take them back. She said a little prayer, hoping for the best. She cradled Peter's head in her lap. Even though close to the fire, she shivered, waiting anxiously for the time when the ordeal would be over. It was little to ask, and she wanted it more than anything else in the world.

The Chevy Blazer Jim drove was the first to reach the clearing. Rikki was close behind and she could make out a large grin on his dirty brown face. It had gone well, she knew.

Jim walked over to the two people with bottles of morphine in his hands, and looked down on their faces. They showed brightly in the fire's light. Peter's eyes were closed. He seemed to be asleep again. Maggie's dark hair was a tangled mess and the path of her tears stood out clearly on her

dirt smeared face. But at that moment, Jim
saw she had a beauty beyond description. She
had given them life, like a mother to
newborns, and it was something he would
never forget.

"I've got it," he said anxiously. "I've
got the morphine. Let's get some into him."

She bowed her head and said nothing.
Her shoulders sagged and she began to weep
softly.

"He doesn't need it anymore."

Jim continued as if he hadn't heard
her.

"I grabbed some needles, too. Chaca
must have been shooting up. Here, you give
him the shot. I'm not good at that kind of
thing."Again she kept her eyes down, not
wanting to see the pleading look spreading
across his face.

"He's gone."

Jim's voice rose, and his heart
pounded. He wanted to move, to strike out,
but he couldn't.

"Give him the shot, Maggie!
Please!"

She could take no more. Tears streamed down her face, and her lips quivered. She cried for both men, the one who was gone and the one who would endure the pain.

Reality crushed Jim Barnes. He dropped to his knees. He began to cry, and scream, and shake his fists, lashing out at everything and nothing. He gripped Peter by the shirt, shaking his limp form violently.

"NO, GODDAMNIT, NO! You're not going to leave me now, you son of a bitch! Not now! Don't leave me, please God, we're so close. It's almost over..." He collapsed down on the Australian, and buried his head into his chest.

"God, not now..." he sobbed.

No one spoke. Maggie and Rikki only watched.

Finally, Jim stood and then started walking away from the fire towards a ledge of rocks that overlooked the valley below. Wisps of clouds crossed the moonlit night and the stars shown bright. The wind began to pick up and Jim never felt more alone as it blew across the desert. At that moment, he felt like the only man on Earth, distraught and abandoned. He wrapped his loneliness around him like a black shawl and drew inward for comfort.

****

The small caravan wound its way to the north across barren stretches of the dusty land. They followed back roads, with Rikki in the lead Jeep, guiding them to safety. Few words were spoken as Jim and Maggie watched the Mexican landscape pass by.

In the back of the Blazer, wrapped in a blanket, Peter Sullivan's body lay still. The joy of their escape was tempered by the loss of a good friend.

They came upon the intersection of two paved roads, and Rikki motioned for them to pull along side. Jim brought the green Blazer up and stopped.

"Senor Jim, my village is down this road. This is where I must leave you. That way," he said pointing to the east, "will take you to El Paso, but it is still many hours away."

"And Riellito? Which way is that?"

Maggie looked at him, but said nothing.

"Straight ahead. You will see the sign in about 50 miles. I thought you wished to go to the States."

"I do," he answered. "But first, I have one last piece of business to tend to."

Rikki Morales nodded. "I guess this is adios, then. I will never forget you, or your friend. You gave me back my life. Someday, maybe I can repay you."

"You don't owe me a thing. Oh, by the way..." Jim said, fishing into his pocket. He pulled out one of the leather bags.

"Chaca said he wanted to pay you for your trouble." He tossed the bag over to the surprised Mexican.

Rikki caught it, and looked perplexed. He pulled on the leather ties, and stared down at enough gold to make him a wealthy man in that part of the country.

"Aye ya yay!" he said, whistling. A huge grin broke across his face as he looked up at Jim.

"Put it to good use, amigo."

"I will, senor. Now I can take care of my family! I did not expect this!"

"I didn't expect any of it either," Jim said with a sad resignation.

"Vaya con dios!" Rikki shouted, and gunned the jeep, racing off to a new life and to the people he loved.

"That was nice," Maggie said, looking into Jim's eyes.

"He earned it. We all did. I have more. You can get a fresh start, away from all this."

"I'm not sure I want to leave everything..." she said, looking away.

"Maggie, we'll talk, later. I feel the same way, but. ..."

"OK. Like you said. Later."

"There's one more place I have to go. We can spend the night in town and take off in the morning. I don't think I can go on much longer."

She patted his leg.

"Do what you have to do. As long as we're together, I'll be all right."

They drove on toward Riellito. The hot sun had crested in the blue sky and the afternoon shadows grew. The Blazer bounced its way north, to the small town that had sheltered them years before.

They finally arrived and Maggie took in the shops and cantinas, watching people hawking their goods. To Jim, it was as if he had never gone. Mexico, he thought, is timeless. Nothing changes.

They pulled up to the old hotel where he and Peter stayed. It was reopened, and even the sign was hanging level. Maggie and Jim walked into the open lobby to the desk. They looked like they had just come from a battlefield, but the proprietor smiled gracefully, because they were Americans.

"Ah, senor, y senora. You look like you could use a nice room with a view of the courtyard! I have just the one!"

"Does it have a shower?" Maggie asked, getting right to the point.

"Certainly, senora. Hot and cold water, too. Can I get your luggage?"

"We have none. It was sort of an unexpected trip," Jim answered. "Maybe you can help us. A good friend of ours was killed in an accident. We need a mortician."

"Ah, yes, senor. Ramon Robles! An honorable man and good friend. Down the street, on the left. I am sure he can help you."

"Thanks. Maggie, why don't you finish up here, and I'll go see Mr. Robles."

"Are you sure...." she started, but was cut off.

"I'll be all right. It's something I have to do. Alone."

"I understand. I'll see you in a bit."

Jim walked back out, and was about to get in the Blazer, when he saw a small bank nearby. It was not good to pay people in gold, he knew. Too many questions would be asked. He wandered over, and after a few minutes, exchanged some nuggets for 'Dinero Internacionale.' The peso was a thing of the past, relegated to cheap wallpaper, as was the U.S. greenback. He looked carefully at the new currency, printed in English, and noticed strips of metal embedded in the soft paper.

"Welcome to the new world," he said to himself out loud.

In a few minutes he arrived at the funeral home of Ramon Robles. Jim pulled the Blazer around to the back, away from questioning eyes, and went inside.

The building was dark. A thick, musty smell with traces of embalming chemicals, hung in the air. There were some small rooms to his left, and a large foyer that held some coffins for sale. Jim felt extremely uneasy, but he pressed on. Just ahead to his right was a large office, very neat and orderly, with a man sitting alone behind a large desk. Jim walked quietly inside, and shut the door behind him.

"Ramon Robles?" he asked.

"Si, senor," the small man said with an uneasy smile, wary of the disheveled stranger who just entered his office.

"I need your help," Jim began as he slumped down into a chair across from the businessman. "A friend of mine, a good friend, has died. You could say it was an accident."

"Ah, yes, senor, there are many accidents these days. Life is very difficult," he said, shaking his head.

Jim was exhausted and he watched the man carefully.

"His body is out in my Blazer. I need your help to see to it that he gets home. I don't want to leave him in Mexico."

"And where is his home?"

"Australia."

"Ah, it is a long way away. It will cost much money."

"I have money. I want his ashes flown home, to a friend of his I will contact later. I will tell you where he lives. He used to talk about him a great deal. Will you do this for me?"

The man searched the tired face of the American. He saw pain and sorrow. His clothes told a story of his troubles. Jim was a man who needed help.

"Senor, I will see that it is done. You have my word. I will make sure your friend gets home."

Jim smiled at Senor Robles. They spent the next hour making arrangements, while two assistants removed Peter's body from the Blazer. He was placed in a side room, near the rear, still wrapped in the old blanket.

When their business was done, the two men shook hands and Jim walked down the dark hall. He stopped in front of the room where Peter lay and turned to go inside. Alone in the quiet place, he pulled up a chair beside the body and began talking to his friend as he had many times before.

"Everything is all set, now. We're both going home. I left a note for your friend Colin, so that he can explain things to your family. I'll never forget you. I know you always felt guilty, blaming yourself for our troubles, but it wasn't your fault. I guess it was fate. You taught me a lot, and you saved my life. But more than anything, you were my brother. I love you, Peter. You'll always be alive in my heart."

Tears came to his eyes as he rose up, and placed his hand on Sullivan's covered face. He stood there silently, head bowed. Then, Jim turned and walked back into the hallway. Standing against the far wall, taking in the whole scene, was Ramon Robles.

"Don't let me down," Jim said softly.

He walked down the darkened hall and passed through the double doors out into the dusk.

When Jim returned to the hotel, he picked up his key and found their room. Quietly he opened the door and stepped inside. On the double bed, lying naked across the turned down sheets, Maggie Stanton slept peacefully, her tired body finally at rest. Overhead, a fan turned slow circles, shifting the strands of hair on her forehead, and a cool breeze blew in from the opened window.

They had returned to the living. It was good to be safe once again.

Maggie Stanton turned over on the soft bed, her long legs sliding up, hugging the contours of Jims Barnes' body. As her arm draped over his shoulders, she awoke, staring directly into his serene face. His clean, sandy blond hair was pulled back, and his skin was shiny, albeit for the stubble of beard that still remained. His body smelled of soap, and the muscles of his chest stood out. His naked legs touched hers, almost as if to assure himself that she was beside him.

Maggie inched forward on the white pillow and softly kissed his lips. His eyes opened slowly, and he studied her face. Jim was about to speak, when she brought her finger up and placed it across his lips.

"Shh," she whispered as her body edged closer, and she raised up. Her white breasts hung full and firm, and they came to rest on his chest as the young woman lay on top of him. He brought his hands up to her face, and pulled her gleaming black hair away, and then moved forward to taste her parted lips. Once again their passion was unleashed.

For an hour, they savored each other, celebrating the newness of a consuming love. They climaxed together, their nerves tingling with the sweet sensation of the other. Now they collapsed in a haze of satisfying exhaustion, embracing tightly. Their hands framed the face of the other lover as they watched each other closely without speaking. Gently, their eyes closed, and they drifted back to the place that would give them rest.

The morning light filtered through the sheer curtains and rays of sunshine warmed their faces. Jim blinked back the sleep in his eyes and leaned up on one elbow.

"What time is it?" he said, shaking his head.

"What difference does it make?" she smiled back. "Do you have some big business meeting to go to?"

"No," he answered, catching her humor, "not now. Probably not ever."

"Good," she said. "We can stay like this forever."

Once again her warm body rolled over on his and she kissed his forehead. Her hand went down between his legs and his arousal was immediate. He entered her, and again they made love, more playful and open then before.

When they finished, Jim looked up at the ceiling as she nuzzled her head to his chest.

"You know, if we keep doing this, I'm going to need some food to keep my energy up. I'm not sure, but I think it's been a couple of days."

"Fine, just fine," she shot back with mock anger. "A couple of rolls in the hay, and you want your house frau to make you some breakfast. I can see where this relationship is heading!"

"Yeah, you're right. It's a new world, I forgot. I'll tell you what. I happen to know where we can get the best Mexican breakfast in this part of the country, and I can do some catching up with an old friend. You get first shower, then we'll be off."

Maggie jumped up and stood at the end of the bed, her smooth brown skin highlighting the supple curves of her body. She looked back at Jim, and gave him a sexy wink, nodding her head toward the bathroom.

"For Chrissakes!" he shouted, laughing and covering his head with the pillow. "I'm at least 10 years older than you. We've got to go easy here or I'll never make it out of this country!"

"Don't say I didn't offer!" she snapped, and skipped out of sight.

During the next hour, they cleaned up and bought new clothes from the vendors in the street. Jim purchased a pair of Levi's, a white, loose cotton shirt, and some leather cowboy boots. They felt so good on his feet after the catch-as-catch-can in his years at the mines that he wanted to sleep with them on, but that was quickly vetoed. Maggie also found some jeans that fit her slim shape, a blue blouse and some boots.

After settling their bill at the hotel, they drove the Blazer out of town, toward the home of Maria Calrone. At first, Jim struggled, trying to remember the way. But then, his memory came back, and he saw familiar landmarks. It wasn't long before they pulled up to the small house.

Playing in the yard was Cecilia, the youngest daughter, who was just a toddler when he was there last. Across the way, inside a ramshackle garage, the two boys, Cesar and Enrique worked under the hood of an old blue Dodge. They stood as the Chevy approached, and Cesar, the oldest, walked toward them cautiously. At 18, he was the man of the house and it fell to him to protect his family. He was also the mirror image of his father, Bernardo.

"Hola, senor," he began hesitantly, trying to search his memory for the name of the face that looked so familiar.

"Hi," Jim smiled, "It's Cesar, isn't it?"

"Si, senor. Do I know you? I have seen you before, but...."

Just then, the front screen door of the stucco house burst open, and Maria Calrone stood on the porch, her hands cupping her mouth.

"Mi Dios, Mi Dios!" she exclaimed through trembling lips, "You are alive, Senor Jim!" She ran forward, and threw her arms around the startled American.

Jim felt a thickness in his throat and he hugged her close, his mind drifting back to better days. A small tear clung to the corner of his eye and he brushed it away quickly. He wasn't prepared for such a warm welcome. In fact, he wasn't sure he would be welcome at all, being partly responsible for the death of Bernardo Carlone.

"Yes, Maria, I am alive. It has been a struggle, though."

She pulled back, and looked at the face that had aged with lines and creases since the day they shared a meal. Jim had lost some of the boyish glow of years past, replaced by a more rugged, mature appearance.

"I understand, senor, I found out much after Bernardo...." She paused, blinking back the tears. Then, her brown eyes flashed and she regained control.

"Come! Have you eaten? You must bring your friend and we will go inside. We have much to talk about."

Jim introduced Maggie and the three went into the house, followed by the two boys and Cecilia.

For the next few hours, Maria fed them a wonderful meal and listened to each word as Jim retold the story of the past four years. The kind woman gasped when she learned of Peter's fate.

"I am so sad. Senor was full of life. He was a good man," she said.

They sat around the kitchen table as Jim told his story. Maria listened but asked few questions. The same wasn't true of her boys, especially Cesar, who wanted to know every detail about the man who had murdered his father. He had a burning anger within him, Jim knew.

"So it was you who killed that pig Chaca?

Jim nodded, and watched the young man carefully.

"I am only sorry I could not be there to help you! I dreamed of that day."

Jim Barnes spoke slowly, and measured each word, so that Cesar would not miss his meaning.

"Killing him was something that had to be done. There was no right and no wrong. I get no enjoyment from it. There is no feeling at all. You have something you must do, also. You must try to become the man your father was and look after your family, or in the end, Chaca will have won, taking everything away that Bernardo built. When we left here, there was a loving, hard-working family, and it must continue."

Cesar watched the American closely. "I will do my job, senor, I promise."

"Good. Now Maria. How are you surviving? Are you getting along all right?"

"Si, Jim. When Bernardo died, his brother helped me with the business, until the boys were old enough to take over. It has been difficult, but we do what we must."

"Good," he said, and his hand searched his back pocket, pulling out another leather pouch. "I have something for you that will make life much easier." He placed it in front of her, and watched the reaction.

"Goodness, Mio! Where did you get this? I can't believe what I see!"

"Let's just say I worked hard for it and it's yours. Your husband helped us when he had the opportunity, and now I am doing the same."

"I don't know what to say, amigo," she answered and once again started to cry.

Maggie patted her on the shoulder and touched the soft skin of her chubby face.

They talked awhile longer, sometimes happy, sometimes sad, remembering the friends and loved ones they had lost. Finally, it was time to leave and the group filed out to the Blazer. The two Americans got inside and Jim started the engine.

"Where will you go now, Jim?" Maria asked.

"You know, I'm not really sure," he answered. "I guess back to try to pick up the pieces."

"I hope you find what you're looking for, amigo. Vaya con Dios. Bless you both."

She leaned forward and kissed him on the forehead.

Slowly they pulled away, waving as they left. Maggie said nothing. It was not the time to complicate or confuse, but rather let life take its course.

"Next stop, El Paso," Jim said to the woman beside him. "Let's go home."

CHAPTER 23

They crossed into the United States in a barren part of New Mexico. Taking advantage of the Chevy's off-road capability, they drove off-road through a gap in a downed fence. Small groups of Mexicans moving north scattered on seeing them approach, thinking the green Blazer was the Border Patrol. Real authorities also paid little attention to the official-looking vehicle.

Finally, they found the Interstate and drove east toward Texas. It was late afternoon. So far, the trip had been remarkably uneventful – exactly as they wanted it. The two passengers talked easily, enjoying their closeness.

"So where do we go when we get to El Paso?" Jim asked.

"You know, I don't know. I'm kind of nervous. And a little scared. I think my sister still lives there with her husband. My parents are probably in Midland."

"Do you want to see if we can find her?"

"Yeah, but not tonight. I've got a better idea. There's an old hotel downtown. It's been there forever and I'm sure it's still there. We could spend the night and sort things out in the morning. It might be the last —"

"Sounds like a great idea to me," Jim said, cutting off her next words. "You point the way. You're the native around here."

They crossed the state line into Texas and headed south. On their left, the hills were filled with homes and the flatlands were spotted with industrial parks and businesses. It would have been just as they left things, but both noticed the abundance of police cruisers and military vehicles at nearly every corner. Oddly, the officials were all parked, as though just waiting for word to act.

Of the faces that Jim could see, few seemed happy. It was if a blanket of gray descended down on life.

The other noticeable difference from years before was the number of motion-sensitive cameras zooming in on everything that moved. All the main intersections had them, along with parking lots and side streets. Big Brother was no longer fiction.

Maggie found the exit to downtown and Jim followed her directions, cutting through the city streets. Homeless people, many with small children, huddled on the downtown sidewalks. Their appearance was shocking, even to a man who had experienced as bad or worse in Mexico. Something was terribly wrong Jim knew. He could feel it in the air.

They pulled the Blazer into an underground parking lot and came to a stop. The hotel was above them. After climbing a flight of stairs, Jim and Maggie entered the lobby. A strange feeling came over the two, as all eyes in the large room seemed to turn, checking out the strangers.

"Is it me, or have you noticed a certain paranoia, too?" Jim asked.

"Strange, isn't it?" Maggie whispered as they walked toward the desk.

The man behind the counter gave them a stiff, uncaring look, and said, "May I help you?"

"Yes," Jim answered, trying to ignore the chill in the air. "We'd like a room for the night."

"I see. Please fill out this card. How will you be paying?"

"Cash," he responded with a slight edge. "In advance. It's still good, isn't it?"

"Why, ah yes. I will need to see your identification cards also, to run through the computer."

"Yes. ... Of course," Jim muttered, stalling until he could think of something.

"Unfortunately, we have had a problem. The lady and I just spent three weeks camping in Mexico and we were robbed. They took everything, including our wallets and IDs."

"Well then, we do have a problem. Government regulations require me to process your cards. Without them, I'm afraid. ..."

Jim pulled out a wad of the new money and looked the man in the eye.

"Look, it's late. We're going to take care of all that in the morning. I'm sure that we can come to some understanding," he began, putting 20s down on the counter.

The clerk watched him carefully count out fifteen of the bills. It was double the price of the room.

"Yes, I do understand your problem and I'd be happy to help. You'll be in room 1410 on the top floor. Enjoy your stay."

Jim and Maggie turned and walked toward the elevator.

"Computerized ID cards?" she said incredulously, shaking her head. "I guess Uncle Sam wants to know where everybody is at all times."

"Yeah. I'm going to have to be much more careful. I'm probably still a wanted man. No doubt there's a file in some database that has my name on it. In highlights. We did cause quite a stir when we left."

"We've both got a lot of catching up to do, but let's start in the morning. All I want right now is a hot shower and room service. That's been my dream for a lot of years."

"Next floor, dreams-come-true," Jim said as the elevator doors closed.

The evening hours passed swiftly, with good food, laughter and the warmth of a loved one filling the quiet time. They talked more about their lives and the people they were before the trouble. Maggie sat and listened of Jim's rise through the fast-paced world of Internet start-ups. He spoke of those times as if they were someone else's life, and in many ways they were. He could no longer feel any excitement for the past, with the exception of the moments when he remembered his family. It was awkward talking about his wife to another woman he loved. Jim usually touched on the subject briefly, and then skipped on. He had no idea where Linda was, if she was all right, or even remarried.

The late night news came on and the two sat up in bed absorbing each word as if savoring bits of chocolate. The world had changed tremendously. Jim was struck by how whitewashed it all was. Obviously, the newscasters' words were carefully chosen. No doubt the country was under control, unlike when he left, but Jim's gut told him the tradeoff was anything but fair. Benjamin Franklin's words were now reality. Americans had given up their liberty for safety, and now, they had neither. If any protests were occurring, the "news" wasn't reporting them.

Finally, having seen as much as they could stomach for one night, Jim clicked off the TV. The lamp was turned down low. In the dim light, high above the city, in comfort neither had known for some time, the two travelers made love and everything else ceased to matter.

In the morning, after languishing in bed over room-service breakfast, Maggie and Jim got dressed and prepared to check out.

But first, Maggie checked the side-table for a phone book, hoping to find her sister's address. The draw contained only a Bible. They both scoured the room, but neither could find a directory.

"Damn it," Maggie said, plopping on the bed, gazing at the mostly empty drawer. "I don't want to pray. I need an address."

With that, the TV flickered to life.

"Welcome to the National Database," a female voice said. "Ready to begin your search."

Maggie and Jim just stared at each other.

Finally, Maggie spoke. "Um. Michael and Gloria Williams."

"City and state, please," the voice responded.

"El Paso, Texas," Maggie said, looking at Jim and shrugging.

A second later, the screen showed the street address. Below that, a map illustrated the way from the hotel.

"I'll be damned," Jim said.

"Better watch what you say," Maggie said. "The Devil might come on next."

They left the hotel and walked to the waiting Blazer.

"Hmmm," Jim said. "You know, I hadn't even noticed, but this thing has Texas plates on it. That's a break. We wouldn't get far with Mexican tags, that's for sure."

"Chaca got it here and he used to drive it on his trips. I guess it was easier to get back and forth across the border."

"Nice thinking, Emilio," Jim said softly, and the two got in.

They crossed town and came to her sister's house. It was in the suburbs on a quiet residential street, and Jim pulled up in the driveway and stopped. Maggie took a deep breath, and the two got out. She knocked on the door, and waited. Finally, footsteps approached and her older sister opened the door.

"Oh my God!" she screamed, and began to loose her balance, as if she were fainting.

Jim quickly grabbed her arm and steadied the stunned woman.

"Gloria, I'm sorry to shock you like this. I'm sure it's quite a surprise. May we come in?"

The plump, middle-aged woman regained her senses and put her arms around her younger sister, hugging and crying.

"We thought you were dead! No word, nothing. There was no way to find out what was going on in Mexico. It was bad enough here. Oh, God, let me look at you!"

Maggie introduced Jim to the still-shaking woman and they entered the house. It was quite large, one-story home, with four bedrooms. Pictures of their two children hung above the fireplace.

"My husband, Michael, is a doctor. He works in the Trauma Unit down at Memorial Hospital. He was on night shift, so he should be coming home any time. You WILL be staying with us, I hope?"

"Yes! I mean, I suppose so. ..." Maggie answered, looking at Jim.

"That would be very kind," he said.

Gloria brought out some food and the three sat in the living room talking. The girls took over the conversation, firing questions at each other, leaving Jim to sit quietly. He didn't mind. He could see how good it was for Maggie to talk about her family. She radiated with excitement. Thoughts of his own wife and daughter filled his memory and he hoped he could call them soon.

After a while, the door opened and in stepped a tall, thin man, with stooped shoulders and graying hair. He wore glasses and had the look of a man who had seen a lot of life, and death, in his work. Immediately he spotted Maggie, and broke out in a large grin, racing over to hug her.

"Jesus! It's been years. We thought you. ..."

"I almost did, but we'll tell you about that later."

Jim stood up and extended his hand.

"Jim Barnes. Nice to meet you, doctor."

"Mike Williams. Just call me Mike. I don't feel much like a doctor these days."

Jim nodded and they sat down. The two men took an instant liking to each other, as they were similar with their easy, quiet manner.

"You know," Gloria began, "the kids are back in school now, so we can talk in peace and quiet. Why don't we go out to the back porch and fill in the gaps."

They all agreed and the four went outside. Maggie spoke first, and her sister and brother-in-law sat silent, enthralled. Jim began to tell his story, cautiously at first, not fully trusting anyone but the woman next to him. Then he opened up. The people in front of him never took their wide eyes off the man. When he finished, there was a long pause in the conversation.

Finally, the doctor spoke up.

"How can we help?"

"Well, I have to get some things together. I have no identification, no wallet. Nothing."

"You probably don't have an implant, either," Mike said.

"A what?"

"An implant. It's a computer chip placed under the skin of the right hand. It has all the pertinent information about you, and your family, your job, etcetera that the government needs to know. They were required a couple of years ago. No exceptions."

"Where do I go to get one?"

"If I were you, I wouldn't. They have unbelievable ways of tracking everyone now. You'd throw up a red flag immediately, and it would only be a short time before they knew who you were."

"Son of a bitch. ..."

"Maggie, you'll be all right. That's one of the first things you should do. The penalty is prison, and seizure of property, if you don't have one."

"They can go to hell," she snapped.

"No, it's not like before. You don't say those things. Hell, I spend half my time down at the hospital patching up people who stepped out of line. Some even got themselves killed. You must be very careful."

"It looks like I still have big troubles," Jim muttered.

"Well," Mike said, leaning forward, speaking in hushed tones, "there is another way. Frankly, I'm sick to death of the whole thing, and I don't give much of a shit anymore. We had a guy come in to the Trauma Center last night, a transient, about your size and description. He had no family, and they've got him up in the morgue, awaiting cremation. When I go in, I'll see if I can get his card, and computer chip. That should work for you for a while."

"I don't know what to say. I don't want you to jeopardize your family," Jim said.

"They'll never find out. Besides, it's done all the time. There's always a black market for such things. I'm not worried."

"Someday, maybe, I can repay you."

"After what you've just told us, you're a man who deserves a break or two. Welcome home."

They talked for the rest of the afternoon, until the kids came home. Jim and Maggie settled into their room and tried to organize themselves until dinner. It was a cool fall day, and the breeze blew through the window. It was quiet and they held hands, savoring the peace. But Maggie could see that Jim had something on his mind, something he was avoiding, and she had a pretty good idea what it was.

"Don't you need to make a phone call?" she asked firmly, watching his face as he tried to avoid her penetrating brown eyes.

"Well, yes. I do," he said. It came out as an apology.

"Look, Jim. It's OK. I know what you have to do and I love you for being the kind of man who doesn't walk away from his loved ones. You and I could easily disappear, but it would never work. There are too many questions, and not enough answers right now. We have to change that. I don't have any idea what's going to happen between us. All I know is that I love you, and I want to be with you, if that's possible. If it isn't, well, then I'll have the memories."

"Maggie Stanton, I love you very much and I don't want any more hurt in your life. I want to hold you, and never let you go. But, I have to find out. I don't know how long it will take, or when I'll be back."

"You mean if," she interrupted.

"Yeah, I guess. I just know I have to do it alone and we'll see where that takes us."

"You should make your call now," she said, her eyes holding back the moisture that was building.

Jim nodded. "You know, I've been thinking about it. Now that we live in a

Brave New World, I don't think I want to use your sister's phone. I'll call from that shopping center we passed down the road."

Maggie put her arms around his neck and they held each other close. Neither one wanted to let go, but they had little choice.

It was getting dark outside when he pulled up to the supermarket. There was a bank of what were at one time pay phones, but now they resembled computer kiosks and Jim parked nearby.

A familiar voice greeted him. It was the same woman from the hotel TV.

"Welcome to the National Database. Please select a service."

The small screen showed a dozen options. He could search the Internet, transfer funds from bank accounts, send an e-mail, order a taxi pick-up and more.

Jim rolled his eyes. A simple phone call, that's all I want, he thought.

Luckily, that was an option, too. Even better, in this Brave New World, it seemed the call was on the government's dime. Of course, nothing is free, Jim thought. The trade-off being the government could monitor every selection offered.

He pressed the screen on the "Make a Call" box.

"Thank you. Please enter the number," the woman instructed.

Slowly, carefully, he screen-tapped the numbers that were burned into his memory through years of captivity. Then, he waited.

"The number you have reached is no longer in service," the woman announced. "Would you like to continue?" Two boxes popped up on the screen.

He tapped "Yes."

The menu screen returned. "Welcome to the National Database. Please –"

"Oh, shut up," Jim said.

"Thank you. Engaging silent mode."

The screen did have an option for searching addresses, but hoping that not everything had changed, Jim tapped "Make a Call" and then hit 0.

"Operator. May I help you?"

He hadn't expected to speak to a breathing human. "Yes, ma'am," Jim said. "I'm looking for a Linda Barnes. It would be in the 313 area code."

"Do you have a city, sir?"

"Well, no, I don't. She's moved, I think."

"I'm sorry sir, but there's not a lot I can do without a city."

"Look, this is very important. It's an emergency. I've got to find her. Can't you scan the database for her name?"

"OK. Let me see what I can find. I have four 'L. Barnes' and three 'Linda Barnes.' Scan your card, and I'll download the information."

"Sorry," Jim said. "I left my card at home. Could we do this the old-fashioned way?"

"I hope I remember how," the operator said, laughing.

Jim jotted the information on some paper he'd brought along. When she finished, her voice stumbled for a moment.

"What was the original number you were calling?" she asked hesitantly.

Without thinking, Jim answered. "750-2378."

"Um, sir. Are you sure you don't have your card? The system is flagging this. What's your name?"

A cold chill ran up and down Jim's back and he tapped the "End Call" button.

As quickly as he could, Jim called the numbers the operator had given him but came up empty.

His name, it seemed, was too common. Suddenly, Jim seized a new idea. The National Database had no trouble giving Jim his neighbor's number. He punched it in

Standing there in the dark, listening to the phone ring, his thoughts raced. One thing he knew for certain was that he didn't want anyone to know he was alive, other than his family.

"Hello?" came an older woman's voice through the kiosk speaker.

"Hello, ma'am. This is Thomas Reed; I'm an attorney in Texas. I'm looking for an old neighbor of yours; a Linda Barnes. An aunt has died, leaving her some money, and. ...'

"Oh, she hasn't lived here in years. The last I heard, soldiers took her away."

Jim Barnes froze, while the woman continued.

"I do have her daughter's number. She used to baby-sit for us, and we've kept in touch. Of course, her last name isn't Barnes, now."

Once again, Jim was shocked. Then he realized how much time had truly passed. His girl was a woman now. Again, he tried to steady himself.

"Let's see, here it is. Kelley Jamison. 467-4655. I hope that helps."

"It does. Thank you for your help."

He leaned against the aluminum kiosk and stared at the night sky. I guess I've missed a lot, he thought to himself. Then he turned and tapped Kelley's number. The phone rang several times.

"Hello?" came the voice of a sleepy young man.

"Ah, Kelley, Kelley Jamison please."

"Just a second. She's in the other room."

After a minute, a woman's voice came on the line. "Hello?"

"Kelley," was all he said.

Across the distance, he could hear a gasp, and Jim knew immediately that she was aware it was her father.

"Kelley, listen to me, honey, it's very important. Don't say my name, not to your husband, not to anyone, until I tell you it's all right. Promise me?"

"Yes. Yes. Oh my God," she stammered, still stunned.

"Kelley, there's so much to talk about, so much to say. We'll do that soon. But right now, it's very dangerous. You must do exactly what I say and no one can know I'm alive. Do you understand?"

"Yes, but. …"

"No buts honey. Now, give me your mother's number. Does she live nearby?"

"No, ah, she has no number. They. …"

"She doesn't have a phone?"

"She's in prison. In New Mexico, a town called Belen. Actually, she's in a hospital in town. Dad, she's very sick. It's horrible. I want to be with her, but the authorities won't let me."

"She's in a hospital? What the hell is going on?" Jim stammered, enraged, nervous, perspiring.

"They took her away when you disappeared," Kelley answered, her voice cracking with emotion. "They wanted to get to you."

"Sweetheart, stay calm, OK?"

"OK, daddy. When will I see you?"

"Soon, honey, soon. First, I have to go to your mother."

"But, daddy. ..."

"Look, it'll be all right, Kelley. Now, don't worry. Please do as I ask. It's better that everyone thinks I'm dead right now. You be strong, and I'll see you soon."

"I love you, daddy. God, I missed you. Please don't go away again."

"I love you too, baby. Just wait. It'll all be over soon."

Jim ended the transmission and drew in a deep breath. His wife has been in prison for four years – the same sentence he had served. Linda was about to be pardoned, Jim vowed.

He got into the Blazer and started the engine. He brought the Chevy up to the stop sign at the far end of the parking lot, waiting to pull out into traffic. He glanced in the rearview mirror and saw something that made his heart race. Cruising slowly in front of the kiosks he just left was a police car, with two men looking all around. They missed him, but not by much.

Jim Barnes' jaw tightened. Rage boiled up in him and once again he had the look of a killer.

"You want me, you bastards?" he said, spitting out each word. "You're going to get me!"

CHAPTER 24

For the next three days, Jim Barnes planned. He studied, consuming as much information as he could about the technology now used. His years of associating with technical experts taught him to delve into the small. Any system could be cracked, because humans created those systems.

Maggie was at his side, watching in subdued silence as he focused on the task ahead. She was well aware of his wife's situation and knew that he would be leaving shortly, toward a confrontation that promised to be explosive. A dark veil of anger descended on the man she loved, and once again, he was transformed into a person capable of extreme violence.

"Were you able to pick up the business cards?" he asked as they sat at the kitchen table in her sister's house.

"Yes. I put them in the briefcase, beside the computer printouts and file folders. I must say it looks like you never left the 'establishment.' Your new suit will be ready at the tailors in the morning."

"Good. If a suit and tie can offer me a little cover, so be it. I'll play by their rules."

"I went down to the Federal Building and applied for my ID card," Maggie continued. "Now I'm a person, I guess. Christ, it was horrible. No one would believe that I could live in Mexico for 10 years and not be wanted for something in this country."

She told Jim about the process – bureaucrats, photographs, fingerprints. They even suggested a lie detector test, but because the man was near a lunch break, they skipped it.

"I'm scheduled to go in for my implant in two days, once they get all my records sorted out."

Jim said, "At least you'll be able to remember who you are. I keep forgetting that I'm supposed to be John Raymond Quinn now. By the way, the guy Mike found did a beautiful job on the ID. It looks just like me."

"Sometimes it pays to have connections in the underworld," Maggie answered.

Jim nodded. He looked down at the paper in front of him and began checking off the notations of things to be done.

"Any problems exchanging the gold at the bank?" Jim asked her.

"You wouldn't believe it," she said. "They were befuddled. It seems the money-for-gold forms went out with covered wagons. They wouldn't stop with the questions, either. But it's amazing how men loose their train of thought when a woman's blouse is unbuttoned a little. I got the cash, finally. It's all that new money, though. I imagine I'll be hearing from the I.R.S. soon."

"I'm surprised they didn't just take it all right then. They figure it's theirs, anyway. I guess it's better to do it slowly, to prolong the pain. More job security. Can I fit it all in the false bottoms of the luggage?"

"If we pack it tight. The lining of the case should deflect any scanners, too. Once again, it pays to have friends."

Jim finished with the last item on his pad and looked up at Maggie. "That's it, then. Tomorrow's the day. It should take me about seven hours to get to Belen. If I leave early."

"You're sure you can't stay another day or two. We could go somewhere, alone. Someplace quiet."

Jim stood up with the pad of paper in his hand and walked over to the fireplace. He picked up a lighter and lit the paper's edge. In seconds, it was engulfed in flames, and he tossed the pad on some old ashes. Then he looked back across the room at the woman waiting for an answer.

"I have to go. I don't know what's waiting for me there, but I've had this awful feeling it's very bad. Anyway, I'm no good like this. You know, I understand what happened to me. But there was no reason for Linda's life to be destroyed. Something happened. Something sinister that goes well beyond the bounds of human decency. She was no threat to anyone. If it's the last thing I do, I'll find out who was responsible."

"And then what?" Maggie asked, studying his face.

Jim turned and stared into the flames.

"Then I'll deal with it, just like I did before, if for no other reason than I'm good at it. I learned well."

"When's it going to end, Jim? When will it stop? Maybe the question is, will you be able to stop?"

"It's going to end when my life returns to a sense of balance, and when accounts are squared. I'll have to be the judge of that. No politician or jury or rule or regulation will tell me when everything is all right. I've seen too much to believe any of that bullshit. I will know and then it will be finished."

"How long do you think I can wait for you? Should I just put my life on hold? A month? A year? Ten years? You are a part of me now. You have a place that will never be filled by anyone else. It's not easy to see it slipping away. I feel so helpless."

Jim walked over to her and she stood to meet him. His strong hands rested on her small shoulders.

"When it's safe, I will contact you. I don't want you involved in this any further. You're all right now and I want it kept that way. If we can be together, we'll know at that time. No doubts, no 'what ifs.' I have to know. For me and for you. I love you too much."

"Then that's the way it will be. No doubts." She lifted up on her toes and they kissed.

That evening, Gloria Williams prepared a large meal and everyone gathered around the table, sharing stories and animated conversation in front of a roaring fire. The kids talked about their teachers and schools, and of all things vitally important to their young, innocent lives. Jim and Maggie listened attentively, for it was good to drift back into memories and, for the moment, not think of the reality before them.

Dr. Mike Williams watched Jim carefully as he shared the meal with his family. For three days they had talked, sometimes alone, sometimes with the women. In short time, they had come to trust each other.

When the dishes were put away and the children sent off to bed, Jim and Maggie decided to go for a walk. Jim bade farewell to the Williams, knowing that he would be leaving very early, much sooner than even Maggie realized.

They walked for hours in the moonlight, hand-in-hand, savoring the feel and closeness of the other. The conversation touched on the past briefly, still less on the future, for it was the moment that they lived for and it would not last forever.

The home they returned to was bathed in darkness, and silently they slipped into the room that would be theirs alone for one more night.

With gentle, knowing hands, the two undressed each other and fell back on the crisp white linen.

****

Maggie Stanton searched the blackness of the bedroom for the sound that brought her awake. Standing above her, looking down, fully dressed in slacks, blue shirt, and tan leather coat, Jim Barnes prepared to leave.

"What?" she said softly, "It's too early. You can't leave yet. What about the luggage, your things?"

"It's already done. You sleep too soundly."

"No, you move like a ghost."

"Maybe," he smiled. "Maybe that's good." He sat down on the edge of the bed, and stroked her face with the tips of his fingers. "It's better this way. I don't like long good-byes. Please tell Mike and your sister how much I appreciate what they did. I won't forget it. I should know something soon. When I do, I'll call. I promise. It may take a day, a week, a month, but I will call."

Maggie smiled. "That sounds just like a man, leaving a woman's bedroom. You're all alike."

"Trust me," Jim smiled back. Then he took on a more serious tone, "If things don't go well, if I should die, the last thought I'll have on this earth is of you. You must believe that."

"I do," she said.

They held each other close and kissed one last time. Then Jim stood up and was about to turn away, when Maggie stopped him.

"Here," she said, holding in her hand a small, pink envelope, the size of a thank you note. "When you're ready for me, open this. But not until then."

He took it from her and rubbed the paper between his fingertips. Then, Jim smiled once again, and started for the door.

****

The green Blazer ran well, gliding down the interstate toward New Mexico. For a truck, the ride was smooth. On the radio, a Country station played the tunes of George Jones and Randy Travis, which were fine with Jim, although he would have preferred the Beach Boys. But there were few towns in that part of the state, and fewer still radio stations. So, he accepted what was available, not really listening anyway.

Just on the other side of Las Cruces, the authorities set up a roadblock, checking identification cards. It would be the first test of the workmanship of Mike's friend.

After a casual glance at the card by a bored soldier, and a quick pass over of the computer chip embedded in his hand, Jim Barnes was back on the road, heading for a part of his life that was a distant memory. In many ways he felt like a stranger, about to meet someone who existed only in his mind. After four years, he didn't know if Linda would be the same woman heknew and loved for so many years. He had changed dramatically, to say the least, and it was a safe bet that she was different, also.

As the afternoon sun beat down on the Chevy, he continued north on Interstate 25, past the browns and greens of the barren land. Belen was south of Albuquerque, and the miles went by quickly. The New Mexican sky was clear, and gusts of wind produced dust devils on the land beside the highway. Small tourist stops dotted the exits, but Jim was not interested. Beyond food and fuel, his mind was focused miles up the road.

He entered the city limits of the town about six o'clock in the evening. It was too late to attempt to see Linda, and it would be foolish, anyway. There were many things he needed to know before venturing into the hospital.

Jim saw a motel on the main drag heading into Belen. that looked presentable, and pulled off coasting to a stopped. Inside, an old, balding man with a weather-beaten face, was watching the news on TV behind the counter.

"You have a room available for a couple of nights?" Jim asked, watching as he stood up.

"Mister, I'd say you pretty well have your pick," he said with a slow drawl, his eyes scanning the parking lot.

"Good. How much is it?"

"Thirty-five dollars a night for one person, 25 for two, if I can watch!" His face lit up at his own joke.

Jim laughed. "Just one, I'm afraid. No thrill tonight."

He finished filling out the check in card, then paused, staring at the old man in a faded Western shirt.

"Aren't you going to ask for my identification card?"

"Nah, Piss on it! Sometimes I do and sometimes I can't be bothered. It's bad enough playing with this funny money, but to keep tabs on everybody for them assholes in Washington is where I draw the line."

"You're not afraid of getting caught?"

"Mister, I'm 76 years old. The worst they can do is kill me, and I'm not far from my grave right now. So I say bring 'em on, and take your best shot!"

Jim eyed the old man with admiration. He had grit, like a lot of westerners.

"If everyone had your guts, we'd be a helluva lot better off. I guess most people figure they have too much to lose."

The man took the registration card and his money and looked Jim straight in the eye.

"Not for long, sonny, not for very Goddamned long! They're losing it, they just don't realize it yet."

They talked for a while longer and Jim picked up some maps of the city. The old man pointed out the hospital, and other landmarks around town, including the best place to get a meal. Then, the tired traveler got back into the Blazer and drove down the parking lot, past the pool, to room 24. He took all his things inside, and sat down on the bed. It was just past seven in the evening, a good time to call the hospital to see if he could get more information. After that, he planned to get some food and drive past the building, to check out the area.

Jim smiled as he picked up the receiver. A normal phone, he thought. I like this place. He dialed.

"Belen Memorial Hospital. May I help you?"

"Yes, this is Doctor Richard Bell. I'm calling from Michigan. You have a patient down there, a Mrs. Linda Barnes. The family has asked me to contact her, and see if I can be of any help. Do you have her room number?"

"Just a moment, doctor, let me see. Mrs. Barnes is in the prison ward, room 322.

I'm afraid I can't connect you. Calls aren't allowed."

"I see. Tell me, is there anyone there I can talk to concerning her condition?"

"Well, the staff doctor in that section has gone home for the evening. I'm not sure the nurse could help you. Maybe if you called back tomorrow."

"Yes, well, I'll do that. I just hoped I would have some news for the family. ..."

"Well, doctor, there is a notation on the screen. I'm not sure it's the kind of news they will want to hear, though."

"Please, what is it?"

"Well, she's in one of the six rooms we reserve on that ward for Hep C patients."

Jim drew in a quick breath, and a stabbing pain shot through his chest. He almost dropped the telephone, but managed to recover enough to end the conversation.

"Thank you for your help. I'll call back tomorrow."

Slowly, he dropped the handset, and fell back flat on the bed. He brought the palms of his hands up to his tired eyes, and cried out.

"Jesus Christ! What have we done to deserve this? No. …God, no! Please don't do this! Don't take her."

He sat in the darkened room, his emotions pouring out in an uncontrolled stream of anguish. Everything that was pent up inside burst out, and in the end, he was exhausted and spent.

Later that night, Jim Barnes drove around Memorial Hospital three times, taking in every detail of the place that was home to his gravely sick wife.

In the morning, Jim awoke early and prepared for the trying day ahead. As he showered and shaved, his eye caught sight of the suit laid out on the bed, and for a moment, he flashed back to the time when every day began like that. Back then, his life seemed certain and sure. The routine provided comfort in a turbulent world. Then, he became a part of the turbulence, unknowingly, unaware, and he couldn't make it stop, no matter how hard he tried.

When he finished dressing, Jim stood before the full-length mirror and stared vacantly. There was a time when he was vain about his appearance, dreading the thought of a wrinkle, or being caught without his Rolex watch. He was a GQ man, living the good life, grabbing all he could get. Now, he saw a reflection of a man with purpose. He would use the tools at his disposal to accomplish what he set out to do: find his wife. That was all that mattered.

Finally, it was time to leave and he set out for the hospital. He was not nervous or scared, even though the possibility of being caught was very real. It would be a dangerous place, for sure, but like the old man said, what can they do? A large part of his life lay sick, possibly dying, anyway. Beware the barbarian with nothing, he kept thinking, for he has everything to gain and nothing more to lose.

Jim parked the Blazer, picked up his briefcase and set off for the front door. Once inside, he looked around, casually taking in everything. Three nurses huddled at the reception desk, and an old security guard stood in the corner, watching TV in the lobby. Everything looked normal.

Down the hall he could see a row of elevators and he moved to the first one going up. As the floors passed, he took a deep breath and slowly let it out.

When the doors opened, Jim stepped out onto the third floor, and quickly looked around. The fewer people he talked to, the better. Starting out to his left, he watched the room numbers raise, and knew he was heading in the right direction. He passed the nurses' station where a woman and a male nurse argued over who would give a certain patient his medication. Around the corner and further up the hall, he finally saw a glass door, with a young, roly-poly policeman sitting in front of it. By the look of him, he was not one of Belen's finest, and Jim made the quick decision to proceed.

As he approached, the guard looked up and struggled to get to his feet.

"I'm sorry, sir, you can't go in there," he said.

"My name is Quinn. I'm from the Center for Disease Control in Atlanta. I have to see a patient. Weren't you informed?"

"Ah, well, no, I wasn't. Do you have some form of ID or something?"

Jim lifted his eyebrows with impatience and set the briefcase on the chair. As he opened it, the young man could clearly see some official-looking computer printouts and a number of other 'important' documents. Jim pulled a card out of the small pocket in the lid, and held it up for the policeman to see. The black print was raised, and it looked very real, complete with seal, thanks to Dr. Mike Williams.

"Yes, well, OK, but maybe you should check in."

Jim tossed the card back into his briefcase and closed it. He cut the man off quickly.

"Look, I'm very busy. We have an epidemic on our hands with Hepatitis C and I have no time to chitchat. I have urgent work to do. Now, are you going to let me in? Or do you want me to go over your head?"

The guard opened the door for him. As he watched Jim go, the guard called out, "You'll find the surgical masks outside each room."

Jim waved his hand in the air and kept walking. There were a number of nurses and doctors on the floor, but each seemed too busy to care or question him. He passed wheelchairs and carts, and patients limping down the hall, leaning on canes. Finally, up ahead in the corner, he could see Room 322. He stopped and for the first time, felt his nerves begin to loose control. The heart sped. He set the heavy briefcase down and fitted the surgical mask over his head. Then he opened the door.

Lying across the room near the window, with the shades pulled low, allowing little light, a frail woman slept, covered to the neck with blankets. He looked at her face and turned away. Then he looked again, certain he was in the wrong room. But as he gently closed the door and moved nearer, the horrible truth fell upon him. It was Linda.

The woman before him was a skeleton, pale and gaunt, with sores and red blotch marks on her head. Her once-beautiful hair was thin and stringy, and gray overpowered what was left of her natural color. The hands that had caressed him lay folded across her chest, bony and white. Her eyes, those beautiful eyes that had captured his heart, were ringed with dark circles and lined with creases.

An inch at a time Jim moved forward, wanting to cry out, but nothing came from this throat. Then he was there, at her side, and he stopped, not daring to breath, watching, listening, and waiting.

As if an inner voice called to her, Linda's eyes fluttered open. She looked straight ahead, and then rolled her head to the right, focusing in on the man staring down at her. She blinked once, then twice.

"Jim?" she whispered. "Is that you? No, I must be dreaming."

Tears welled up in his eyes and he sank down on the bed beside her. His hand came up, and lightly brushed the hair away from her forehead.

"It's me, Linda. It's Jim. I'm here now. It's not a dream," he said through sobs.

"My God, you're alive," she answered as loud as her raspy voice would allow her. "Oh, Jimmy."

He bent down, and her arms came up around his neck. They held each other tight, their tears touching the cheek of the other. Gently, he rocked her, not wanting to let go of the woman he loved, the mother of his child.

"I always knew you would return," she whispered in his ear. " I knew it was something horrible that took you away from us."

He pulled back and she could see the aging of his once boyish face.

"It was beyond horrible," he said, his chin dropping to his chest. "It was a living hell."

She brought her thin index finger up and placed it on his lips.

"But you're here now and that's all that matters. We have time to talk. Right now, I just want you to hold me, and don't let me go."

They stayed that way for many minutes, undisturbed, pressing their face against the other. After a while, they began to talk, to fill in the blank spots of two lives that should have been spent together. Linda was very weak, but she understood every word Jim spoke, and lay with tears streaming. At times she flashed the same anger and spirit that was her way, and Jim felt good.

They were interrupted just twice, when an orderly came in to change the bedpans, and a nurse to check her blood pressure. It was as if both people sensed something special was happening between the man and the woman, and backed away, not wishing to disturb them.

As Linda struggled with her own story, returning to the day he disappeared, and continuing on to her time at the prison, Jim's emotions rode the roller coaster of hatred, anger, frustration and impotence. He listened carefully to all the names, and places, and events that had brought her to that room. He was etching them in his memory.

Hours passed, and the coolness of the late afternoon breeze gently shifted the blinds. They spoke every word, every sentence, until there was no more left to say. And then they found more.

Finally, Linda looked up through eyes struggling to stay open, and with the last of her energy, began to bring the conversation to an end.

"Jimmy, now you must listen to me, and promise to do as I say. I'm dying. We both know that. The pain is beyond description, even with the medicine. ..." her voice drifted off.

"I have endured it for one reason, and one reason only; I prayed for the day when I could see you one last time. That day has come, and now I'm happy. I'm ready to go."

Jim shook his head, not willing to accept the words that were coming out of her mouth.

"No, hon. No! Don't say anymore."

"I've heard the doctors talking. It might be a week, maybe two, but no more than a month. I could accept that then, but now things have changed. Because you're here I, I...can't live without you anymore. I don't want to be alone, but you can't come back, not to this place. It's too dangerous. I'm sure they're still looking for you."

Tears fell from his eyes, along the strong line of his jawbone and onto the blankets that covered her. Jim Barnes listened, unable to move, wanting to cry out in protest, but he found no words, no voice.

"I'm going to go to sleep now. For the first time in a long while, I feel at peace. And, after I say good night and close my eyes, I want you to help me stop breathing."

"No, Linda, No! God, don't ask me to do that!"

"You will because you love me, and I love you. Everything is all right now."

She pulled his head down to her breast, like a mother holding a suckling baby, and gently kissed his forehead. He lay there holding her body, sobbing into the blanket, listening to her gentle sighs as she faded off to sleep.

"Good night, sweetheart. I love you and I'll be watching over you.

Time passed in the still room, and he drifted off as well, searching for past memories that would take him away from his grief and sorrow. Noises filtered in through the walls, but they were alone, truly alone, the only two people on earth.

Later, when there was nothing more to do, he gripped a clean, white pillow and held it down over his wife's sleeping, peaceful face, fulfilling her last wish.

CHAPTER 25

A black Lincoln pulled away from the command center in Albuquerque. It was late but the lone passenger in the back didn't mind. His wife was back in Washington D.C., getting an early start on the Christmas social scene. For now, he would no bitching, no complaints, no snide remarks about living in the boondocks, far away from the centers of power and glamour. Mrs. Colton had returned to the society and position for which she was born and bred, and the general was a contented man. The evening promised to be peaceful.

The driver skillfully maneuvered the large car through downtown traffic. Lights brightened the shops and stores, but very few shoppers strolled the walks. Citizens were still hesitant, uncertain of the future.

The general had reinstated order, but at Faustian price. For the spark, and spirit of the many people going about their business was gone, replaced with a subdued resignation. They made their way, but with a yearning for another time, when the choices were theirs to make, and not the centralized monolith that had been created.

As he relaxed in the soft tan leather, Jennings Colton waxed philosophically on his life and career. For him, it was the best of times. The general accomplished the mission his superiors sent him west do to and now they talked of a new posting in the east. That, of course, would make his wife happy, and relieve him of a degree of pressure, for they had not been able to relate to the independent-minded Westerner.

Where they expected grateful thanks for imposing the new version of order, they received, instead, muted hostility. No matter how many times they heard the message, the people weren't convinced that Washington had their best interests at heart, and that things would work. The general, on the other hand, was the product of that system. There was no doubt in his mind that Washington, and the East Coast centers of power, knew what was best. He could not connect with Joe Six-pack, who retreated in horror at the dark shadow that was encompassing every aspect of his life.

The car turned east and climbed into the hills overlooking the city. General Jennings Colton lived on top of a mountain and his view was wide and unrestricted. He lived on a splendid estate, complete with pool, tennis courts, gardens, hiking trails and a servant's cottage. And it was all locked away behind a guarded gate at the bottom of a steep, quarter-mile driveway. From his vantage point, everything below seemed just fine and he was proud to be an American.

The Lincoln slowed to give the large metal gates time to open. The guard inside, watching television with his feet up on the desk, snapped to attention and saluted. His gesture went unreturned. The driver pressed his foot on the accelerator and began the winding traverse of the steep grade, with the hood of the vehicle pointing toward the heavens.

When they came to a stop in front of the four-car garage, the General waited for his driver to open the door, and then stepped out.

"O'Reilly, it's not necessary for you to wash and polish the car tonight. Take the golf cart down and relieve Miller in the guard shack. Tell him that will be all for tonight."

The private snapped a salute. "Yes, Sir!"

As Jennings Colton walked up the stone stairs toward the front door, he stopped and looked back out over the rocks and shrubbery of the rugged mountain, toward the city.

Mission accomplished, he thought. His lungs took in the clean night air. His climb to real power back in Washington would begin soon.

****

Two miles away, in a small, Spanish-style apartment complex in the foothills, a man patiently watched the arrival of the General through the night vision equipment attached to his telescope. It had been part of Jim Barnes' daily routine for nearly two months. His view through the second story window was unobstructed, and hidden from anyone who might have been looking back. In the dark apartment, the man noted every movement, and ruefully smiled as the pattern he had witnessed replayed itself once again, from the light in the study, to the time close to 11:30 when the general would retire to his bedroom.

Jim stepped back, still staring at the mountain. Scattered around the cluttered room were a dozen or more books on computers, which had absorbed a great deal of his time. He immersed himself into the details of his past career, updating himself on every new development, ensuring himself that he could overcome any problem, any glitch. Also, there were numerous articles and bits of information on the man who ruled Sector 47; his likes, dislikes, office, staff, home. If it's wise to keep friends close and enemies closer, Jim Barnes was a sage.

He bent down to pick up his watch, which lay on top of the social pages of the Albuquerque Journal. It showed a small picture of Mrs. Jennings Colton smiling gaily at a society fund-raiser to help pay for the Cotillion Ball. Mention was made of her upcoming trip back to the nation's capital.

Jim snapped the watch around his wrist. He still had a few things to do before three a.m., when his plan would begin to unfold.

Earlier that day, Jim took a bus to the seamier side of Albuquerque, and closed out his lease, under a fictitious name, on a mini-storage garage. Inside, only the light green Blazer formerly owned and registered to Emilio Chaca was parked. It had been months since he had driven it, but the engine fired immediately. Near his apartment complex, he pulled into the parking lot of a large strip center that featured twenty-four hour movie classics. Cars were always parked there, and one left for a long period of time would never be noticed.

Now, it was after midnight, nearing two thirty in the morning. The apartment that had been home for two months was once again immaculate. It was an upscale complex, comfortable, and similar to units he rented in his younger days. Jim was careful to make arrangements for vacating a few days before, and he promised to send the landlord a California address where his damage deposit could be mailed.

When all the remaining papers had been burned, with the ashes disposed of, and the refrigerator emptied of his last Diet Pepsi, Jim Barnes stood alone in the quiet room. He flashed back to another time when accounts had to be settled and his heart began to pound faster in his chest. His hands were steady, though. For a moment, the memory of a frail woman, lying near death in a hospital bed, flickered across his mind, and the anger and loathing that consumed him resurfaced. But it was not a time for emotions. There was work to be done. He picked up the hiking boots near the brown footstool, sat down, and laced them. They were well worn from his trips into the surrounding mountains. Jim Barnes knew every trail, every ledge, and every resting place in the rugged hills. He had become a familiar sight to the many enthusiasts who loved the sport for exercise and the feeling of freedom.

Finally, when everything was done and all details attended to, he placed his two keys on the kitchen counter, and quietly slipped out.

With the turn of his wrist, the engine of the Blazer roared and he started off toward the base of the mountains about four miles away. Nestled against the hill, away from any nearby houses, a small electronic switching station stood. It was at the end of a hill on a dirt road, surrounded by a wire fence. Within minutes, he arrived, and turned off the lights. Jim rolled down the window, and listened for any approaching sounds. All was quiet. The plan was about to begin.

He opened the Blazer's door and put his left foot on the running board. His eyes stared straight ahead at the building and his jaw set.

"One, two, three!" he shouted, and slammed his foot down on the gas pedal. The rear tires spun, and the old truck lurched forward. Jim's eyes settled on the speedometer, and his pulse quickened. Fifteen, 20, 25 miles per hour. The Blazer charged the small frame structure. When the needle hit 30, he took one last look at the bulls-eye, and then launched himself through the door. He landed on the sandy dirt, and rolled until his body stopped. He sat up just in time to see the Blazer smash into the building, nearly demolishing it.

Sparks shot up in the air, like a Fourth of July celebration. Then, darkness descended once again, and all was still.

Quickly, he jumped to his feet, and raced over to some branches he had left earlier by the side of the road. In minutes, all tracks and other markings disappeared. He flung the branch further down the hill, and set off for a residential street about a mile away. When he passed by a dumpster behind a small dry cleaning store, he removed the torn and dirty sweatshirt he wore, and buried it down among the garbage.

He walked down the street, past a dozen houses, until he came to a place where cars were parked on both sides. Waiting for him there, locked, packed, and loaded with gas, was the year-old Ford Bronco he had purchased from a newspaper ad when he arrived in town. It was black, with gold pinstripes, and it melted into the dark New Mexican night. In seconds, he was back on the road, heading for the place at the base of the mountain.

When he finally arrived at the small clearing, he shut down the engine and the headlights. Again, he listened for any unusual sounds, but heard nothing. Jim opened the door, and slid the driver's seat forward. Reaching inside, he pulled out a hiker's knapsack. He stole one more look around, and started up the treacherous path, hiking more from memory than sight.

Minutes ticked by. Inside the house, General Jennings Colton slept peacefully in the large, king-sized bed that was his alone. His bedroom was immense, and ornate, with expensive furniture filling the space. Billowy curtains draped gracefully on the walls, and the mahogany vertical blinds in the windows allowed the light from the stars into the room. Everything was quiet, except for the click of the electronic clock changing numbers and the rattle of the brass bed frame as he turned over. The general's breathing was rhythmic. Orderly, always orderly.

Suddenly, from the darkness, he could feel cold steel pressed against his throat. His eyes shot opened. At the same time he heard a metallic click, and something cold grip his wrist. Then it happened again, and the brass on the large bed rattled. He had been handcuffed to the frame. Panic set into the old soldier's frightened face.

"What IS this!" he cried out, gathering himself to take command. "What's going on here?"

The intruder stepped back, his dark clothes still hiding him from the blurred vision of the general, who moments before slept secure. He slid a nearby chair close to the bed and settled back, holding the gleaming steel blade of the hunting knife at both ends, as if contemplating his next move. Nothing was said. He sat still, and watched the general grope in the dark.

"Who are you?" Jennings Colton demanded, his senses coming to full attention as the danger he faced became more apparent. His eyes were wide, and the fact that the stranger did not answer further frustrated him.

Then, in a voice cold and clear, the silent man spoke, hardly raising the volume above a whisper.

"I'm the man you've been looking for," he said.

"What? Who?" shouted the General, thankful for finally getting a response.

"Listen, mister. I don't know what your game is, but you are in big trouble. BIG trouble! I have security all around here, and..."

"No, you don't. The guard down the hill is asleep. Frankly, General, it surprises me that a man with your enemy's list could be so careless."

Colton's nerves were on end. It was obvious the man knew what he was doing.

"Look, mister, ah... I didn't get your name," he said trying to calm down, to let his intellect begin to work.

The eyes of the stranger bore in on his captive, and he spoke softly.

"Barnes. Jim Barnes."

Then, when he saw the fear grip the older man, he added, "I think you know my wife, Linda."

Jennings Colton, for the first time since his days in the war, broke out in a full sweat. His lips and mouth twitched nervously, and he brought his left hand up to wipe away the perspiration.

"That was a long time ago," he began, trying to recover.

"Time flies when you're having fun. At least, that's what my late wife used to say."

"Yes, I heard about her death. Tragic. I gave specific instructions that she was to be released a year ago. I can assure you, heads rolled on that one."

"Yeah, " Jim replied coldly, "I guess people have a way of falling through the bureaucratic cracks. A file lost, a misplaced memo. Next thing you know, something bad happens. It's hard to pin down the person responsible. And then, nothing really happens anyway, except maybe a reprimand in a personnel file somewhere. That's kind of why I wanted to talk to you, to register a complaint. I didn't think it was a very good idea to go down to your office and put a note in the suggestion box."

"Ah no, ah, under the circumstances, I can see your point," Colton said, trying to bring the conversation to the level of two people negotiating. That was his forte.

"Anyway," continued Jim, "we'll come back to that in a minute. Right now, I want to tell you a little story about some things that happened to me over the last few years, and maybe help you understand my situation. You got a minute? No meetings to run off to, or anything like that?"

"No," the general said. "Please, go ahead."

For the next 20 minutes, Jim Barnes reviewed the last four years of his life, from the day he left California to the night he said good-bye to his dying wife. Jim knew the general would be unmoved by his tale, but he wanted the man to hear it. Finally, Jim finished.

"That's an amazing story, young man, simply amazing. Of course, we had no idea…"

"No," Jim interrupted, "I'm sure you didn't. It was your job to make judgments. Unfortunately for all of us, you made the wrong ones." He took the knife by the tip of the blade, and flipped it once in the air. The General noticed.

"Well, Mr. Barnes, I'm sure we can get this whole thing straightened out."

"Yes, General, I'm sure we can. Tell me, though, when you issue orders and make commands, does the thought ever occur to you that one day you might have to account for your actions and your judgment, or do you just figure the system will always protect you?"

"Well, naturally, we have review boards, superiors. Everything we do, we are accountable to someone higher in rank."

"You see, that's just what I mean, General. You answer to the people above you, but never to the little guy down below. From your superiors, you get a poor performance evaluation. From me, well, it's more serious than that."

Fear shot through the old soldier, as he watched the face of the man beside him who spoke those words.

"Look, I'm sure we can come to some arrangement, there's no need for..."

"Wrong, General. There is great need. I need you to agree to the arrangement I have in mind," Jim shot back to the man who was not used to being spoken to in such a manner.

"My life, unfortunately, has changed in so many ways that even I no longer recognize it. I'm tired, very tired. I just want to go somewhere quiet, and be left alone. I don't want any forms, any tax notices, any subpoenas or the like, destroying the rest I think I deserve. I just want to disappear. Completely."

"I don't follow you. How can I help?"

"Being the commander of this region, you have an access code to the National Database in Washington. As I'm sure you are aware, that gives you an enormous amount of power over all of us. You have the ability to gain entry into the catacombs of the computers back there, to add, delete, modify, and so on. I want to borrow that power for just a little while. Through that door at the end of your bedroom, is an office with a direct, secure link up. I want to use your computer for a little while. In return, I will leave here tonight, and never come back. You will go back to your work, and I will fade away into statistical oblivion, without a trace. Do we have a deal?"

Jennings Colton's mind raced, figuring all the angles before he answered. It was no wonder his stupid men couldn't catch this fugitive, he thought to himself. He was clever, and cunning, and he did his homework. The dark stranger waiting for his reply was no match for them, but HE was another story.

"You've got a deal, Mr. Barnes," said the general, smiling. "Maybe in some way it can make up for the tragedy in your life."

"Well, I appreciate that, Jennings. Now, there is one other thing. When you give me the code, I want it right the first time, digit by digit. Otherwise," he continued, his tone hardening, "I'll have to come back here and slit your throat from ear to ear. Believe me, General. One time, and one time only."

Colton's eyes were wide. "I understand perfectly. Please, get me that piece of paper and pen on the nightstand, and I'll write it down. We don't want any mistakes."

Jim placed the paper in front of him, and watched without speaking.

In a few minutes, he was in the home office. The hardware was impressive, Jim had to admit. It was a mini command center. At first he was overwhelmed, but then his knowledge took over, and in a short while he had the database searching for the information he wanted. If people only knew the vast range of information Washington had on them, there would be a bloody revolt in this country, Jim thought.

Out in the bedroom, Jennings Colton listened as Jim worked at the computer. Sitting on the nightstand, just inches from his outstretched left hand, sat a small, oval device no bigger than a key chain fob. The single button would set off alarms all over the house and transmit an SOS signal to his staff at the command center.

The general listened, making sure his intruder was still clacking at the computer. Then he lunged for it and smiled as his hand reached around it. His eyes stole furtive glances over his shoulder as he pressed the button. But there was no sound, nothing. It was completely dead.

"I'll be a son of a bitch!" he mumbled.

Finally, the light in the office went out. According to the National Database, Jim Barnes did not exist.

"OK, General, I think we have everything settled. Now, as I am a man of my word, I am going to leave the key to the handcuffs on the table by the door. I'm sure with a little effort, you can pull that big bed over and free yourself. Meantime, I'll just be on my way."

Colton looked at him, relieved, and began to speak.

Jim cut him off.

"Oh, there is something else. You know, if there is one thing that life's taught me, it's that ANY man, no matter how big or powerful, can be killed. I think history backs me up on that. All you need is someone dedicated to the task. Take yourself, for instance. I'm sure when you went to bed tonight, safe and warm, you had no idea you would wake up with a knife at your throat. You assumed your world was secure, just like I did years ago. But you were wrong. I paid a very hefty price for my error. I don't want you to do the same, just in case you get any ideas about re-negotiating our deal."

"Oh," the old man replied with grave sincerity, "you don't have to worry about that. When General Jennings Colton makes a deal, that's it. I'm a man of my word."

"Fine," Jim said smiling back at the man. "It's been a pleasure doing business with you. I'll say good bye now."

He slipped quietly down the darkened hall and disappeared into the night.

Jennings Colton lay on the bed, straining to hear footsteps. When he was sure the intruder was gone, the rage building up inside the career public servant bubbled to the surface, and the air was rife with invectives.

"You miserable little bastard punk!" he began, just getting warmed up, as he stood up from the bed, and began to tug it closer to the key with his one free arm. "I'll have your Goddamned balls on a platter by noon! Who the hell do you think you're dealing with? Some piss-brained traffic cop issuing tickets? You're ass is mine, and when I get through with you, what I did to your wife will be a cakewalk compared to what's going to happen to you!"

Finally, he reached the table and snatched the key. Even in the dark, he was able to free himself from the bed in seconds, taking the loose handcuff and firing it at the wall. Then, he slammed the bed back into its original position across the room, always the orderly one, and raced outside.

The old legs wobbled as Colton flew down the long flight of stone stairs leading to the garage. He stopped for a moment, gasping for air, trying to think what to do next. Communications were dead, so he couldn't call his driver. He was too far away to shout to him. He was probably sleeping on the job, anyway.

Then he spotted the black Lincoln and raced around to the driver's side.

He jumped in, hoping the keys were in the ignition.

"Yes!"

In seconds, he had the engine revving and he squealed backwards, braking suddenly, then took off down the drive. His eyes were bulging and temples pounding from the fury he felt.

The audacity of that punk!

The heavy car began to pick up more speed.

He grinned a wicked smile.

"Barnes, I'll have your ass sooner than you can say..."

His words stopped suddenly, as he attempted to brake. The pedal went straight to the floor with all the resistance of soft butter.

In the instant before a man reaches the end, it is said that all things become clear. By the stunned look on General Jennings Colton's face, he had arrived at that moment.

"SHITTTTTTT!"

The word echoed out into the night, to be carried by sound waves over the vast domain he ruled, just as the black Lincoln plunged over a sheer, rocky cliff, and exploded on impact, bursting into flames.

Near the base of the mountain, Jim Barnes stopped, and looked back over his shoulder. The general flew off the road just about where Jim figured he would.

Small brush fires erupted everywhere in the rugged terrain and bits of metal still rattled as they came to a stop.

He took in the stunning sight with cold detachment. In that crisp hour before dawn, he stood silently.

Then as he turned to leave, he muttered, "I hope you were watching, honey."

****

The black Ford Bronco passed through the rolling hills of southern Indiana, winding its way north. The crossing that began years before, changing the lives of everyone it touched, would soon be over. One day, the driver hoped it would be a distant memory.

He pulled off the old two-lane country road into a ramshackle service station.

"Fill 'er up, mister?" came the cheerful drawl of a young farm boy, happy in his first job.

"Sure, son. Hey, have you got a pay phone around here?"

"Yup, over behind the ice machine," he said, pointing.

"Great, I'll be right back."

He picked up the old receiver and dialed an El Paso number he located the day before, but was hesitant to call. It was still early in the morning, Texas time, and the phone rang twice. Finally, a sleepy, soft female voice came on the line.

"Maggie?" was the only thing he could say.

"Jim? Jim, is that you?"

"Yeah, it's me."

"Oh, my God! Where are you?"

"North. Quite a ways north. In Indiana."

"What..."

"It's over now, Maggie. All over. Remember, I told you I would know when it was time."

"I remember. I know you can't say much, but is she all right? Is she...?"

"She's dead. It was very bad. I don't think I'll ever forget it."

Maggie broke out in tears and the sobbing carried across the telephone line.

"I'm sorry, Jimmy. Truly I am. I wouldn't wish for it to be this way."

"I know that, and I love you for it."

"Did you open the pink envelope I gave you?"

"No, ah, I didn't. I need some time, still. I've got a few things to do back home. And I need to be by myself for a while to sort it all out."

"I understand, Jim, take all the time you need. Just know I'll be waiting for your call."

"I hope so, Maggie, God I hope so. Good-bye. I love you."

Jim Barnes gently placed the receiver down and leaned forward, touching his forehead to the stainless steel. He stood like that for a while, tears forming up in his eyes, until he heard footsteps coming up behind him.

"You all right, mister?" asked the concerned young man, whose fresh face mirrored his own many years back.

"No son," he answered, wiping away the tears, "but I will be."

EPILOGUE

The blinding fury of the winter storm subsided, and stopped with the first light of dawn. White snowflakes sparkled in the evergreens like diamonds on an emerald velvet cloth, and fell softly to the ground, finishing the journey that started the dark night before. The air was alive with the sounds of nature, as all things living began to come forth from hidden shelters.

Up, off the ground, movement could be seen among the branches and twigs of the pines. Soon, the face of a bearded man appeared, his hollow eyes searching the forest around him. It was still fiercely cold, and he would make no movement to leave the protection until the time was right.

Shivering beneath an old army jacket with a small blue flag containing the Southern Cross sewn above the breast pocket, he silently made the decision that had eluded him for many months. In his heart, his penance was complete, for he had finally found the strength and desire to live. There would be no more questions, for he knew that answers were hard to come by, and illusory, at best. Finally, the tired man understood that it was enough to just be, and move on.

Slowly, his joints stiff from the bitter cold, he felt for the pocket of his jacket, and clutched a small pink envelope, creased and torn, with no writing on the outside. His fingers closed around it, and he felt warm again.

The envelope fell open at his touch, revealing a single piece of paper inside.

Gently, he pulled it out, and read the words.

"What took you so long?"

ABOUT THE AUTHOR

Thomas Parks is the married father of three children living in Scottsdale, Arizona. He would welcome your comments on this work. Contact him by email at tparks1@hotmail.com